FOCUS ON DECEPTION

KENDRA PECCI

Yellow
Canary
Press

Cover Design by Maldo Designs

Developmental Edit by Rachel May, Golden May Editing, LLC

Line Edit and Proofread by Earley Editing, LLC

First Edition, 2025

Digital: 979-8-9931431-0-1
Paperback: 979-8-9931431-1-8

Kendra Pecci, www.kendrapecci.com

Yellow Canary Press

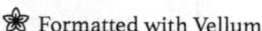 Formatted with Vellum

To those who never stop chasing their dreams.

"You can waste your lives drawing lines.
Or you can live your life crossing them."
— Shonda Rhimes

1

S tella Meyers slid into the sleek Mercedes and took a moment to run a gloved hand over the supple leather of the passenger seat, a discreet smile touching her lips. This level of luxury was new to her. She felt like she was in a cockpit, not a car. Every part of her wanted to start hitting buttons, to program the seat to conform to her body, and change the ambient lighting to fit her mood. This car could do everything.

She glanced at her watch and marked the time: 12:37 p.m. "Stop gawking. Time to go." She punched the ignition, and the engine purred.

Stella backed out of the parking space and watched Max take her spot. Same model car, same plates, only the ones on Max's were fake. The valets shouldn't notice. Max tapped his watch as Stella pulled away; she was due back within the hour.

As she navigated the crowded streets of the marina, Stella envisioned the job ahead one final time. The two biggest risks were talking her way past the guards at the gate and disarming the alarm. If she could clear those hurdles, she would be home free. Stella visualized herself succeeding each step of the way. This was no time for fear; she'd planned the job down to the last detail. By the time she hit the highway, she knew nothing would stop her from getting her prize.

The clock on the display read 12:41 p.m.

Stella opened the sunroof and let herself enjoy the gorgeous spring day. She blared The Struts' "Could Have Been Me" in her ear on repeat, and raced down the highway, hyping herself up during the twenty-minute drive to El Paraíso. The Mercedes needed to dust itself off after wasting time in a garage, and the speed helped calm her nerves.

Doing a job in broad daylight bordered on recklessness, but the security at El Paraíso left her no choice. Some of the world's wealthiest people called the community home for at least part of the year, and they demanded first-rate protection. Cameras captured everyone coming and going from the sole entrance gate, manned by one of the top security teams in the world. Nestled against a mountain range to the north and a sea to the south, the landscape provided the final barrier against unwanted visitors. El Paraíso was a fortress designed to make getting inside impossible.

Stella loved a challenge.

When the chance came to be the first person to break into El Paraíso, she grabbed it. Six months of preparation taught Stella everything she needed to know about Sebastian Hayes, his security, and his art collection. She'd planned for every contingency and prided herself on being able to switch gears on a dime. Stella smiled to herself and floored the accelerator; she was ready for anything.

As she pulled up to the gate, Stella cast a quick glance in the mirror to check her disguise. The whole persona worked; she didn't even recognize herself. She'd briefly joined the cleaning crew here two months ago to stake out the job. Then she'd blended in by dressing the part, keeping her eyes averted, and speaking only when necessary.

This time, she pulled up in Mr. Hayes's car, the picture of a senior executive assistant. Her skin shone a healthy bronze, her jet-black hair was concealed under a blonde wig sleeked back into a stylish low knot. But her clothes really gave her an edge: a push-up bra enhanced her cleavage, and a leather top zipped low would draw attention away from her face. She wore leather driving gloves and pink-tinted heart-shaped Cartier glasses with diamond studs—all of it combined with a slight Czech accent to match Sasha Novak's fake passport.

Stella lowered her window. "Señora," he greeted with a nod.

Already, she could see the outfit doing its job; the guard struggled to meet her gaze. Stella pasted a smile on her face and handed over her passport for identification. She'd manufactured a message emailed earlier in the day saying she would come to collect some files for her boss. It should be a quick exchange.

"You are here for Mr. Hayes?" he asked.

"Yes." She kept her answer curt. It wouldn't do for her to give him any attention.

"We received notice that you would arrive today. How long will you be here?"

Stella glanced at her watch and replied, "As little as possible." She tried leaving it at that, but the guard didn't budge. "I expect no more than thirty minutes." Satisfied, he checked her identification one last time, and then buzzed her in. She reached for the passport, but the guard shook his head.

"We'll keep this while you're on the property." She glared at him, but he wouldn't relent. "Policy for all visitors." Stella waved her hand to dismiss him, rolled up her window, and drove through the gate.

Stella stayed in character, never knowing when a camera might catch her expression, but she celebrated in her mind—she'd passed the first major hurdle. If something went wrong now and she had to ditch the job in a hurry, the only thing she'd leave behind was an untraceable passport.

She drove to Hayes's villa and turned down the long, winding drive, heading to the west side of the house. Once the garage came into sight, Stella hit the programmed button beneath the rearview mirror. The door opened to reveal the only empty slot left in the four-car garage.

Security might keep strangers out, but the car belonged here—the Mercedes was home.

Stella pulled into the garage and promptly closed the door behind her. She grabbed her imitation Hermes Kelly bag and exited the car, heading straight to the door leading inside the house. There she eyed her next hurdle: the alarm.

Alarms didn't normally concern Stella; she used a handheld computer to hack into them and shut them down. But that wasn't an option at El Paraíso. Here each alarm system had multiple codes for different levels of access, tracking everyone who was coming and going. Only Sebastian Hayes's personal code would disable the alarm and turn off the internal cameras. If she used her computer to disarm the alarm, she wouldn't know if the code it found would shut down the internal cameras or just provide her with access to a portion of the estate. That was a risk she couldn't take.

When Stella took the job on the cleaning crew, she broke into the property manager's office and lifted Sebastian's personal code from the database. Her deep dive into his background showed his hubris—Mr. Hayes thought himself untouchable. She gambled he would neglect to update his password routinely.

Stella glanced at her watch and marked the time: 1:02 p.m. She took a deep breath, paused, and typed in the code she'd memorized.

The alarm beeped and the light turned green. She closed her eyes and suppressed a grin. She was in.

But were the cameras disabled?

Stella walked into the house as if she owned the place, acting the part of a professional on a routine visit. She kept her sunglasses on and pretended to chat on her phone as she crossed the expansive hallway to Sebastian's office. If someone was filming her, she wanted it to look like she knew where she was going; this was all routine.

Sebastian Hayes fancied himself a patron of the arts. He practically launched careers for several young artists by purchasing their early work and promoting them to his friends and colleagues, watching their value skyrocket. His collection was extensive, making the place more like an art gallery than a home.

But that suited her needs perfectly. No large windows faced the walls displaying artwork. The gallery rooms were closed off from the elements; the light funneled through the rooms in recesses from the top and bottom of each room, making her movements invisible to anyone who might be watching from the perimeter.

Stella made her way through the gallery hallways until she approached Sebastian's private office. The door was closed. If the system hadn't changed since her recon work, the door should be unlocked now. She concentrated on her movements, never breaking stride while she chatted away to no one on her phone, and turned the door handle, letting herself into the room. A quick glance at the camera trained on her target showed her the light was off. She kept up the ruse as she moved around the office to Sebastian's desk, looking for any additional cameras. There were none she could see.

Stella dropped her phone back into her bag, raised her sunglasses to the top of her head, and took in her target.

She'd been prepared not to like this painting, to see it as a huge payday and nothing else. Her research revealed the artist's reputation toward women was complex, some scholars calling him a misogynist who objectified women in his work. But something changed when Stella first laid eyes on Sebastian's priceless treasure. It was breathtaking.

The painting in front of her was alive with energy. Four dancers gathered together preparing to go on stage, finishing the last-minute touches of readying themselves for their performance. It was awash in brilliant blues with yellow undertones, every detail of the women imbued with energy. Edgar Degas might have been a jerk, but he painted these women so alive she felt like she could reach out and touch them, help them straighten their dresses, and pat their hair before sending them in front of the waiting audience.

Stella shook her head, pulling herself out of a stupor. This was no time to lose sight of the mission; she needed to move.

The cameras being offline was both a gift and a curse. She could work without being filmed, but anyone watching the feed would see the cameras were dark. Since the entire staff knew the Hayeses were on their yacht for at least two more weeks, this could be a problem. She had to be quick.

She checked the walls for signs of additional security devices on the painting. None were visible, but she didn't trust her eyes. Stella pulled a small UV light meter from her bag to scan the painting and surrounding wall. The meter registered nothing.

Stella reached out to touch the side of the painting, caution in every movement. Any interruption now could be explained away, but once the painting was in her hands, that was it. She glanced out the door, her fingers inches from the gilded frame. The hallway was empty. She heard no sound in the house save for her own breathing. It was time to put her work to the test.

As Stella touched the outside of the painting, something buzzed her left hand. She yanked her hand back, whirling around her to see if she'd set off some kind of alarm. Her eyes scanned the book-shelves for another camera or something she'd missed, but she saw nothing. Then her wrist buzzed again, three more times in quick succession.

"Fuck." Stella cursed, checking her watch. Text messages were coming in from her daughter. She had her devices set to Do Not Disturb, but Caitlin's messages could always get through. Stella slapped her wrist to make the messages disappear so she could see the time again. 1:06 p.m. She needed to hurry.

Stella pulled down the notifications. Was this an emergency? The messages were too long to show on her watch; Caitlin clearly had a problem. It was just after 7:00 a.m. in Connecticut. If she was texting this much before going to school, something was wrong.

"Shit," Stella cursed before turning back to the painting. She didn't have time for this right now, but Caitlin came first. Stella grabbed her AirPods, but put only one in. It was vital that she didn't miss any noise in the house. Then she blocked the option for a video call. Caitlin would have a million questions about her getup if she saw her face.

"Mom, I didn't want you to call," Caitlin sighed when she answered.

"I can't text right now, sweetie; I'm in the middle of something. Are you okay?"

"I'm sorry to bother you. I'm sick, but Gram says I have to go to school." Stella could hear her daughter start to cry; not a normal response when she was sick. More telling, her grandmother was a pushover. If Caitlin were sick, she'd be the first person to keep her home.

"What's wrong, honey? Why don't you want to go to school?" Silence answered her. This call was going to take some time.

Stella reached for the painting with both hands, relieved not to feel anything when she touched the frame. She hefted the painting off the wall as her daughter brought her up to speed.

"Amelia doesn't want us to be friends anymore." Stella relaxed a bit. Though she could hear Caitlin crying as she spoke, Amelia was her best friend, and it wasn't unusual for the girls to have dramatic flare-ups.

"Did she actually say that? Or did you misinterpret something?" asked Stella.

"She said it." Caitlin fired back. "She said I didn't know what it meant to be a best friend, so she didn't want to be mine anymore."

"Sounds a bit dramatic, even for Amelia. Did you do something to her?"

"Why do you always think I did something? It's not me."

Stella grabbed her phone off the desk and shoved it in her pocket, then took the Mercedes key fob out of her bag. She kept the conversation going while she headed back to the garage, the Degas in her arms.

"Sorry, I didn't mean to upset you. What happened?" She huffed as she carried the painting. At three feet wide framed, the painting wasn't too large or heavy for her to manage. The real weight was in knowing what the masterpiece was worth. She'd never stolen anything this expensive before. She'd be damned if she was going to damage it.

Stella set the painting down and eased open the door to the garage, activating the automatic lights. A quick glance around the garage bay confirmed she was alone. She hit the trunk button on the key fob and bent to pick up the painting again.

"Remember the new girl? Rachel?" Caitlin spoke in her ear while Stella wound her way through the parked cars to the Mercedes. "I played with her yesterday during recess, and it made Amelia mad. She said best friends don't ditch each other. Now she doesn't want to be friends anymore." Caitlin sighed, the sound echoing through Stella's earbuds; she was beginning to calm down.

"And your plan is to stay home so you won't have to deal with Amelia?" Stella asked. "What will happen to Rachel if you're not there today?" If Caitlin thought her new friend would be ostracized, Stella knew she'd go to school. Caitlin's empathy always made Stella proud.

Stella set the Degas down beside the car, then moved to the trunk. She pulled back the blanket covering the fake she'd had made and lifted it out, setting it next to the original. Stella stared at the two paintings side by side.

The reproduction artist had done a fantastic job. The painting and frame looked identical to the original. With any luck, Sebastian would never know it had been swapped.

Stella placed a hand on the original while she talked to her daughter, making sure she didn't mix them up. "You're right, Amelia might be mean to Rachel if I'm not there," admitted Caitlin. Stella nodded, both to her daughter and to the paintings in front of her, even though neither could see her.

"Exactly. And you don't want that to happen." She grabbed the original and put it in the trunk of the car, covering it with the blanket.

"No, I don't," Caitlin said. "I'd better go to school. If Amelia is mean to Rachel, I want to be there to defend her."

"I agree. Hopefully, it'll blow over quickly. It usually does," Stella reassured her.

"I'm getting a little tired of all of this drama." Stella couldn't agree more. She closed the trunk and picked up the reproduction she'd commissioned. "Sorry for interrupting you. Have fun at the photoshoot. You'll be home Sunday, right?"

"Absolutely," said Stella. "I've got to run, sweetie. I love you."

"Love you, too." Stella let Caitlin disconnect the call.

Stella picked up the replica and took two steps towards the internal door when the doorbell rang. Her eyes went wide, and she clutched the painting to her chest. She spun around, looking for a place to hide it while her mind raced through scenarios that would bring someone to the door. Security knew she was on the premises; this had to be someone coming to talk to her.

A toolbox stood beside the door, almost as tall as Stella. She rolled it away from the wall just far enough to put the painting behind it. If anyone came into the garage, it would be behind the door when they opened it. It was the best she could do. Stella noted the time. 1:15 p.m.

Thinking quickly, she pulled off her gloves and tossed them on the bench beside the door. "Shit." She cursed under her breath. Now she'd have to keep a mental record of every surface she touched because her prints were exposed.

The doorbell rang again, followed by someone banging on the door. She hustled inside the house, touching up her hair, and straightening her outfit as she moved through the sweeping foyer. Stella made a quick adjustment to her bra, pushing her breasts up as high as she could, and opened the door.

"Ms. Novak, I presume?"

Stella recognized the property manager standing in front of her. He ran the entire community behind the scenes. He also kept the database of everyone's passwords on his computer. It was his laptop she'd broken into two months ago to get Sebastian's code to the house. He had to be here about the cameras.

"Can I help you?" She squinted at him a bit and shook her head, looking at him like he was intruding in her space, not the other way around.

"Are you Sasha Novak? Mr. Hayes's secretary?" He held up her passport and waved it at her. Stella felt her heart pick up its pace. She covered the slight tremor in her hands by strumming her fingers on the door impatiently.

"Senior Executive Assistant," she corrected. She reached for her passport and was relieved he released it to her. "You know this. Who are you?" She didn't ask a question as much as demand an answer. She could feel her nerves turning into anger. The best way to throw someone off was not to stay calm, but to let your emotions erupt. Anger at the intrusion seemed the best way to deflect his attention.

"I'm Antonio Alfaro. I run El Paraíso." She stared at him expectantly, not speaking. She wouldn't give him a drop of information she didn't have to. "Can I ask what you're doing on the premises today?"

"I am here at Mr. Hayes's request. He cleared it with your security team."

"He did, but we noticed the internal cameras in the house are off. I was concerned. Has there been a power outage?"

She'd known cutting the cameras off posed a risk, but she didn't have another option.

"I know nothing about these systems."

"May I come inside?" Antonio stepped closer to Stella, pushing the door open further as he spoke. Stella didn't object, but opened the door and motioned for him to come inside.

Stella flipped on a light switch in the foyer, illuminating the chandelier hanging overhead. "Power is fine. There is no problem I can see."

"I'd like to check the alarm system." He moved farther inside the house. She nodded and followed behind him, running through different scenarios if he went all the way to Sebastian's office to check on the cameras. He knew his way around the house. Probably knew every estate on the property as if it were his own. He led her to the interior garage door and opened it, stepping inside to examine the alarm system. "What code did you use to access this door?"

"The code Mr. Hayes gave me." He stared at her for a beat and Stella wondered if this was a test. He didn't think she was going to give him the code, did he? "I will not tell you the code. I have no evidence of who you are."

He scowled at her. "I assure you I have access to all the codes in this community."

"Then I do not need to tell you what it is." She crossed her arms and scowled at him, holding her ground.

"The problem, Ms. Novak, is the code you entered turned off the interior cameras. Only one code does that, and it belongs to Mr. Hayes. We run a very secure system here. Any visitor or guest should have an individual code created for the time they're on the premises. Mr. Hayes didn't do that. It appears he gave you his personal code to get into the home."

Antonio glanced around the garage. Stella couldn't be sure what he was looking for, but she wanted to interrupt his inspection.

"I run everything for Mr. Hayes." She looked at his Mercedes while she said it, proving her point. "He does not have time to put in a request to you every time he needs something."

"You need your own code to this house, especially if you're going to be on the premises while Mr. Hayes is away." He looked at his watch and back at her. "If you could follow me to the main office, I'll submit a request for your private code. This will give you access to the house without disabling Mr. Hayes's internal security system. I'm sure he'd prefer to keep security tight while he's away."

"I have no time for this." Stella allowed herself to get genuinely angry at the implication she wasn't trustworthy. "Mr. Hayes is on a tight schedule and wants his files immediately. There will be no further delay." She put her hand on his arm and guided him out of the garage.

"Ms. Novak, I have a job to do—"

"As do I." She pulled her phone out of her pocket and clicked on Sebastian Hayes's contact, the first one in her favorites. "I know my job is secure, Mr. Alfaro. Is yours?" Stella stared at him as her finger hovered over the icon to place a call.

"No need to interrupt him." Antonio waved her off and walked back toward the front door. "We can settle this without involving him."

She led him to the front door and opened it for him. "I will not come to your office today."

He hesitated, then reached into his inside breast pocket and produced a business card and handed it to her. "Please call me at your convenience, and we will begin the process of getting you a separate code. We'll update Mr. Hayes's personal password as well."

Stella took the card as she ushered Antonio out the door, but she wouldn't accept his solution. "Mr. Hayes will not want a new code. I would have to learn his code and recite it to him each time he forgets it." She raised her eyebrows at him. "There is no scenario where Mr. Hayes does not give me full access to his affairs."

Stella closed the door at the same moment she watched her words hit their mark. She made certain to slide the deadbolt into place with some force, locking him out and re-securing the home. She headed back down the hall to the interior garage door, looking to see how long this exchange had cost her.

It was 1:22 p.m. She was running late. Had Mr. Alfaro left the property, or was he waiting for her outside? Probably waiting. Either way, she needed to hurry.

In an instant, her outfit turned from an asset to a liability. Stella kicked off her heels and went back into the garage, putting her gloves back on, then pulled the painting from behind the tool chest. Moving with more confidence knowing she was no longer carrying a multi-million-dollar masterpiece, Stella sprinted back to Sebastian's office as fast as her short skirt would allow and hung the painting on the wall.

Stella stepped back to check her work. She leaned in and straightened the painting a couple of times, ensuring it was level and hanging exactly as the original had been. She chuckled to herself. The task of hanging artwork was new to her—normally she only took art off the walls.

Stella checked her watch again. 1:27 p.m. There was barely enough time for a quick clean up, but it couldn't be avoided. She wiped down the office doorknob, then sprinted to the foyer and wiped down every surface she had touched. The only spot she couldn't get was the exterior part of the door where she'd drummed her fingers. Loose ends unnerved her, but she couldn't risk being seen wiping the door's outside surface. Hopefully, someone would clean it before anyone discovered the theft.

Stella made it back to the garage, put on her heels, and closed the interior door, rearming the alarm system. The security team would note the cameras had come back online. Stella hopped back into the Mercedes, put her sunglasses back on, and backed out of the garage.

As she'd suspected, she spotted Mr. Alfaro sitting in his car at the back of the driveway; he'd been waiting for her to leave. Stella nodded at him curtly before driving off, glancing only once in her rearview mirror to confirm he was tailing her back to the gate.

By 1:34 p.m., Stella was back at the guard shack, with Mr. Alfaro blocking her in from behind. Stella's heartbeat picked up speed, but she kept her composure in front of the guard. He motioned for her to roll down her window, and Stella waved her passport at him. "Your boss returned my passport already." She looked ahead as if expecting the gate to open at her command.

The guard nodded at his boss behind her, then looked in her car. A second guard came out and circled the Mercedes with a mirror on a pole, looking underneath the carriage. "I thought you were getting some files," he said, motioning to the empty seat beside her. "Are they in the trunk?"

Stella sighed, reached into her bag, and pulled out a flash drive. "It's 2024." She waved the stick at him, then dropped it back into her purse and looked straight ahead. She refused to say another word or make eye contact with the guard, drumming her fingers on the steering wheel. The gate opened.

Her eyes flicked to the rearview mirror as Mr. Alfaro tailed her off the premises. She drove just over the speed limit to deflect suspicion. Only when he finally gave up and peeled off did Stella allow herself to take a deep breath.

Without taking her hands from the wheel, she gave a voice command to her phone to call Sebastian Hayes.

Max answered the call. "Ms. Novak." He made his voice deep and kept to only her name in case she wasn't calling from a safe place.

"Heading back now. Arrival time says 2:03."

"You're late," he said.

"Got a little sidetracked, but I got your files." Stella cut the call and paid attention to her driving, keeping an eye out in case anyone followed. She'd get the car back to the slot in the parking garage, move the painting to Max's car, and be on her way out of the country by dinnertime. The plan was to take a train to Germany and leave from there on Sunday, while Max would stay behind to sell the painting. He already had a buyer for it.

She'd told Caitlin she was doing a shoot for a tourist magazine, so she'd spend Saturday taking photographs in Hamburg. Caitlin was getting older and sharper. Navigating her double life was tricky, but it was worth it. This would be the single biggest payday she'd ever earned. She'd just catapulted herself to an entirely new level.

Stella smiled to herself as she drove, feeling the rush of her success. She loved this life.

2

Stella and Caitlin pulled into the school parking lot as the sun began its final descent into the horizon, Taylor Swift blaring from the speakers, as usual. Caitlin was bouncing with excitement for the night ahead. She popped her seatbelt the second the car came to a stop and shoved the door open. Halfway out the door, she paused and looked back at her mother. "Do you need help with your stuff?"

"No, go on ahead. Have fun tonight." She hollered the last part just before Caitlin slammed the door. Her daughter waved at her and took off running. Tonight was the Fall Festival—Northbrook Academy's biggest fundraiser of the year. The school gym housed an elaborate carnival with games, food, activities, and a raffle rivaling the state lottery in swag the kids could win. Each year, Stella ran a photo booth at the event to stay in good standing with the Mean Girl Moms who ran the school PTA.

Stella reached in the back of her RAV4 and unloaded her gear. She grabbed the bag of costumes, then picked up the Rubbermaid box full of camera equipment. As she eyed the lights and the backgrounds she would have to come back for, she heard the unmistakable sound of high heels clicking on the pavement behind her. There was only one person who wore heels to a school carnival in October.

"Holy fucking shit. Did you see him?" Fiona yelled, still 20 feet away. "He should be the grand prize in tonight's drawing. I'd pay anything to win him." Fiona arrived at the car to help unload, grabbing the lights and putting them on top of the box Stella was holding. "What else do you need me to get?"

"Get the background displays if you can." Fiona reached into the car and pulled out the three different cardboard displays Stella had printed for tonight's event. The kids could pose for pictures in front of a grave, a haunted house, or in an apple orchard if they weren't feeling particularly ghoulish tonight.

"How about these?" Fiona picked up a pair of sunglasses from under the displays and held them up to Stella. "Girl, what the fuck are you doing with a pair of Cartier sunglasses?"

"They're left over from a shoot. They're not real." Stella reached for the glasses, but Fiona deflected her.

"The hell they aren't. I know quality when I see it. These probably cost more than your car." Stella shook her head and laughed it off, pretending Fiona was nuts. It wasn't a stretch.

"Please put them in the glovebox. I don't think they're real, but if they are, someone will want them back in one piece."

"You can't afford to break these. I'll just hold on to them for you." She slid the sunglasses onto her face and gazed toward the setting sun. "I was born to wear these." She pushed them up onto her head, brushing her hair back, and picked up the displays. Stella wondered if she'd ever see the sunglasses again. She was a thief by trade, but Fiona could charm souls from the devil himself.

"Gorgeous," Stella noted. "Now what were you saying? Someone is cute?"

"No, girl, I did not say someone was cute. He's a sexpot. And that is not the half of it. He is the hottest man I've seen in this school—possibly the entire Eastern seaboard. And you've won the lottery because he's teaching Cait's class. You have an excuse to talk to him."

"You won the lottery because you're married to Malcolm, who worships you and lets you do whatever you want," Stella chided.

"I haven't forgotten. I promise I was only thinking of you. What kind of friend would I be if I didn't run and tell you what just looking at him has done to my insides?" Fiona wiggled her hips a bit as she walked.

"Pipe down before someone hears you and thinks you're up to no good," said Stella.

"Yes, Mom." Fiona mocked. "But seriously, he's yummy, and you have to see him for yourself."

"I'm sure we'll meet soon enough. How long is Ms. Beaker going to be out?"

Last week someone had run Caitlin's 4th grade teacher off the road, causing her car to flip several times until she landed at the bottom of a ravine. The whole community was holding its breath to see if she'd pull through.

"No idea. We need to organize something from the kids to give her. In fact, I think that's what Richard was talking about doing today."

"I was just thinking the same thing," said Stella. "Wait, who's Richard?"

"Keep up, girl." She laughed as she pulled open the door to the gym and held it for Stella. Fiona whispered again, quietly this time, "Richard Medina, the sexy new substitute." She waggled her eyebrows at Stella. "And he's single. You have to meet him."

Stella laughed. "Do not try to set me up with Caitlin's teacher."

"No promises," sang Fiona.

Stella met Fiona Adams two years ago when her son Levi was in Pre-K and Caitlin was in 2nd grade. She'd walked into a PTA meeting talking loudly and laughing, every head turning when she entered. As much as Stella tried to blend into the background—critical in both her professions—Fiona liked to be the center of attention. Which was good, because her stunning good looks, posh British accent, and loudmouth that cursed like a sailor meant everyone within a fifty-foot radius knew everything she was thinking the second she thought it.

Where Stella kept everything locked away, Fiona made life fun and spontaneous. Of course, Fiona didn't know the reason Stella controlled her life so carefully. As wild as Fiona liked to make herself seem, she followed a strong moral and ethical code, and she didn't broker any bullshit. No matter how close they were, Stella knew if Fiona ever found out how she really earned her money, she'd drop her in a heartbeat. It was a risk Stella wasn't willing to take. She kept Fiona firmly in her personal world; her real identity safely tucked away.

They found the section of the gym reserved for Stella and set up her booth. Fiona knew the routine from having been on photo-shoots with Stella. As they were putting up the lighting, Fiona elbowed Stella in the ribs. "Here comes Pam." She looked over Stella's head and waved, then said loudly, "What is Levi up to? Gotta run."

Stella looked behind her and saw Pam Fisher making a beeline for her. By the time she turned back around, Fiona was long gone. Stella cursed in her mind but kept her mouth shut. She put on her best fake smile and turned to greet the woman who inspired both fear and awe in the Northbrook community.

"Stella. Good to see you finally made it," said Pam, tapping her watch as she approached.

Stella stifled the urge to roll her eyes. "The festival doesn't start for another twenty minutes. Plenty of time."

Pam was the perpetual president of the Pride of Northbrook Parents' Association, and her husband was on the board. They had three children at the school, and she reminded anyone within earshot that it was their generous donation which had funded this new gymnasium for the high school last year. Nothing escaped her attention, and no one could get anything done in the school without Pam's approval. She embodied everything Stella and Fiona hated about these elite schools, but you couldn't argue with the results. Northbrook was the best education money could buy, and Stella considered it her penance for living a double life to put up with Pam and her groupies to keep Caitlin in the school.

"Have you looked at the schedule of events?" Pam asked, pointing to the paper in her hand. "I want to make sure you get a picture of

Principal Stevens in the dunk tank. She's the grand finale. Due in the tank at eight o'clock sharp."

Stella nodded at her and forced a smile. "No problem. I can shut down the booth a little early. I'll be there."

"She's only going to be there for twenty minutes or until someone dunks her, whichever comes first. It's a real coup to get her in the tank at all." Pam straightened her shoulders and beamed with pride. "I practically had to agree to donate another building for the school to persuade her. We thought building this gym would be enough."

There it is.

"Anyway, I don't want to miss it if someone dunks her. It'll be great for the yearbook, as well as our website to showcase how down-to-earth we are here at Northbrook. Everyone gets in on the fun."

"I'll set an alarm to be safe." For good measure, Stella added, "The gym looks amazing. I'm sure the Lions are happy to have a real gym with a workout room, snack stand, and everything. Thanks, again, for the donation."

"That's right, you missed the dedication. We could have used some professional photos of the students seeing it for the first time. Truly priceless." Pam spotted her next victim and waved. "Let's not miss this opportunity, too. Eight o'clock sharp." She tapped her watch again, and Stella resisted the urge to punch her in the face. She'd never done business in her own backyard, but she often fantasized about breaking into the Fishers' house. The mental image of Pam coming home from a vacation to find blank walls and an empty jewelry box helped Stella get through encounters like this.

As the carnival got underway, Stella got into the spirit of the season and focused on getting as many pictures of the kids as she could, with groups of friends coming in pairs and entire squads to get their pictures taken. Caitlin and Rachel came by and checked in, posing with the orchard background. Amelia really had ditched her at the end of the last school year when Rachel came into the picture, surprising Stella with her stubbornness. But Caitlin and Rachel had hit it off, and it seemed Caitlin recovered nicely from the snubbing she'd received from her former best friend.

Fiona came by with Levi and his friends to get some photos of him in his Halloween getup. Fiona was a master makeup artist, and Levi always had the best costume in town. Tonight, he was dressed as a vampire with his hair sleeked back, realistic razor-sharp incisors, and blood dripping down the sides of his mouth then splashed all over his neck. If Fiona hadn't been with him, Stella might not even have been able to tell it was him. He looked good enough to be put in a magazine with the graveyard background behind him.

When her alarm sounded at 7:50 p.m., Stella shut down the booth and headed outside. With the gym floors still so new, they put the dunk tank on the lawn despite the late October temperature registering a cool fifty-five degrees. Supposedly, the water in the tank was warm, but Stella thought by this time of night it had probably cooled considerably. Pam instructed the DJ to announce the principal's arrival in the tank. Stella couldn't hold back her eye roll when Pam tapped her watch at her arrival.

The DJ gave the audience the play-by-play as Principal Stevens climbed into the tank sporting a wetsuit and a Northbrook Lions baseball cap. Stella took pictures of the crowd, catching the kids hopped up on cotton candy and ecstatic at the chance to dunk their principal. The younger kids were up first. Stella got closeups of the kindergarteners standing not three feet away from the target, their throws either wildly off the mark or too weak to make an impact if they did hit the target.

As the clock counted down her time in the tank, the students aiming for the principal got older, and the pitches packed more punch. When the pitcher for the baseball team stepped up to take his turn, the tension reached a frenzy. Ms. Stevens heckled and trash-talked George Lee when he stepped up to the line. Kids cheered him on louder than the state championship game last year. If anyone could get Ms. Stevens in the tank, it was George.

Stella aimed her camera and took a few shots of him setting up. He threw his first pitch, and Stella swung the camera around in time to catch Ms. Stevens laughing and cheering at his miss. Stella wondered if he'd missed on purpose to drag out the game as long as possible. She decided she'd best keep the camera aimed at the tank to be sure she wouldn't miss it.

Excitement spread through the crowd as George readied another pitch. Stella snapped a picture of Ms. Stevens's eyes widening at the sight of the star pitcher winding up.

"Excuse me." A voice Stella didn't recognize cut through the noise, followed by someone tapping her on the shoulder. "Are you Mrs. Meyers?"

Stella glanced over her shoulder to see who it was, then whipped her head around for another look when her brain registered what her eyes had seen. Her mind went completely blank. The man standing before her looked like he belonged on the cover of a magazine, not at a school carnival.

"Um. No, I'm not," she managed to get out. Then Stella heard the unmistakable sound of George's throw finding its target. The crowd erupted as Ms. Stevens hit the water.

Stella's stomach sank. She'd missed the shot.

She took a couple of pictures of the aftermath as Ms. Stevens resurfaced from the tank, hat off and fully soaked. She also snapped some photos of everyone congratulating and cheering on George. But she lost the actual image of Ms. Stevens hitting the water.

Stella turned back to the cause of her distraction. Standing next to her was a man in a dark suit, a few inches taller than Stella with olive skin, short black hair, blue eyes, and the perfect hint of a five o'clock shadow. "Damn," she mumbled, unsure whether the curse was for her mistake or the only word her brain could come up with.

"Disculpe." He shook his head at her. "My timing is bad. I'm sorry if I ruined your picture."

Stella chuckled to herself. There was only one person who would care about this; it's not like she hasn't upset Pam before. She waved her hand, gesturing to the excited crowd. "Everyone here has a camera on their phone. I'm sure someone caught it."

"Let us hope so," he said. "Have I been misinformed? Someone told me you were Mrs. Meyers. Caitlin's mom?"

"No," she said. She shook her head and stumbled over her words. "I mean yes, I am Caitlin's mom."

"Yes?" He tilted his head when he asked, clearly confused.

"I mean, yes, I'm Caitlin's mom, but I'm not Mrs. Meyers. I'm single." He nodded as if he were beginning to understand. "I'm a single mom." People dispersed, making their way back inside the gym now that the main event was over. Stella motioned for him to walk with her while she tried to recover the conversation. She failed.

"I'm not divorced, if that's what you were thinking. I mean, I'm a single mom, but I've never been married." What the actual fuck? she chastised herself. "Sorry. Not sure why I'm giving you my dating history."

"I would love to learn more about your dating history." He grinned at her and let his eyes trail over her body. Stella felt the heat rise in her cheeks as they walked.

"It's a short story." Stella laughed. She found her footing and looked him in the eyes with more confidence now. "So, yes, I am Caitlin's mother. Stella Meyers." She extended her hand to greet him.

Before he could take her hand in return, Pam appeared at her side, pulling on Stella's arm like one of the kids. "Did you get it? Did you see the look on her face when the ball hit, right before she went in? Let me see." She leaned over Stella's arm to peek at her camera.

"I am sorry; this is my fault. With all the excitement, I got confused and interrupted her at the wrong moment." He wasn't lying, but Stella felt bad that he was throwing himself under the bus for her. Pam wasn't someone you wanted to cross.

She tried to diffuse Pam. "I'll find someone who got it on video. I can fix it in my editing studio."

Pam looked like she wanted to stab Stella, but she kept herself in check in front of the handsome stranger. "If there is anything I can do to make it up to you, please do not hesitate to ask." He smiled at her and turned his charm to full volume, all but kissing the back of her hand.

"I understand," said Pam. "We all make mistakes. Some more

than others." She cut her eyes to Stella, then turned back to the gentleman. "Good to see you, Mr. Medina."

Stella raised her eyebrows hearing his name. She watched Pam strut away in a huff, grateful for the distraction so she could get her thoughts in order.

"Mr. Medina? Caitlin's teacher?" Her heart sank as the pieces of the puzzle fell into place. This was the sexpot Fiona had been talking about. She shook her head. Stella kept her private life and public life separate for her protection. Dating anyone associated with the school —parent or teacher—was fodder for the gossip mill. Stella didn't want to be on the PTA's radar.

"An inauspicious introduction, to be sure. I'm Richard Medina." He extended his hand to her, wanting to complete the introduction Pam had interrupted. Stella noticed elegant cufflinks peeking out of his suit.

She let him take her hand and allowed herself to briefly fantasize about photographing him. This man would make a beautiful model. "I'd heard they'd found a permanent sub. Welcome to Northbrook."

"I wish I'd come under better circumstances. I'm happy I'm here with these incredible students, but what a horrible way to come into a job."

"The kids are going to need your support through this. Kids this age aren't accustomed to tragedy." She looked around the gym and gestured to the surrounding opulence—designer clothes, $250 shoes, iPhones in every pocket. "At least, not these kids."

"I'll do my best to carry them through this," he promised.

"How can I help you, Mr. Medina?"

"Please call me Richard." He smiled, and Stella felt her heart pick up speed. Calm the fuck down, Stella. He's off limits. "I only wanted to introduce myself. With the circumstances of my being brought into the classroom, I thought I'd meet as many parents as I could—the sooner, the better."

Stella set her camera down and caught Richard looking at her equipment. "Are you a professional?" he asked.

Stella nodded. "I donate my services to the school whenever we have events like this to help them raise a little more money. I get to connect with the kids and get out of doing anything else for the PTA." Stella nodded in Pam's direction. "You've met our PTA president, Pam Fisher."

"I've heard it's an active organization. Does a lot of good for the school." He let the statement drop, leaving Stella an opening.

"Sounds to me like you're well informed." She laughed. "And I can tell you, whatever you've heard, it's probably worse in real life. I'd tell you to stay away from them, but they'll get their hooks in you soon enough. A single man teaching at this school is fodder for the gossip mill."

"That must be some lightning-fast gossip if you've already learned I'm single." He laughed at her, and she knew he'd caught her.

"Well, Fiona Adams is my best friend. She knows everything and everyone."

"Ah, I recall meeting her." Richard nodded with a smile as he made the connection.

"She's hard to forget. But don't let the blonde hair fool you; she's smarter than all of us put together. It just comes in a stunning package."

"Dark hair is more my type," he replied, meeting her eyes again. He smiled at her, and Stella felt her defenses slip again. She let the comment drop, but she couldn't deny how her heart fluttered.

"Anyway, if there's anything you need for the class, please let me know." Stella spotted Caitlin across the gym and waved her over. Caitlin bounded over to them. With Caitlin's jet-black hair and dark eyes, she was the spitting image of her mother. "If Caitlin ever gives you any trouble, don't hesitate to reach out." Stella put her arms around her daughter and hugged her from behind. "She's a handful."

"Mom! I am not." Caitlin protested.

"Just kidding. You know how much I love you." Stella rocked her from side to side while she kept hugging her, purposely embarrassing her in front of her new teacher. "Shall we clean up, sweetie?" Stella moved to gather her things. Richard helped them pack up the costumes and disassembled the backgrounds standing at her station.

"Thank you; you don't have to do that."

"Looks like you could use an extra set of hands. I don't think there are any parents left to meet, anyway."

"Saved the best for last?" She eyed him as he put a fur wrap into the costume bag.

"Precisely." They fell into a comfortable rhythm as they cleaned up, Stella and Caitlin both giving him directions when he needed it. Within five minutes, they had it all boxed up, and like a true gentleman, he helped them carry it all out to the car.

"Thanks again for taking the blame in front of Pam. I owe you one," Stella said once they'd finished.

"My fault entirely. It was the least I could do."

Richard waved at Caitlin as she got into the car. "See you Monday morning, Caitlin." He turned back to Stella, pausing before he spoke again. "Is there any chance I can have your number?" He grinned at her, a twinkle in his eye visible even in the dark parking lot. "In case Caitlin gets out of hand." He tried to look stern, but they both knew what he was asking.

Stella let her gaze fall to his lips and imagined what it would be like to kiss someone like him. She smiled at the thought, but then shook off the image. Her life didn't have room for someone new, especially not a Spanish supermodel who taught her daughter's class. "The school knows how to reach me if there's any trouble."

Stella drove home, letting Taylor Swift's voice fill the car and drown out her thoughts. She didn't want Caitlin to see the smile she couldn't seem to wipe off her face. She switched the song from Getaway Car—a personal favorite—to Love Story. She wanted early, optimistic Taylor singing in her ear for the ride home.

3

S tella sat at her computer, hot on the trail of her next target. Since they'd been together, Max had always produced the hit list for her heists. His lifetime of experience and contacts in the darkest corners of society meant he could identify and vet a target faster than anyone. She did the research and recon work, but Max brought the big jobs to her doorstep.

Since she'd had so much fun grabbing the Degas, she decided it was time to level up her game and develop a target list on her own. Learning how to select her own prospects was a skill she wanted to have. For the last few months, she searched the society pages of international gossip columns, lurked on popular social media accounts, and researched who had the best private art collections. She had come up with a few names that interested her.

Today her focus was doing a deeper dive into one of her potential marks: Gerald Martin of Paris, France. Gerald was an international financier with a love of fast cars, fine wines, and an art collection that rivaled a national museum. He also had a trophy wife from the US named Mandy, who loved covering herself in diamonds. Stella guessed she was the weakest link in Gerald's security system.

She was reading an article about Gerald's new yacht and how

much time he and his wife liked to spend traveling the world on it—leaving their home in Paris empty—when the doorbell rang. She waited to hear Caitlin or her mother's footsteps, but none came.

"Probably some asshole trying to sell me windows again," she muttered to herself as she pulled herself out of her chair and marched to the door.

She approached the door and furrowed her eyebrows as she swung it open, ready to dispatch the person quickly and get back to work. "I already voted, and I don't need . . ." She halted, the words caught in her mouth.

She lost her voice for a moment, disoriented from seeing the man standing on her doorstep. Those beautiful blue eyes. Caitlin's teacher stood in front of her, sporting a button-down shirt, khaki pants, and a navy-blue overcoat with a leather satchel hanging across his body. He looked like a version of Clark Kent without the glasses; ready to turn into Superman and save the world.

"Mr. Medina?"

"Still so formal?" Richard's shoulders dropped, and the smile disappeared from his face. He seemed to deflate.

Stella reached for him and shook her head. "I'm sorry. Old habits are hard to break. Richard, isn't it? Is everything all right?" She opened the door and looked into the house behind her. "Do you need Caitlin for something?"

"No, actually. I'm here for you."

Stella looked behind her again, trying to get her brain to engage. It shouldn't matter if anyone saw them talking; he was her daughter's teacher, after all. Still, her internal alarm blared: Proceed with caution!

She stepped back into the house and gestured for him to come inside. "Please come in." She had more control inside the house than out in public. She wiped her hands on her jeans to get rid of the perspiration forming in her palms. "Can I get you something to drink?" She walked into the kitchen as she spoke and pointed for him to take a seat at the breakfast bar.

"I'd love some water, thank you." He rummaged in his satchel while she got them both ice water. "I apologize for coming by unannounced, but you didn't give me your number."

"I remember. I think this is why." Stella laughed. "But I'm glad you tracked me down."

She handed him the water and sat beside him at the bar. "What brings you here today?"

"I have something of yours." He held up the Cartier sunglasses Fiona had absconded with at the carnival last weekend. "I'm told these belong to you?"

"Not me," said Stella. Richard tilted his head, a look of confusion on his face. "I mean, I don't own them, but I am responsible for them."

"You really do have a way with words."

"Sorry, I'm not normally this tongue-tied. I'll take those. Thank you." She took the glasses and set them on the counter. "Last I saw these, Fiona declared me unworthy of owning anything this fine."

"I confess she gave me your address. She said you needed these immediately, but she couldn't make the trip today. I volunteered to bring them instead." Stella couldn't decide whether she wanted to strangle Fiona or kiss her for delivering this man to her doorstep.

"I think we've been set up." Stella felt heat rise in her cheeks. "This wasn't an emergency."

"Well, she insisted, and I was happy to help." Richard took a sip of water and relaxed into his chair. Stella fidgeted with the expensive glasses, averting her eyes from his. *What's he doing here?* She didn't know if the question came from her overly cautious nature, or from the nervous energy running through her.

"I'm fairly certain Fiona wanted to keep these for herself. She really doesn't love my fashion sense." Stella looked down at herself, dressed in what Fiona called her uniform: jeans and a black turtleneck. "No idea why."

"I think they suit you perfectly. Sometimes the smallest detail can really make a statement." He picked up the glasses and opened them, motioning to Stella. "May I?"

Stella nodded. Her breath hitched as he leaned forward and carefully placed the glasses on her face. "Every beautiful woman deserves the perfect adornment." He locked eyes with her, his face inches away. "Stunning."

Stella blinked several times rapidly, trying to break the spell he cast over her. She needed to gain control of this conversation. She pushed the glasses to the top of her head. "You seem to know a lot about fashion. I don't know a lot of men who talk about accessories. At least outside of my photo shoots." She fished for any reason to dismiss the stunning man next to her. *Please be gay.*

"I come from a family where appearances matter," said Richard. "Although I left that life behind, some lessons are hard to unlearn. My mother was always more interested in what someone was wearing than what good they did in the world."

Not gay. "Damn," Stella mumbled.

"Pardon me?"

Stella let his question drop. "Is that why you wear these?" Stella reached out and took his wrist in her hands, turning it to show off the blue mother-of-pearl and gold cufflinks at the end of his shirt sleeves. She saw the name Turnbull and Asser stamped on the side. "You wore them to the carnival."

Richard nodded. "Very observant of you. I guess I haven't quite given up every aspect of my misspent youth."

"Heirloom quality cufflinks seem like something worth holding onto."

"My thoughts exactly," said Richard.

Stella released his hand but let her gaze linger. "We make a good team," Richard said. "We both recognize something valuable when we see it."

Stella took a sip of her water, putting some physical distance between them. She racked her brain to say something witty or charming but came up blank. She hadn't flirted in over a decade; she didn't know what to say or do.

The sound of the garage door opening interrupted them. Stella hadn't realized her mother had left but silently thanked her for rescuing her.

Caitlin must have heard the door, too. She emerged from her bedroom and bounded down the stairs, stopping short when she saw her teacher sitting at the breakfast bar with her mom. "Mr. Medina?" She looked at her mother. "Am I in trouble?"

"Not possible," Richard reassured her. "You're one of the best students in the class." Stella watched her daughter's face light up. "I simply stopped by as a favor for Mrs. Adams. I needed to deliver something to your mother on her behalf." Caitlin made a face at this. Apparently, Fiona's schemes didn't even pass muster with the fourth-grader.

"Gram's got groceries. I'm helping her unload." Caitlin headed to the garage to help bring in the bags, and Richard took it as his cue to leave.

"I'd best be going." Richard rose and slung his satchel back over his shoulder, heading for the door.

"Thank you for dropping these off," said Stella, tapping the sunglasses still perched on her head. "I appreciate it." She moved to open the front door, but Richard touched her arm.

"I'm glad Fiona sent me here today, whether or not it was an emergency." Richard dug in his satchel and pulled out a pad of Post-it notes and a pen.

"I've never met anyone quite like you, Stella Meyers." Stella felt her knees go weak. "I respect your privacy, but I also can't walk away knowing you have no way to reach me." He scribbled on the Post-it note. "Here is my number. Use it anytime." He stuck the note on her sweater, leaned in, and whispered in her ear. "For any reason."

Stella watched him get in his car, her hand covering the number he'd placed just above her heart. Only after his car disappeared did she close the door and lean against it, briefly shutting her eyes. *Thank you, Fiona!* She slipped the note into her pocket for safekeeping.

As her mother and Caitlin unloaded the groceries, they both peppered her with questions about the visit. "Caitlin says her teacher was here?" Rita smiled at her as she asked.

An image of Fiona texting Rita about her plan flashed through Stella's mind.

"You knew he was coming, didn't you?"

"Gram." Caitlin gasped. "Is that why you wanted me to go with you? To leave them alone?"

"I don't know what you're talking about. Here I am trying to make sure this family has enough food to eat, and you accuse me of scheming against you." They worked as a team in the kitchen, getting everything put away in short order. "But since you mentioned it, did you give him your number?" Rita asked.

"I did not." Rita sighed at the same time Caitlin groaned. "I barely know the man." Stella looked to Caitlin for backup. "Besides, you don't want some strange man taking me out on the town, do you?"

"He's not a strange man; he's my teacher. And he's a hottie!" Caitlin folded and put away the grocery bags. "Have you ever even been on a date?"

"Of course I've been on dates. How do you think I got you?" They didn't talk about Caitlin's father, but she knew the essentials. Stella had enough secrets, she didn't need to keep that from her daughter as well.

"I'm ten now, Mom. That was literally a lifetime ago."

Rita raised her eyebrows and nodded. Apparently, she agreed with her granddaughter. "It really is time, Stella. Caitlin and I are all grown up and ready for you to do something for yourself. Aren't we?" Caitlin rapidly nodded her agreement.

"And you think I need a man?"

"We think it's okay for you to let loose a little and at least give yourself a chance at love."

"Love? We just met."

"You'll never find love if you're not even willing to talk to a man," teased Rita. "I think it's time you took a risk, don't you?"

Her mother normally preached caution, trying without success to get Stella to stop taking the risks she did in life. But stealing felt safer than opening her life to someone new.

Stella turned to Caitlin. "You really wouldn't mind if I talked to him?"

"Not at all. If I were old, I'd talk to him."

"Thanks for the vote of confidence," teased Stella. "I'll consider it. Now what's for dinner?"

Rita opened the fridge and stared at the items they had just put away. "Actually, I don't know. I didn't have a list ready when I left, so I only bought the staples. I think it's a DoorDash night."

"Did you just run out of the house the second Fiona texted you?"

"Pretty much." Rita laughed. "And my plan would have been perfect if I could have convinced Miss Thing here to join me."

As they got their dinner delivered and enjoyed their evening together, Stella couldn't shake Richard from her thoughts. She'd never had the desire to let a man into her life. In her experience, they weren't worth the effort.

But this man? She couldn't deny how handsome he was. And he'd hinted the attraction was mutual. Maybe she could jump through a hoop or two. She'd let Fiona come into their lives and kept everything in order. Fiona had no idea what she did for a living, yet they were inseparable. If she applied the same rules to Richard as she did to her best friend, it might be possible to let someone new into her life. Eventually.

Before she went to bed, Stella texted Fiona to give her a piece of her mind.

> Stella: I cannot believe you're all conspiring against me. Getting my mom in on the ruse? And she tried to recruit Caitlin!

She didn't have to wait long for her reply.

> Fiona: Whatever are you talking about? I am completely innocent. 😇

Stella clicked the exclamation mark on her reply.

> Stella: Innocent my ass! At least I got my sunglasses back, bitch.

Fiona sent back a GIF of Matthew Perry giving the thumbs up saying, "Totally worth it!"

Laughing, Stella hopped in bed and opened her laptop. She was leaning toward sending a text to Richard, but she wanted more information about him. She ran his name through a search engine, which hit on the announcement at Northbrook about him stepping in to replace Ms. Beaker after her accident. There were a few other hits on the name, several of them in Spain, where she learned he was from. She was surprised to learn he was forty-three years old. *Man's aging well.* He looked younger in person.

She spent an hour going through social media platforms and saw he had a private Facebook account, as well as a public Instagram profile. There were enough photos on IG to confirm she had the right account, but he mostly liked to post pictures of food, wine, and even what books he liked to read. Basically every 40+ year old's idea of social media, but no real red flags stood out to her. He seemed to be a normal guy.

Her mom teased her about not taking risks, but Stella had too much to lose to let a stranger into their lives. In an abundance of caution, Stella created a fake profile for herself on three of the most popular dating apps and searched them for any sign of him. If he was using a fake profile as well, she'd never find him. But his name didn't come up on any of them, and typing in his general description, things he appeared to like from his IG posts, and even searching for international men living nearby didn't yield any results resembling him.

As she closed her laptop, she realized she was out of excuses. She grabbed the Post-it note from her nightstand and stared at his number. "Take a leap, Meyers," she said to the empty room.

Stella typed Richard Medina's contact information into her phone and sent him a text.

> Stella: Thank you for bringing me the glasses today.

Since it was nearly midnight, she didn't expect a reply, but he responded before she had time to close the app.

Richard: Stella Meyers, I presume?

Stella: That's right. How many women did you deliver sunglasses to today?

Richard: It was a long list. Your friend Fiona really gets around.

Stella: Then how did you know it was me?

She laughed at herself; she was having fun.

Richard: I delivered glasses all afternoon. But I only gave one woman my phone number.

Stella clicked the laughing emoji as a reply.

Richard: Thank you for trusting me with yours.

Stella: I already regret it. Go easy on me.

He clicked the same laughing emoji to her note and replied with a single word.

Richard: Never.

4

Stella wound her way through the tight spaces between tables and waved when she caught Max's eye. He always arrived first to check a place out before entering, even if it was only for a lunch date with friends. Max kept his life small, intentionally cautious about everything he did, and taught Stella to do the same. She scanned the tables as she passed them to ensure she didn't know anyone.

He stood and hugged her as she arrived. "I'm glad you wanted to meet here today. We haven't been here in a while." She picked up the menu and pretended to look at the specials, though they both knew what she would order. Max signaled for the waiter.

"I will have the Grilled Chicken Breast Paillard," said Max. He paused and glanced at Stella, who nodded, laughing. "And she will have the Seafood Risotto."

They handed the menus back to the waiter, then Max added, "And bring us a bottle of the Ruffino Chianti, please. 2020." He nodded and left them alone.

"I don't order that anywhere but here. Nonna Vita's means Seafood Risotto. Always has."

Max had taken Stella here the first time they met eleven years ago. She'd ordered the dish because it was expensive, and she'd wanted to get back at the wealthy British man who'd caught her lifting a wallet at The Met and made her return it.

Max had spent the entire lunch trying to dissuade her from continuing on the road she was on, but Stella wouldn't listen. She'd had no job, no money, and a baby on the way. She was desperate. She was also pissed off at the world, and in her mind, stealing from the same social circles as the asshole who had dumped her once he found out she was pregnant balanced the scales a tiny bit.

That lunch had sparked a friendship that would tie them together for the rest of their lives. Max became her mentor and taught her everything he knew, helping her minimize risks and come home safe after every job. In time he filled the void her father's death had created, and Stella, Caitlin, and Rita became the family Max never had.

The waiter served their wine. Stella raised her glass for a toast. "We're celebrating today, aren't we?" she asked.

"Indeed. We both had an extraordinary day. Cheers to us."

"To us." Stella tapped her glass to his. The largest payout from the Degas heist finally hit her account this morning, after months of waiting for it to be cleaned. She'd created several fake photoshoots to help explain the inflated balance in her account, and Max had left considerable percentages of it out of their direct control until even more time had passed.

Getting caught wasn't an option.

The waiter returned with their food and placed Stella's favorite basket of bread on the table, leaving them to eat in peace.

"We've had a good run lately," Stella said, giving Max an opening.

The Degas heist had brought her professional life to a new level. She knew she was ready for the big leagues now. All she could hope was that Max had lined up another job that would both challenge her and allow her to show off her skills. She also wanted to tell him about her own target list. Stella was at the top of her game, and she was ready to take on the world.

"We certainly have," said Max. "I think it's safe to say Caitlin's college funds are secure, as well as anything else you could want for the rest of your life."

Stella sipped her wine, letting the statement sit for a moment. It wasn't what she had expected him to say.

"If I live modestly," she admitted. "But I'm not sure I want to live modestly. At least, not forever." She swirled the Chianti in her glass, breathing in its aroma before indulging in another sip.

Max shook his head at her. "Pretend all you like, but you're already uncomfortable with the opulence of Caitlin's school and the community in which you live."

Stella set down her glass and tilted her head at him. "What's on your mind? Why did you bring me here, really?"

"To celebrate. I was honest about that." Max touched his napkin to either side of his mouth, then set it in his lap. "It truly has been an extraordinary year for you, Stella. You must admit you've achieved a level of success virtually unheard of in our world. By all measures, you are the best at what you do. And your net worth is more than enough to keep you and Caitlin comfortable for life."

Stella locked eyes with his and lowered her voice, barely audible above the crowded restaurant. "This stopped being about accumulating wealth a long time ago."

"I understand that. Better than anyone."

"Then why are you talking about money?" She leaned back in her chair, considering him for a moment. "Why do I get the feeling you're not here to offer me a new job?"

"You're mistaken. That's precisely why we're here. I'd like you to give this your full consideration."

Stella shifted in her seat, fully engaged now. "What is it? Something like the last one?" A wave of adrenaline rose within her. She loved the chase more than the payoff, and hearing about a new prospect was the ultimate high. "I've been working on some prospects, too. I want to learn that side of the business." She shook her head, trying to slow herself down. "You go first. What's on your radar?"

"A job seemingly written for you." Stella nodded for him to

continue. "This opportunity will take every ounce of your skills, your planning and preparation, and your unique ability to improvise and gut your way through it, if necessary."

"Sounds exciting." She smiled, hardly able to sit still at the thought of being back in the game.

"It certainly should be. The way you handled yourself at our last outing showed you're ready for this." He sipped his wine again, letting the compliment break her defenses. "I'd like for you to be able to put those same skills to use every day, with a generous bump to your bank account that you can actually spend rather than squirrel away from Uncle Sam."

Stella shook her head, confused. "Wait, what are you talking about?" She leaned in closer, making sure she heard him correctly. "A legit job?" Max didn't respond.

She dumped her napkin on her plate. Within a moment, someone appeared at her left elbow and cleared the table, then asked if they'd like dessert. Stella shook her head. "I'll take an espresso, and he'll have a decaf cappuccino." Stella waited for the man to leave before she asked Max to clarify. "What the hell are you talking about?"

"I'm talking about an opportunity as unique as the one you took last spring. Something to push your limits, keep your mind and body sharp, and allow you to put your skills to good use," said Max. "And yes, it's legitimate."

"You don't want me to go work for the feds, do you?" she whispered.

"Certainly not." Max shook his head, but Stella knew she was close.

"Then what? More importantly, why? A nine-to-five job is the last thing I want right now."

"Because it's time." He reached for her hand and squeezed it. "It's time to stop taking these risks. I can't bear the thought of you ending up like your father."

She winced and withdrew her hand from his. "I am not my father," she said through gritted teeth. "Not even close."

"No, you're not. Not yet," he said. "But there is a point where your number comes up. You should understand that better than anyone. Expressly because of how things ended for your father."

"He did it to himself. He broke his own rules; I would never do that."

"And yet you drove into one of the most protected communities in the world—in broad daylight—to get your prize. You think that was a good decision?"

"It worked." Stella shot back. "The bank balance speaks for itself."

"Sometimes bad decisions have good outcomes." Stella flinched at Max's words. "You know as well as I do you were inside too long. They knew the cameras were off and approached you. It's a miracle you weren't apprehended."

"I'm the miracle."

Max didn't take the bait. "One slip and I would be taking Caitlin to visit you in prison today instead of sitting in our favorite restaurant." He leaned in and whispered the rest to her. "Or worse, visiting your grave."

She stared at him; her face flushing as the humiliation of her mistake hit her. She fought against the shame and turned it into fury. He was punishing her for being good at her job. "This is ridiculous. I'm fine. Why are we even having this conversation?"

"Because you scared me." He banged his finger on the table, enunciating every word. He took a deep breath and gathered his emotions before continuing. "I have always felt responsible for you and Caitlin. I know I brought you into this world, even when it was my sole intention to dissuade you from the path you seemed intent on when we met."

"You didn't—"

He raised his hand to interrupt her. "Don't fool yourself. I take responsibility for what has become of you. Sometimes that gives me tremendous pride. Other times, it scares me to death. Watching you take these risks—even when the gamble works—unsettles me. Deeply." He leaned back to make room for the approaching server to put his cappuccino in front of him.

When the waiter walked away, Stella pounced. "I don't like being doubted. Coming from anyone else, I'd walk out of this restaurant and never look back."

"I'm doubting fate. Not you," Max clarified. "Technology is changing faster than we can keep up with. Everything we're saying could be being recorded by our phones right now. There are cameras everywhere. At some point, that's going to catch up with us." He leaned in and assured her, "I don't want you to stop being who you are. In fact, what I have in mind requires your skills. It would allow you to keep your senses sharp without putting your life on the line. You should earnestly consider it." He sipped his cappuccino, letting her process what he'd said.

Stella took a deep breath and held it for several seconds, then released it slowly. She followed strict rules and controlled every aspect of her life to keep her family safe. She prepared for every possibility, and when things did go wrong, no one was better at thinking on their feet and getting out of a sticky situation than Stella. All the pieces of her life were in perfect sync. The Hayes job proved it. She was ready for the next challenge, not to retire.

She closed her eyes and shook her head, trying to remember how much Max loved her. He always had her best interest in mind, even if he still treated her with kid gloves. "Out of respect for you, I'm listening." Max smiled and reached into his breast pocket to pull out a plastic card, sliding it across the table to her. It was solid black with no writing or markings on it. She turned it over in her hands a few times. "What's this?"

"An invitation to meet with Marcus Williams, owner of Onyx Intelligence Group."

Stella looked at the card some more, not sure what to think. "This is blank."

"Touch it to your phone as you would a payment."

Stella pulled out her phone and unlocked it, then tapped the card to her screen. The phone beeped, and a contact flashed on the screen before a website opened.

Stella lifted the phone and read the information aloud. "Onyx

Intelligence Group. Your last defense against the unknown." Stella tapped around the website and found it lacking. Someone with so little information on their website probably didn't need to advertise their services. She wondered why they had it in the first place.

"You know this guy?" she asked.

"Quite well."

"Has he done jobs for you?"

"I can't say," said Max.

"I'm not the only one who's good at keeping secrets."

"You learned from the best," Max agreed. "We worked together in the past. Marcus's skills are invaluable in our world. And he has access to information almost no one has."

"Why does he need me?" Stella tried to put the pieces of the puzzle together. Did he want her to do a job for him, with information he gives her? Except Max said it was a legitimate job. She shook her head. "Do you know what the job is?"

"I know he was looking for someone with a particular set of skills, and I thought of you. I also know this would be a company position. Lucrative salary, 401(k), health benefits—everything on the up-and-up. I can hazard a guess as to what he would want you to do, but it's not my place to say. If you're interested, he's expecting your call." Stella raised her eyebrows at him. "It goes without saying he doesn't even know your name. You'll have to use my name to schedule the meeting."

Stella trusted him implicitly. She also knew he had a lifetime in this business before she came along and had participated in jobs she might never learn about. If he believed she should talk to this man, she should at least consider it. "I'll think about it."

"That's all I ask," said Max.

Stella heard her phone's text ping and she glanced at the screen. She was half hoping it was a message from Richard, but no such luck. It was from a number she didn't know, and the message didn't even make sense.

Unknown: I have an opportunity for you.

A link was attached. She swiped it to delete and report it as junk.

"Anything of interest?" asked Max. He cocked an eyebrow at her and smiled.

"Spam," said Stella. "What's the grin for? What have you heard?" Stella put the phone back in her bag to finish her espresso.

"I hear there's a new man in your life." Max looked genuinely happy for her; his eyes gleamed with it.

Stella denied it. "I don't have room in my life for a man. Talk about taking risks."

"You could make room for a relationship. You have an opportunity to imagine a different life for yourself. One where you're truly safe."

"I don't want to give this up. I get to do a job I'm damn good at that makes me feel alive. That's worth more than all the money on the planet. And damn straight more than a 401(k)."

"Please tell me you'll think about it."

Stella couldn't hide her disappointment. "This isn't the lunch I wanted to have." She finished her espresso and relished the clarity the caffeine brought her brain. "I didn't even get to tell you about the research I did. I found a pretty good prospect on my own."

"I'm not surprised. You're more than capable of running that end of the business. I will always help you if you decide to continue. But please give this some serious thought. Have one conversation with the man. My gut tells me the time is right."

"My gut says the opposite."

"Don't mistake stubbornness for intuition. Clear your mind and set aside your ego, then meet with the man. You'll know what to do only when you have all the information."

She nodded. "I'll consider it. It's the best I can do." Stella stood and gathered her things, then leaned over and kissed him goodbye on the cheek. "Thank you for lunch." Stella waved and walked away, letting Max settle the bill. He'd thrown her for a loop today, and the price was the cost of their lunch.

As she walked out of the restaurant and wrestled her coat on,

Stella's phone beeped again. She glanced at her watch and saw a message from Richard. A smile spread across her face.

Maybe fate was stepping in. Two weeks ago, she was photographing a school carnival and wondering about her next heist. Now she was getting texts from Caitlin's teacher and grinning like a schoolgirl. Maybe she could let someone new into her life. Without giving up her job; her identity.

She had everything under control, no matter what Max thought.

5

S tella stared at the screensaver on her laptop, lost in thought. She'd hoped to dig deeper into Gerald Martin's life before logging off for the night, but she kept getting distracted. The black card Max had given her sat on her desk, calling to her like a siren song.

She'd promised Max she'd consider his proposition, but in the week since their lunch, she'd actively avoided thinking about it. Every time her mind drifted back to their conversation, she drowned it out. She played music, sought out Caitlin or Fiona to distract her, or quieted her mind with long runs and yoga sessions. She was being childish and stubborn, behaving like a petulant teenager, but she couldn't help feeling insulted by Max's offer. Why would she quit when she was at the top of her game?

"Fuck it," she mumbled to herself. "Let's get this over with." She reached for the card, shaking her head at the inanimate object. She woke up her laptop and fired up Google. It was time to research Marcus Williams, owner of Onyx Intelligence Group.

Within ten minutes, Stella's mood switched from detached, to curious, to fully engaged. She didn't like anyone getting the best of her, but Marcus was an elusive target. She expected him to be cautious about his identity, but this was next level. He owned a successful business, so surely, there had to be some information about him online? Standard searches showed almost no trace of the man, and searching for his company didn't go any better.

Up for the challenge, Stella decided to come at Marcus from a different angle. She searched for personal and corporate tax records, city leasing agreements, and state and federal court documents, pulling any name associated with Onyx Intelligence Group or Marcus Williams. She lost herself in the work, going down every rabbit hole she could find.

Stella's tenacity paid off. A picture of Marcus took shape among the scraps of information she pieced together. Her phone beeped the now familiar popcorn alert and pulled her from her research. It was Richard's dedicated text tone.

> Richard: Up for a chat?

She looked at the information she'd found. She'd learned Marcus was in his late thirties, had served in Afghanistan, and had a degree in Computer Science. She had some photos of him with some friends while they were deployed and learned his wife and daughter had been killed in a car accident when his little girl was a toddler.

It was a start.

> Stella: Almost. Finishing up some work. Give me ten minutes.

They'd graduated from texting to talking on the phone every night this week, getting to know each other better. Stella felt comfortable with the budding relationship; they were taking it slow. He only knew what she was willing to share, and despite taking her breath away whenever she saw his face on the screen, she maintained her control. Stella poured herself a glass of wine and FaceTimed Richard from her bedroom, ready to take her mind off Marcus Williams.

"Hope I didn't interrupt you. What were you working on?"

"Just researching some potential clients. Believe me, I'd much rather talk to you." Stella loved how easy it was to tell the truth without revealing who she really was. "How was your day? Did the kids drive you crazy?"

"Nothing I can't handle. They're a good bunch." Caitlin loved having him as a teacher. Stella suspected his charm went a long way to keep the kids in line.

"Did you always want to be a teacher?"

"No. When I was young, I wanted to rule empires, just like my father—at least that's what I thought he did."

"Not a king, then?"

"King of the financial world, maybe." Richard took a sip of wine, and Stella let the pause linger. They hadn't talked about their childhoods yet, and she was in no hurry to rush this conversation.

"I remember one time, when I was quite young—four or five at most—my parents were attending some fashionable event, and I snuck out of bed after the nanny had put me down and broke into my father's office. He must have left the door unlocked. I don't remember knowing how to pick the lock then."

"But you learned later?" Stella asked.

"Everyone should know how to pick a lock. But back then I was only an amateur criminal."

Stella held her smile in place and nodded, careful not to react to his turn of phrase. "So, you ditched the nanny and were in his sacred space. What was it like?"

"His office was grand to my young eyes. The desk backed up to a wall of windows overlooking our estate. The walls were floor to ceiling books, with one of those rolling ladders to help you get to the top shelf. I loved climbing that."

"Sounds like heaven."

"It really was. And across from his desk was a fireplace. He loved looking into the fire when he took calls. As soon as the temperature allowed, he'd order it be lit anytime he was home."

"What a beautiful place to work."

"I eventually realized I liked his office more than his work." Richard laughed at the thought. "But that night, all I wanted was to be him. I pulled some books off the shelves and stacked them in his chair so I could see over his massive desk. I picked up his phone and chatted away to no one, even opened several of his files and drew on some of them, trying to sign documents just like he did."

"I bet you were the perfect forger."

"In my mind it looked exactly like his. Of course, I couldn't read yet, much less write."

"I can see you sitting up there, taking calls and ordering people around as you signed contracts," said Stella. "Sounds adorable."

"He didn't see that way." Richard dropped his eyes and swirled the wine in his glass. "I fell asleep at the desk and woke to the sound of him yelling loud enough to raise the dead. He made more of a mess in the office than I did, tossing everything around while he screamed, waking up the whole house. He wanted to murder me."

"That must have been terrifying."

"Hard for me, but worse for the nanny. He fired her on the spot. I rather liked that one."

"Probably because you could sneak out so easily with her." Stella smirked.

"Maybe so," said Richard. "But I stopped idolizing him after that. I didn't want any part of what went on in that office."

"What's your relationship with him like now? If you don't mind my asking." Stella wondered if they'd patched things up. He didn't work in the family business, but she hoped they were proud of the man he'd become.

"We were never close. I attended boarding schools and university, and visited on breaks, but he only cared about his work. I think once he realized I wasn't going to follow in his footsteps, he dismissed me. He had a heart attack at that very desk three years ago."

"I'm so sorry. And your mother? Is she still alive?" Richard nodded, and Stella pressed for more. "Are you close with her?"

"Not really. She stepped into his shoes and took over his companies. Turns out, she was more of a cutthroat business mogul than he was." Stella couldn't understand a mother not wanting to be close to her child, even as an adult. "What about you? Caitlin adores her grandmother. Are you as close as it seems?"

She took a sip of her wine and thought about how she wanted to steer this discussion. They were crossing a line. Richard wanted to know more about her, but letting him in exposed her. She forced her voice to remain steady. "Now we are."

"Not an idyllic childhood then?" he surmised.

"We were an unconventional family." She smiled at the memories that played across her mind. Her parents adored her, and Stella loved being the center of their universe. "We didn't have any real money, but there was a lot of love in our house. And a lot of fun."

"That sounds idyllic to me."

"It really was until I was ten. Then it all fell apart."

"What happened?" Richard tilted his head, a look of genuine concern in his eyes.

She paused, lecturing herself to slow down and not say too much. She chose her words carefully. "That's when my father died."

Richard set down his drink. "Oh, Stella, lo siento. I'm so sorry. That's terribly young to lose a parent. May I ask how he died?"

She took a deep breath and settled into her body. She had to say something, and it needed to be close to the truth. This was a matter of public record, keeping it from him wouldn't serve any purpose. "He was killed by the police when he was attempting to rob a bank. During the raid, one man was injured, two more escaped, but the police killed my father."

Richard's eyes widened. "That must have been quite a shock for you and your mother."

"It was the turning point in our lives." She let her eyes drift offscreen, seeing it all play out in front of her again. Waking up to the sounds of her mother's screams, everyone in town learning what he'd done. He broke his own code that night, and Stella and her mother paid the price.

"I always wanted to know what the hell he'd been thinking."

"He probably wanted to give you a better life."

Stella's heart swelled that Richard would come to her father's defense.

"I'm sorry to pry. You don't have to talk about it now."

"Actually, it's nice to finally talk about him. There was so much shame around how he died, I forget how great it was when he was alive."

Stella shook her head a bit, almost in disbelief at what she was saying. "I've never told anyone outside family what happened. You're a curveball in my life. I'm not quite sure what to make of you."

"The feeling is mutual, believe me." And she did believe him. Whatever was happening to her, it seemed to be happening to him, as well.

Stella tapped the screen on her phone so she could see the time. It was after midnight. "We'd better go to bed."

"Now that's a tragedy," Richard said. "Us going to bed in separate places." Stella's eyes widened a bit, but she didn't disagree. "Speaking of which, can we do this in person sometime soon?"

Stella feigned ignorance of what he was asking. "You mean a date? Are you asking your student's mother on a date, Mr. Medina?"

"I am asking a beautiful, brilliant woman on a date, Ms. Meyers. But if I have to quit to go on a date with you, I'll resign tomorrow. Just say the word."

"No, no." Stella held up her hand in protest. "Caitlin would kill me if you left."

"Then how about throwing the rules out the window and going out with me?"

"What are you thinking?"

"Let's make the first date something unconventional. We can even do something the gaggle of gossips at the PTA would approve of."

"Now I'm intrigued."

"Let me make the arrangements and get back to you. For now, clear your calendar for Saturday. Would that be okay?"

"I'll have to run it by Caitlin," Stella said. "I won't do anything she's uncomfortable with." *No matter how I feel about you*, she added to herself.

"I wouldn't want it any other way," he agreed.

Stella raised her wineglass and toasted him. "Thank you for a wonderful evening." Stella clicked off the call and downed her last sip of wine. She set the glass on the bedside table and fell back onto her pillows. Then she picked the phone back up to text Fiona.

> Stella: You're never going to believe this, but Richard and I are going on a date!!! 😊 🤍

Her phone beeped immediately. She could almost hear Fiona screaming from her house.

> Fiona: NO FUCKING WAY!!!
>
> Where are you going?
>
> When?
>
> What are you going to wear?
>
> I want to know EVERYTHING!!!!"

Fiona never texted more than a few words at a time. Stella complained about it, so now Fiona did it intentionally to bug her.

> Stella: Give me a second to respond, will you?
>
> Fiona: I'm waiting as patiently as I possibly can. Type faster!
>
> Stella: No destination yet. He said he wanted it to be unconventional. I still need to ask Caitlin about it. I don't know what she's going to say.
>
> Fiona: She's going to say she wants you to be happy. No question about it.

Stella reacted by clicking a heart on the message.

Fiona: I want to know everything the second it happens. Don't you dare leave out one detail!

Stella: Will do.

Fiona: I'm the one who brought you two together, you know. You can name your first child after me!

That got a laugh out of Stella.

Stella: Let's see how the unconventional date goes first, ok?

Fiona sent a GIF of a man and woman in bed together, the man stroking the woman's hair and kissing her forehead. Stella had to admit they looked a lot like her and Richard. How did she find these things?

She replied with a GIF of a man in bed with a Saint Bernard kissing him and slobbering on him.

Stella: This seems more like it.

She put her phone in sleep mode and plugged it into the charger. She would deal with Fiona tomorrow.

Stella stared at the ceiling, wide awake. She'd never seriously considered dating someone since Caitlin was born. Fear lurked in her mind, demanding she proceed with caution.

But happiness filled her heart, giving her permission to be excited. Richard Medina checked all the boxes. If she could keep her private life locked down, she might be able to make room to have a little fun with the gorgeous substitute.

6

t's not a real date. It's just an outing. Stella talked to herself as she paced in her closet, looking for clothes appropriate for an "adventure." She picked up the phone and texted him, trying for the last time to get an idea of where they might be going.

> Stella: Any hints? I don't know what to wear.

It took a minute for him to respond. Finally, her phone dinged, and Stella grabbed it.

> Unknown: We'd make a great team.

> Stella: Doesn't answer my question.

The popcorn noise—Richard's personal signal—sounded and she realized her mistake. She looked back at it and saw she'd replied to a phishing text. She quickly deleted it, then read his note.

> Richard: I recommend something tight-fitting but warm.

She hit the question mark reply on his note.

Stella: Tight-fitting?

Richard: Only for your comfort. Trust me. Put on the sherpa leggings all the mothers around here wear and your uniform turtleneck. You'll be fine.

Stella: I'm guessing we'll be outside?

Richard: You could say that.

She threw down the phone and grabbed her faux sheep-lined leggings, a little upset he knew she'd have a pair in her closet. Maybe she wasn't as different as the Northbrook moms as she pretended to be. She checked the weather on her phone and saw it was going to be sunny with a high of sixty-three degrees today. She thought the leggings were going to be overkill, but she tried to trust him.

She grabbed a bag and threw in an assortment of gloves—fleece gloves, down mittens, and a pair of ski gloves—two hats, a fleece headband, her balaclava, and smart wool socks. Finally, she tossed a large flannel shirt into the bag she could use as a light jacket, if needed. She could survive whatever he had planned.

Stella went downstairs when the doorbell rang. 8:00 a.m. Right on time. She smiled and opened the door to find Richard standing on her porch, greeting her with a cup of coffee in hand.

"Good morning," he said. "This is for trusting me with your Saturday."

"It's looking good so far." Stella laughed, accepting the coffee and taking a sip. Her whole body seemed to relax into the drink when the dark roast hit her system. She turned and waved goodbye to her mother. "Be home . . . later?" She turned to Richard and let him answer.

"It'll be the end of the day," he said. "We have a bit of traveling to do."

"Tell Caitlin I said goodbye when she wakes up, please."

Her mother nodded and let them get on their way.

Richard was correct about traveling to reach their destination.

They passed the time raging about politics, worrying about what the future looked like for Caitlin and her classmates, as well as sharing their favorite books, what music they enjoyed, and the places they most wanted to travel. She tried not to read too much into it, but her relaxed demeanor and calm mind showed her she was having a good time, whether she wanted to admit it or not.

After almost two hours in the car, Richard took a turn off the beaten path and brought her to a small airport in the middle of nowhere. She looked around a bit and saw a few outbuildings, a huge field with an inch or two of snow accumulation leftover from the first dump of the season, and not much else.

"Is this it?" she asked. "Or do you need a pit stop?"

"This is it. Welcome to Ellington Airport." As he said it, the drone of a turbine engine sounded nearby. She leaned over to look out the front windshield to see a small twin-engine airplane coming in for a landing, not 100 yards from their car. She shook her head, trying to make sense of what she was seeing, still not sure what they were doing here. Then she spied a group of people walking out to meet the airplane as it landed. Instead of passengers carrying luggage, she saw a group of people covered head to toe in gear—helmets on their heads or in their hands, and colorful packs on their backs. It could only mean one thing.

"We're going skydiving?" she asked, unable to wipe the smile from her face.

"I promised an adventure. Have you ever been?"

"No." Stella shook her head in disbelief. "This is perfect."

They gathered their things from the car, deciding to bring her entire bag of extra clothes so they could help her pick out the best things to stay warm. Although the temperatures were mild, it wasn't as bad as it could have been for a Saturday in November.

Richard explained what to expect as they walked to the main building. "We're doing tandem jumps today—where you're strapped to an instructor. They don't normally do them in the winter, but I called, and they were happy to make sure two of their instructors could come today."

They headed toward a building with a sign that read: *Connecticut Parachutists, Inc. Since 1962*. Once inside, Stella and Richard were greeted by a lovely woman named Jan, who ran the front office for the club. She had them fill out a bunch of paperwork, essentially saying this was a dangerous sport and they could die participating in it.

"Life is short," said Stella. "Let's have some fun."

They signed the paperwork everywhere Jan asked them to, and initialed their lives away, or so it seemed. She also took down their weight and gave them a brief overview of how the next hour or so would go. Finally, they watched an introductory video about jumping, again noting it was a risky sport. The video might have been trying to intimidate them, but Stella could see the smiles on the jumpers' faces and hear how excited students were after they landed. Rather than feeling intimidated, she felt increasingly excited.

After they finished checking in, Jan escorted Stella and Richard to a classroom for them to meet their instructors. "You're the only students we have today, so there's no waiting," she explained. "In the summers we're packed, and this entire center is buzzing with students in various stages of training, but this time of year, it's mostly fun jumpers out having a good time."

Jan introduced them to their instructors, Mo and Chris. Mo would take Stella. She had over 1,500 jumps, was a tandem master and an AFF instructor, and loved to shoot video. Stella saw a tattoo of a parachute on her wrist when it peeked out from under her shirt sleeve. She loved her already.

Chris would be Richard's instructor. He was about Stella's height and looked not much older than Caitlin. He smiled and shook their hands, and assured them both he was old enough to do this. Jan teased him when she introduced him, filling them in on his background since he was too humble to share. He had 3,500 jumps, was an AFF instructor and tandem master, and was also a pilot and the manager of the Drop Zone.

"He might look younger than any of us, but he's the best there is."

Stella knew what it was like to be underestimated because of your looks. She liked Chris immediately.

Chris carried out most of the briefing. They had good weather today, so aside from being cold they would be able to make it all the way to 13,000 feet to do their jump. They would free fall for almost a minute before they would need to open their parachutes around 5,000 feet. Chris and Mo would be there to do most of the work, but Stella and Richard needed to understand the basics in case something went terribly wrong.

After issuing some brief instructions centered on arching their backs as hard as they could during free fall, Stella and Richard put on their jumpsuits and the harnesses they needed to attach themselves to their instructors. Before she headed to the plane, Stella pulled her phone out of her bag and shot a quick text to Caitlin.

> Stella: You're never going to believe this, but he's taking me skydiving! I'll text you when we're finished, but wanted you to know what we're doing. I love you!

She snapped a quick selfie with Richard, Chris, and Mo and quickly hit send, then waited for Cait's reply. All the talk of signing your life away had her wanting to hear from her daughter before their jump.

Cait's replies came in rapid succession, as always.

> Caitlin: Cool
>
> Isn't it too cold? 🫠
>
> Have fun
>
> I'll text Fiona and let her know, too. She's going to be jealous

Finally, she sent the text Stella was waiting for.

> I love you!

Stella hit the heart reply and typed it back to her.

Stella: I love you, too!

Then they were ready to head to the airplane.

They crammed into the small plane with four other people, giving a total of eight passengers on this load. The ride was full of people laughing and having a good time, teasing Stella and Richard about making their first jumps in the middle of winter.

At about 9,000 feet, Mo tapped Stella on her shoulder and pointed to her altimeter; it was time to get ready. Encouragement from the other jumpers helped ease her racing heart—everyone cheered and gave them high fives as Mo and Chris connected their harnesses to Stella and Richard and cinched them tight. Stella felt closer to Mo than she'd ever been to another human with her clothes on.

She watched the experienced jumpers get ready to go first. They threw the door open, filling the plane with freezing cold air. Three of them crawled outside the plane and held onto a bar above the door, all crammed as close as they could be together. Then the fourth person crouched in front of the group and grabbed the chest straps of the person in front of him. They counted together and left the airplane in one clump. Stella burst into a smile watching them disappear.

Then it was her turn. She waddled with Mo along the middle of the plane until they reached the door. She glanced out the door and saw a brilliant blue sky dotted with white clouds beneath them. Her pulse raced as they moved into the doorframe.

Mo shouted in her ear, "Head back," and physically pulled Stella's head against her right shoulder. "Cross your arms." Stella put her hands on her shoulders across her chest. Then Mo counted them off. "One, two, three!"

They leaped from the door and Stella let loose a scream of joy so loud she thought Caitlin could hear her back home.

Stella kept her head back as they fell and watched the airplane flying away from them, hoping to catch Richard and Chris as they jumped, but she lost sight of them. She felt a slight tug and then Mo tapped her on the shoulder, signaling she could relax her head and release her arms; they were stable enough to fly.

Stella's brain raced to process everything as quickly as it could. She noticed she had a bit of tunnel vision, only able to see what was right in front of her. She felt like she could see the entire state of Connecticut. She was so overcome with joy she barely noticed the sound of the wind roaring in her ears, or the cold air biting the exposed parts of her face.

Within a few seconds of falling stably, Stella felt Mo execute a twist and turn them around in the sky. They made one circle in one direction, then stopped and circled back the other direction. By the time they stopped again, Stella could see Richard and Chris flying in front of them. Stella could see a smile plastered on Richard's face, and she knew she looked the same. They waved at each other, and both laughed before the instructors put some space between them.

Stella fell for a few more seconds but then felt the over-whelming urge to check her altimeter. She glanced at the device attached to her chest strap and saw they were at 6,000 feet. Almost to break-off point. Mo spun one more time, then tapped Stella on the shoulders to signal she put her arms back across her chest. As Stella brought her arms into position, she felt Mo pull the ripcord. Her feet kicked out from under her as her body was pulled from a flat to an upright position, the giant parachute overhead now supporting them both.

The world went from loud and windy to quiet and still in an instant. The only sound left was the whipping of a small flap above their heads. Mo unhooked a set of handles from the risers and gave them to Stella, showing her how to use them. She let them twirl around a few times under canopy, spiraling down in either direction to get a feel for how it flew.

Mo pointed out the windsock and the snow-covered gravel pit they were aiming for. As they approached, she instructed Stella to lift her feet.

Mo yelled, "Flare," in Stella's ear, and they pulled down their parachute handles in unison. The parachute tipped up and felt as though it came to a stop, letting them both step onto the ground with no more impact than if they'd stepped off a curb.

"Holy shit. That was amazing," yelled Stella, laughing.

Mo quickly unbuckled her harness and set her free. "Holy shit is right. You did it! Your first jump." She cheered and high-fived her.

Stella could feel the rush of adrenaline in her system, amping up her emotions and sharpening her focus. This was the same way she felt after a job, when she knew she was out of danger and had her prize. She hadn't thought anything else on earth could make her feel that alive.

Stella and Mo stood to the side of the pit while Richard and Chris landed. They landed almost gracefully. She had imagined skydiving to be like bull riding—full of testosterone and beating your body up while you did it. She'd been wrong. And judging by the smiles on everyone's faces, Stella thought this euphoria was more likely the norm than the exception.

Once Richard detached from Chris, Stella threw her arms around him and squealed. "That was amazing. We just jumped out of a plane!"

"I knew you'd like it. You're a daredevil at heart." He put his arms around her and leaned down to kiss her, but Stella quickly deflected and kissed his cheek, instead. She couldn't contain her smile, every part of her buzzed with energy and excitement. But she managed to keep her composure; she didn't want her first kiss with Richard to be in front of a group of strangers.

Richard put his arm around her and walked her back to the main building. "Now, how will we top this?" Richard asked.

"I have some ideas," Stella said with a laugh.

On the ride home Stella and Richard talked through every second of their jumps, giddy from what they'd done. As they laughed and recounted their stories, Stella realized what made this moment so special was having someone to share it with. She was used to chasing an adrenaline rush and pushing herself to her limits, but she always did it alone. Max was her mentor, not her partner. He didn't do the jobs with her. And Stella kept Fiona in the dark about her real life.

She had mind-blowing experiences, but she couldn't tell anyone about them. This was the first time she could share an experience like this with someone else.

By the time she made it home, the adrenaline high had worn off, and she was beginning to hit the wall. Stella grabbed her phone to text Max before she chickened out or collapsed. She looked at her unread messages and saw a note from a new number.

> Unknown: No one knows you like I do. Let's connect.

Stella wasn't stupid enough to click the link attached. She deleted it and reported it as junk, then clicked on Max's pinned profile and shot him a note.

> Stella: I'll meet with your friend.

After today, Stella realized that opening herself up to new possibilities could be intoxicating. She was willing to see where this would lead.

7

After their skydiving adventure, Stella let down her defenses enough for Richard to spend time with her family. Max met Richard at Thanksgiving, giving him an A+ when he showed up with a great bottle of wine and then jumped up to help clean the kitchen after the meal. It was his first Thanksgiving in America, and Richard didn't know anything about the tradition, but he understood what a kitchen full of dirty dishes meant. Rita almost swooned when he stepped in to clean, relegating her to pointing where things went while she sipped her wine, not allowed to touch a dish.

Richard was slowly making his way into Stella's heart. Despite the secrets she kept, he seemed to know who she really was underneath the public mask she wore. When Richard looked at her, he saw more than a single mother, or even a photographer whose work kept her hidden behind a camera lens. Richard knew there was a fire burning inside her that no PTA meeting or magazine photoshoot could satisfy. When he looked into her eyes, Stella felt him chip away at the walls she'd built around her heart.

She felt alive in ways she'd never felt before. It terrified her.

She was falling for him—there was no denying it. If she wanted to even consider a future with this man, she needed to explore the opportunity Max had given her and see if Marcus's security firm held any future for her.

Stella arranged to meet Marcus on Sunday on her own turf—Roger Sherman Baldwin Park—a crowded marina in the summer and host of the annual Greenwich Town Party. This time of year, though, it was nearly deserted. They should be able to meet discreetly without anyone observing them. Stella had never had a conversation about her true profession with anyone except Max. She didn't take the risk lightly.

She had five days to learn as much as she could about the man and the company he ran before she exposed herself to meeting with him.

Even in the best of circumstances, online research was no substitute for tailing someone in person. She wanted to see where he lived, who he hung out with, and get a feel for his routines. But to do that, she had to figure out what he looked like. Marcus had wiped any pictures of himself since his Army days, and revealed nothing about his current life online. Stella had almost nothing to go on, and the clock was ticking.

Wednesday morning, Stella drove to one of her storage facilities. She kept the tools of her trade in two different places: one right outside the city and one in Newark. They were mostly mirrors of each other, rented under different names, and both had enough costumes, makeup, and vehicle magnets to help her get into almost any building in the city and surrounding suburbs.

This storage room was closest to the city and held everything she needed for jobs in this region. She made sure her storage units were in places a bit run-down with spotty security, something she and her fellow storage renters valued most in a facility of this type. The average renter here was most likely running in the same circles Stella did, or worse. She was convinced there were bodies buried in some of these units, which was exactly why she used them. She knew she was safe when she was running the cleanest game of anyone around her.

She knew Marcus's office was at 30 Rockefeller Plaza, one of the most iconic buildings in town. She'd gone by the office two days prior and snooped around the building, taking photos like a common urban photographer. In reality, she had been getting the lay of the land. She wanted to see Onyx's offices, find the entrances delivery personnel primarily used, and watch how closely the security guards monitored people coming and going. Getting a general feel for the rhythm of the building with its tenants and visitors involved hours over multiple days, learning their routines and the places they frequented.

During her initial recon, Stella saw a lot of ways for her to get into Marcus's office without raising any alarm bells. FedEx and UPS routinely made deliveries, and she could easily use one of the uniforms she had for them to get inside. But she thought it better to distract them with an errant pizza delivery. She didn't know the names of the people who worked at Onyx and didn't think it likely they'd get a package delivered to the wrong person. Better to show up as a DoorDash driver with the wrong info to avoid suspicion.

She put on a blonde wig with short spiky hair and a nondescript black T-shirt to go with her jeans. She caked foundation on her face, aging herself at least ten years, and added brilliant blue eyeshadow to her lids. Finally, she threw on black Chuck Taylors and added some fake nails almost too long for Stella to use her hands. Sometimes blending in wasn't as important as forcing an observer to see only what she wanted them to see.

She threw a different shirt, lightweight coat, and baseball cap into a backpack in case she wanted to switch looks while she was out and packed her Nikon. She put makeup wipes in the bag and grabbed an ID and credit card set she hadn't used in a while. Finally, she checked her reflection in the full-length mirror, then went through every pocket of the backpack to assure she had everything she needed— and nothing she didn't. Satisfied she was prepared for almost any eventuality, she locked up the storage unit and headed for the city.

Stella got off the N line at 49th Street and walked to Famous Ray's Original Pizza, picking up three large pizzas on her way to Marcus's office. She ordered the pizza under the name of the Lazard Group, a huge tenant occupying several floors in the building. If anyone got too enterprising, they could direct her to the correct offices. It was all the cover she'd need.

By the time she arrived at Marcus's office it was 12:15 p.m.—perfect time for a lunch delivery. She took the elevator to the twentieth floor and got off in full character. Stella clocked the entrance to Onyx Intelligence Group the moment she stepped off the elevator, but she intentionally wandered the halls of the office a bit, pretending to look for the company on her receipt. She made a show of poking her head into the two other firms on the floor, a real estate company and an engineering group. She was likely on camera and wanted to make sure it looked like she was looking for the person who'd ordered the pizza.

Finally, pretending to be exasperated, Stella went into Onyx Intelligence Group with the food, and found a young man willing to help her. "Did y'all order some pizzas today?"

He shook his head. "I don't think so."

Stella pulled her phone out of her back pocket and unlocked it, staring at the DoorDash app as though it had any useful information on it for her. "Someone named Krystal Jones?"

The young man shook his head. "Not here. Sorry." She made a face somewhere between pissed off and about to cry. In her experience, men didn't like to see either of those expressions on a woman's face. "What am I going to do? It says it's right here. The little dot is flashing right here." She held up the phone quickly then turned it back to herself. "Suite 2050, right?" She pulled back and glanced around, as if they would have the floor number painted on the wall. For extra measure, she spun around in a circle. "Where the hell is she?"

As Stella feigned anger at the mix-up, her phone vibrated in her hand. Richard's face flashed on her screen. Why was he calling her now? He was supposed to be at school. She cursed herself for neglecting to put the phone in DND and declined the call, trying to refocus on the young man trying to help her.

"Was that her?" he asked. Stella shook her head no.

"My dumbass brother. Probably needs money. Don't we all?" She knew the image of the man on the screen did not match her character's idea of a deadbeat brother, but she hoped he hadn't seen Richard's picture too closely.

"Sometimes those apps get locations wrong. We're all on top of each other, so if she's under us or above us, it might show her here," he said. "Can you call her?"

"I'll try. Thanks," Stella said. Her phone buzzed the second she stepped out into the hall. Richard was calling again. She declined the call and texted a quick reply.

> Stella: Can't talk right now. Everything OK?

By everything she meant Caitlin, but she didn't want to be rude.

She pretended to make a phone call, stressed to hear Richard's reply vibrating in her ear as she spoke to an empty line pretending to talk to her pizza customer. His timing was terrible. Stella held the phone, pretending to listen while she prayed Richard would stop texting, then turned around, and looked through the glass door of Marcus's firm, keeping her eye on the man who'd helped her. She said again, loud enough for him to hear. "What the hell am I supposed to do with three pizzas?" After a pause, she clicked off the call, mad as hell.

Stella looked down the hall again and then back into Marcus's office. She threw open the door and marched back to the man's desk. "You want some pizzas? They canceled the order; said I was late. I'm not late; they gave me the wrong address. I can't be walking around with three pizzas." He politely declined, so she raised the volume of her voice and hollered at everyone in the room. "Anyone here want some free pizza? You'd be doing me a favor."

It had the desired effect. A few heads popped up from different computer terminals in the office. Some of them were looking at Stella, others at the young man she was standing near. As someone approached her, saying they'd be happy to take them, Stella clocked a man who had to be Marcus Williams coming out of the back office. He wore olive slacks with a gray sweater, short twists, and a well-kept beard. Now she knew what he looked like; she wouldn't let him out of her sight again.

"Thank you, sweetie. I appreciate it." Stella handed the pizzas to the young woman who agreed to take them off her hands and thanked them both for helping her. She saw Marcus pause at someone's desk, no longer interested now that the issue was resolved.

She waved goodbye as she walked out of the office and returned to the elevator bank. Once inside, Stella pulled her phone out of her pocket to check Richard's text.

Richard: Had a free moment. Can you talk?

She hit the button for the fifteenth floor. She needed to get to some place less crowded.

She walked into the women's restroom on the fifteenth floor, thrilled to see it was empty. She ducked into a stall and hung her backpack on the peg while she called Richard back. He answered on the first ring. "I'm in the middle of a job. What's up?"

"I didn't mean to interrupt. I was on my lunch break and wanted to run something by you." He paused but Stella let him continue. The sooner this call ended, the better. "How about we go into the city tonight? We can grab some dinner and then see the Christmas tree at Rockefeller Center. I've never been. Pam Fisher told me it's a must-see."

Stella wasn't sure what bothered her more: Richard wanting to visit the exact building she was in right now, or Pam Fisher talking to her boyfriend.

Or the fact she'd just thought of him as her boyfriend.

"I'm already in the city doing a photoshoot."

"Great. I can meet you when you're done."

While this was a complication she didn't need, he sounded excited. Stella didn't want to disappoint him. She had no idea how late Marcus would work, though. He'd already cost her hours of research and a full day trying to figure out what he looked like, she wasn't going to lose track of him now.

She also had no good way to explain her car being parked near the storage facility. She didn't even have her wallet or real identification on her.

This was far more complicated than she liked.

"I'm sorry, but tonight really won't work. We can do it this weekend." She warmed up to the idea as she said it. "We'll make a day of it —lunch, shopping, looking at all the holiday decorations. We can even go ice skating beneath the tree. It'll be a real New York Christmas. How does that sound?"

Richard agreed and Stella was grateful to end the call and get back to the task at hand. She quickly ditched her disguise and changed into her normal clothes. She took off her wig and ran her fingers through her hair, then put on the baseball cap she'd brought. She ripped off her fake nails and used the makeup wipes to get most of the junk off her face. When she confirmed she was still alone in the bathroom, she used the mirror to ensure her face was clean and her hair had survived the wig. Ten minutes had elapsed since she'd entered the bathroom as a delivery woman, and she was ready to emerge more or less as herself.

Stella had some time to kill before Marcus was likely to leave the building. Pizza sounded good after hauling it around and smelling it for the last half hour, so she got some for herself, then hit a bookstore and a coffee shop to help pass the time. By 3:00 p.m., she took up residence near the main employee exit of the building. She knew what Marcus Williams looked like now, making it easier to clock him leaving the building and tail him.

She pretended to read her book, kept her coffee cup full, and watched people come and go for the next three hours. Finally, at 6:10 p.m., Stella saw Marcus leave the building with two of his colleagues. He bid them farewell and headed to the 50th Street subway station.

Stella slipped into the crowd, hopping in the same car as Marcus but standing at the opposite end. She put in her AirPods and pretended to be scrolling on her phone while she watched him out of the corner of her eye. When he got off at 86th, Stella hung back until the last second, exiting as the doors closed to give her maximum separation from him. She followed him to 87th and Broadway, then kept her distance as he walked the last two blocks home. Stella watched him walk into The Normandy at 140 Riverside.

Stella planted herself on the corner and watched the windows to see if Marcus was visible from the street. He could have lived in an apartment facing the other buildings, but she reasoned someone with his level of success probably invested in a view of the Hudson.

Two minutes after entering the main building, Stella's instincts were proven correct when Marcus Williams framed in a fifth-floor window while he closed the blinds for privacy.

She had him in her sights.

Stella devoted another hour to watching people come and go in the building and even scouted ways she could get inside. These pre-war buildings usually came with a trash area for the residents accessible from the service elevator. It shouldn't be too difficult for Stella to gain entry to Marcus's apartment through the back door.

She headed back to her storage facility to switch her IDs and grab her car, confident she'd discover everything she needed to know about Marcus Williams by the end of the week.

8

S tella arrived at Sherman Park ahead of schedule. As she headed to the bench they'd picked for their meeting, she surveyed the area. Her hunch had been correct: the park was nearly empty on this brisk November afternoon. There were some boats in the harbor and a few people tending to them on the pier, but no one was loitering in the park. She pulled out her camera and photographed the area—the sculpture, the harbor, and a full 360-degree view of the park. If Marcus had someone planted in the park to watch them, she wanted them caught on film.

Satisfied the area was clear, Stella sat on the bench and set her backpack beside her, waiting for Marcus to arrive. She pulled out her Kindle and pretended to read while she listened to the sounds of the park, alert to any change in the environment. After twenty-five minutes of waiting and intermittently tapping her Kindle, Stella heard a car pull up into the parking area and a door slam closed. Stella checked her watch and smiled to herself. 12:23 p.m. He was late.

Stella heard Marcus approach the bench but didn't turn to look at him right away. "Sorry I'm late," Marcus said, staring straight ahead.

"Do you feel good about this place?" she asked. She caught his nod in her peripheral vision. "Can we speak freely?"

"I think so." He sat on the bench, her backpack between them. "I'm Marcus Williams." He extended his hand, and she shook it, relaxing. "Sorry I'm late."

"Stella Meyers," she said. "It's okay. Traffic is always unpredictable, even on the weekends."

"I wish I could blame traffic, but this was on me. I lost my car key." He shook his head. "I never do that. I tore the place apart, but no luck. I finally gave up and grabbed an Uber."

"I'm sure it'll turn up." Stella heard the popcorn tone go off on her phone; Richard was texting her. She cut the sound off, then put it on DND for good measure. She didn't want to be distracted during this meeting. "Sorry." Marcus nodded.

She shifted in her seat a bit, turning to face him. She took the time to study him, up close and personal.

"Thank you for agreeing to meet," he said.

"It was Max's idea. I trust him completely. If I didn't, I wouldn't be here."

"I understand. This isn't something I normally do, either."

"So how can I help you?" she asked.

"I told Max I was looking for someone to bring into my company. Someone with a specific set of skills. He recommended you."

Stella knew they were sizing each other up. Both had something to lose by even having this conversation. Still, Max's recommendation carried a lot of weight. She looked at the man sitting next to her and wondered how he knew Max, and what, exactly, Onyx Intelligence Group did for their clients. Or themselves. "I confess I don't really know what you do. I tried to check out your website, but it's vague, to put it mildly."

Marcus nodded. "We like it that way. We get clients from referrals, not from Google. But we need to have some presence online, so we keep it up."

"We're going to have to trust each other a little if we want to even consider working together," Stella said. "What can you tell me about your firm? What role do you see me playing in it?"

"We provide cyber security for our clients. We stress test their security systems to see if there are any vulnerabilities," said Marcus.

"There are always vulnerabilities."

"Exactly. Up to now, our work has focused on technology—software, hardware, and security systems. We break into their companies in as many ways as possible to show them where they need to shore things up. And then we do the shoring up."

"That gives you incredible access to their systems."

"Yes, it does. We have an impeccable reputation. We access all their systems, analyze them, then go in and shut down any holes we see so no one else can get in."

Stella paused. They were about to cross a line, and she wanted Marcus to cross it first. "I assume when you're doing that, you can also build in some backdoor access that only you have." Stella looked out on the harbor and let the accusation sit between them. They were both at risk here, and she wanted Marcus to know she understood enough to see the full scope of what he was discussing. "How is it they don't understand the position they've put you in?"

"It's taken years of work to build trust between us and our clients. We continually go in and monitor their systems, with nothing amiss. Any information we gain from our access is leveraged in ways no one could ever trace back to us. We make certain of it." Stella nodded her understanding but remained quiet. "We benefit from knowing the inside operations of so many major international firms."

Stella crossed her arms and tilted her head at him. "How would I fit into this? I'm a decent end-user, but I don't know the first thing about tech security."

"I have that covered," Marcus assured. "What I don't have is anyone good on the human side."

"Go on," Stella encouraged.

"The industry is changing. As companies bring new technologies online and rely more and more on those systems to run their business, vulnerabilities through those systems are decreasing."

"Really? That seems counterintuitive."

"There'll always be issues with both hardware and software, but as the world gets more advanced, we see more people with the skills to both exploit those gaps or close them down. A massive vulnerability is developing in the real world of security. No one is watching who is coming and going in a building, especially when they're 'supposed' to be there." He used air quotes to make his point. "No one pays attention to the food delivery guy or the cleaning crew, not beyond initial background checks."

"You mean people like me," Stella said.

"Precisely. People are so focused on the technology to both save them and put them at risk, they're not paying enough attention to the old school people who can find a way into a building simply by walking through the front door."

"And you want to have someone like that on your team?"

"Damn right I do," said Marcus. "We provide the best cybersecurity in the world. I make certain of that. And if we don't have someone on the ground able to test their blind spots to humans breaching their security, then we're not doing our job."

The idea intrigued Stella. Marcus's tech prowess and her cunning could be a good match. He paused and looked down at his lap, then raised his eyes and stared at the harbor. She could see him working up the nerve to say something.

"May I be frank?" he asked. "Max told me you were the best at what you do." He pulled his phone out of his pocket. Stella saw him open a file, and a video appeared on the screen. He pushed play and passed it to her. "I have some concerns."

Stella looked at the video as it played, her eyes widening. No sound came out of the video, but it was clearly a shot of her getting off the elevator on his floor. The first shot was time stamped 6:23 p.m. on Tuesday night. She saw herself get off the elevator and head down the hall. Then walk back again and go to the bathroom. She raised her head and caught his gaze but said nothing.

Marcus let the video continue. It jumped to the next day at 12:15 p.m. Stella emerged from the elevator again, this time carrying boxes of pizzas. The video cut one last time to her inside Onyx's offices, learning the pizza order had been incorrect. Marcus cut the video off and pocketed his phone.

"Are you mad I looked into you?" asked Stella, finding her voice, and going on the offensive. "You can't expect me to put myself on the line without knowing anything about you."

Marcus shook his head. "No, I'd expect that. But with all due respect to Max, I'm looking for someone better than this. We can't have you popping into people's companies and getting caught on the most basic security cameras."

"Then why have this meeting at all? Why didn't you save us both time and cancel?" Anger simmered to the surface. This asshole judged her without even meeting her and then had the audacity to imply she wasn't good at her job. She felt like she'd failed a test she didn't know she was taking.

"Like I said, Max is a good friend, and I respect him. I'm beginning to understand why he thinks you're ready to quit."

Stella looked and felt like someone had slapped her in the face, her blood pressure rising. "I don't exist in the shadows like you do. I'm always going to be caught on film or run into the property owners. You saw those because you were looking for me." Stella grabbed her backpack, and tossed it over her shoulder, rising as she spoke. "My job is to not get caught. And when people don't expect to see me coming, when they aren't scouring their cameras for me, they don't see me."

Marcus rose to his feet as well. "I'm sorry if I wasted your time. My clients are some of the leading companies in the world. I need someone who can get into a place even when someone is looking for it." He reached out his hand to shake hers.

Stella took his hand and passed something to him while she shook it. "I wouldn't want you putting yourself at risk." She turned and walked away, allowing herself a small smile once she had her back to Marcus.

She counted three steps before she heard him exclaim, "What the hell?"

Stella kept walking, a full smile breaking across her face now. She didn't need this asshole criticizing her. She heard him utter a few more expletives and then race after her. She felt his hand on her shoulder just before he pulled her around to face him. "Where did you get this?" He showed her the key to his car that she'd just handed back to him.

"As I said, I don't exist in the shadows. I do end up on security cameras sometimes, and I have to interact with people every day, but when I want to get into a place undetected, I do it." She turned to walk away again but he stopped her.

"How did you get this? I ride my bike to work or take the subway. I keep this key in my foyer." He paused, putting the pieces together. "You broke into my apartment? When?"

"Maybe you dropped it," Stella said innocently. "After all, you don't think I have what it takes to work with you."

Marcus laughed out loud. "I take that back." He shook his head, smiling at her. "Max knows what he's talking about."

"Always." Stella smiled again. They fell in step with each other, walking toward the parking lot to Stella's car.

Marcus pulled out his phone and requested an Uber back to his house. He helped Stella put her backpack in the car and held her door while she climbed inside. "What do you say? Will you join us?"

"I'll consider it," said Stella.

"Even after I made a complete ass out of myself?"

"You're very good at your job, Marcus. But I'm good at mine, too. You've given me something to think about today."

"Same here." Marcus held up his key. "Will you please tell me how you got this?"

Stella shook her head and smiled. She pushed the ignition button. "I'll be in touch." Marcus stepped out of the door and closed it for her. Stella waved at him and watched him walk back to the edge of the lot, waiting for his ride. "Smug bastard," she mumbled.

She grabbed her phone out of her bag and checked her texts before leaving. Richard had been trying to get in touch with her for an afternoon coffee date.

> Stella: Sorry for the delay. Coffee sounds good. Caitlin has soccer practice this afternoon. Let me see if my mother can take her, and then I'll get back to you.

Before she pulled out of the lot, her phone dinged. Her brows furrowed when she looked at the message. She didn't recognize the sender's number.

> Unknown: I don't like being ignored.

What the fuck does that mean? She looked again at the number of the sender and couldn't place it. She hit delete on the bottom of the message and then marked it as junk for good measure. Someone was playing games with her; she wasn't inclined to take the bait.

9

On the drive home, Stella debriefed Max about her meeting with Marcus. He laughed at her trick with the key, impressed by her showmanship. He didn't push her to make a decision now but thanked her for taking the time to meet with him and at least see what the job might entail. She ended the call with the promise that she'd give the job real consideration. It was the best she could do.

As she pulled into her garage, she heard her text alert go off. It was the generic ping, another spam. Stella grabbed her phone out of the console to read the note.

> Unknown: I've been patient with you up to now. We have business to discuss.

She was about to swipe it and delete it when another note came through. This one was from a different number, but it had the same tone.

> Unknown: Respond now or you will pay.

Stella had no idea who this was or what they were talking about. Habit dictated she delete these messages and report them as junk, but as her finger hovered over the message, something forced her to pause. She left the messages on her phone and headed into the house.

Her phone pinged again seconds after she stepped into her office. She glanced at her phone, and read the simple text.

Unknown: Open me

There was a link attached.

Fuck that. She felt certain this was from the same source who had just threatened her.

Every part of Stella was tight and on high alert. Something nagged at her to click on the link in the message. She had survived over a decade of breaking the law without getting caught by listening to her instincts. If this message put her on edge, she was going to pay attention.

At the very least, Stella suspected the link would contain a virus. Based on her racing heart, she would be happy if that was all it contained. She knew any interaction she had with this message and embedded link could open a channel where someone on the other end trace her keystrokes on her phone or computer, access all her information, and connect to her network from her phone. She needed to be cautious.

She reached for her phone and pulled up Marcus Williams's contact, letting her finger hover over his number. She checked the time. He was probably still in his Uber.

She put the phone down. She'd told him she never got caught. If this were an innocuous spam note, she'd look stupid for asking him about it. If it was worse—if someone had a bead on her and was threatening her—she'd look incompetent. Either way, she'd lose all the credit she'd earned in upstaging him.

She thought of calling Max, but what would she tell him? She'd gotten a funny message? He'd tell her to call Marcus, and that wasn't happening. She clicked off the phone and tossed it onto the desk. She would handle this herself.

She needed a way to open the message without infecting her computer or her network. She knew her systems were secure. She used a separate computer to do any research she had on her thefts and always used a VPN to hide where she was searching from. But if she opened this message and there was a virus on it, she could infect everything. She needed something clean, with zero information about her on it.

Stella grabbed her phone and keys and went to find her mother. "I'm going out. Can you take Caitlin to soccer practice today? I'm not sure how long I'll be gone."

Rita nodded. "You and Richard going out?"

She'd forgotten she was going to text Richard about getting together today. "N-no. I have something I—I need to tend to."

"Everything okay?" she asked. Rita respected Stella's boundaries, but Stella knew she appeared more scattered than normal.

"All good. Just need to do something." Stella left, not wanting to continue this conversation.

She headed to the Apple store in Greenwich. She needed a new computer to open the link without putting her data at risk. She wouldn't use it on her network, wouldn't connect it to her phone, or attach her identity to it in any way. Stella could access whatever link someone wanted her to see and fully protect her information. She didn't know whether she was paranoid or a genius, but this was the best plan she had.

After getting the computer, Stella drove to the public library. She checked into an individual study room, which would be her private space for the next three hours.

Stella closed the door to the study room and verified no one could see her through the small window next to the desk. She spent the next fifteen minutes setting up the computer. She created a new Apple ID and email for the computer, skipping the computer's prompts to sync with any of her other devices. She wanted this to be a clean slate.

Finally, Stella pulled up her cell phone and looked at the message again.

Unknown: Open me.

Following the command was a link. Stella carefully clicked on it and waited for it to open a small window. She could see the full link address here, and the phone gave her options to open the link, copy it, or share it. Her fingers hovered over the share button. Would sharing it tie the link to her? She shook her head; it wasn't worth the risk.

It took three tries to get the address typed correctly into the browser. She took a moment to take some deep breaths. She felt like she was on a job when she reached the point of no return. Nothing had happened yet. She hadn't done anything irreversible. She wanted to be sure of her next steps before she committed to opening the link.

She forced herself to do some box breathing to slow her heart rate and clear her head. Breathing in for four seconds, holding for four, letting it out for four, and holding again for four. She increased it one second each time until she was up to eight. Once finished, she felt completely in control of herself. She was ready for whatever this link led to.

The instant Stella clicked the link it directed her to a site with only a video on the page. The thumbnail on the video simply read *Play me*. Same simple messaging as the text.

Stella dug into her backpack and pulled out her ancient earphones, glad she'd saved this pair after they'd upgraded to the wireless AirPods. The hardwire would allow her to listen in private without attaching her device to the computer through Bluetooth. She checked the window next to her again—all-clear. Satisfied no one could see her, she hit play.

Stella's eyes widened, immediately recognizing the scene. She sat in stunned silence as she saw herself sitting in Sebastian Hayes's Mercedes at the gate at El Paraíso. She didn't think a stranger would associate the woman in the car with the designer shades and blonde hair as herself, but clearly someone knew it was her.

She watched herself hand her ID over to the guard and talk to him for a few seconds before driving off. The video cut to a shot of the Hayes house from behind as she drove into the garage. That shot was from far away, the video zooming in enough to obscure much of the scene. But she knew it was her.

A similar shot caught Stella leaving. This time, the camera grabbed a good shot of her profile as she lowered the garage door and drove away. She watched the property manager follow her out of the driveway on her way back to the gate. The video flipped again, showing her at the gate with the guards circling her car, looking under the carriage, and harassing her a bit while she waited for them to open the gate. She could almost hear what they were saying as it unfolded.

Her mind raced as she watched each scene. Half of her brain was occupied with the questions of who had sent her the video and how they had possibly found her, while the other half calculated whether the footage could lead to her arrest.. Were the images good enough to hold up in court? Was she identifiable through the disguise and grainy video?

There wasn't anything in the video showing her taking the painting or making the switch. Right now, it felt more like conjecture —circumstantial evidence at best. She relaxed a bit.

But then the video cut to the next scene. She watched the Mercedes pull back into the garage, Max waiting in a car nearby. This was shot from outside the parking garage but was up high enough to catch them on the fourth floor of the building. It had to be either a drone or a camera from across the street aimed at the exact place where Sebastian Hayes parked his car. This shot was the most damning of all.

Stella watched the screen, already knowing what the video would reveal. She exited the vehicle and popped the trunk, then moved the painting from Sebastian's car to the rental Max had pulled out of the same space. Max wasn't visible on film, but anyone could see she was carrying something from one trunk to the other. Stella thanked herself for having the painting fully covered by the blanket.

The video was plenty damning, but the painting wasn't shown in it. Someone would have to know what they were looking at to be convinced it was Sebastian Hayes's Degas.

Stella thought the video would end now, but the timer on the screen showed otherwise. "What else could there possibly be?" she asked the empty room.

The screen flipped to a series of screenshots of headlines about stolen art, jewel theft, and several other unsolved crimes. Some were hers, others not. They were spread out across the globe and, from what she could see, covered the last three-to-four years. It wasn't a comprehensive list of her work, by any means, but it covered enough.

"Holy fuck," whispered Stella to the empty room. "I've been made."

As Stella sat with this realization, her cell phone pinged. She picked it up and saw another text from a new number.

> Unknown: I have a job for you.

Stella threw the phone on the table as if it were on fire. She paced in the tiny room, struggling to figure out what to do next. She'd never been confronted with anything remotely like this before. To her knowledge, she'd never been on anyone's suspect list, much less someone being able to tie a crime directly to her. A million questions raced through her mind.

Who was this person? What did they want from her? Was it someone she knew, or a stranger? How did they get this footage? What were they going to do with it? The barrage of questions hit her, and she had to sit down again. *Think, damn it!*

Stella picked up her phone to call Max. He'd been in this business long enough to know what to do. But as the phone rang, she froze. She clicked off the call and shot a text off to him quickly before he could call her back.

> Stella: Accident, sorry. I'll call soon.

Max did not appreciate the term "butt dial." She couldn't talk to him in this state of mind, with this much uncertainty. The easy thing would be to tell Max and get his advice. She told herself she didn't want to alarm him, but deep down, she knew it was pride.

And besides, she had to consider her phone compromised. She couldn't be sure she hadn't already opened one of these messages and infected her phone. She needed to be smarter than that. Clearly, she'd screwed up somewhere along the way and calling him to bail her out felt wrong. He'd given her so much. He'd built his life around her these last ten years. She didn't want to repay him by admitting she was an idiot.

Her mind flashed to their meeting for lunch at Nonna Vita's and his concern for her safety. He thought she'd gone too far on the Hayes job, been too bold, and she'd argued with him. She'd enjoyed the rush and gotten away clean. To call him now and admit she'd fucked up this badly . . . That wasn't a call she was prepared to make. At least not until she'd done some work to figure out what was going on.

She grabbed a notebook out of her backpack and clicked play on the video again. She was going old school with the tech—there would be no electronic files of her notes. There wasn't a ton there in terms of the actual heist. Stella felt almost certain she couldn't be charged from the video alone—without evidence of what had been in the trunk of the car under the gray moving blanket. But someone absolutely knew who she was. That was the message they were trying to send. She'd received it loud and clear.

The guard interactions were disconcerting but not surprising. She knew she'd been on film since they kept cameras trained on the gate. Anyone coming or going by car or on foot had to use that entry point and would be captured on film. If the police had a shred of evidence she'd stolen the Degas, Stella felt certain Antonio Alfaro would have shown up on her doorstep to arrest her, himself. He had not been happy with her that day. No, this footage showed someone had hacked into their system and grabbed this video.

She wrote down a couple of notes. Did Sebastian Hayes know she had switched the paintings? That was an immediate concern. If he knew, and he'd sent her this video instead of sending the cops after her, then he wanted something from her.

She got up and paced the tiny room again, trying to sort fact from conjecture.

"Does he know about the switch? Why wouldn't he send someone after me directly if he knew?" Since she wasn't on her home computer or network, she risked searching for information about it online. She opened an incognito window for what little good that did and put in a few prompts about a stolen Degas.

Search engines spit out what she already knew. The pieces that had been stolen in the infamous Isabella Stewart Gardner Museum heist in 1990. Les Choristes was stolen from a museum in Marseille in 2009, but it had been later recovered. The chalk drawing of Ballerina Adjusting Her Slipper, which was stolen from a man's safe in Cyprus in 2014. Stella had reviewed all of these before she took this job. None of them had updates, and no one mentioned a new theft from a private collection. If Sebastian Hayes knew his painting had been switched, he hadn't reported it publicly.

She played the video repeatedly, looking for anything amiss. The footage she kept replaying was the parking garage. That was the most damning since you could see her take something out of Sebastian's trunk and put it in Max's rental car. The only saving grace was that you couldn't see what it was. It just looked like a box with a gray blanket over it.

Why did that keep coming to her? She free associated words on the notepad that flashed in her mind. Garage. Switch. Entire scene. High. Drone? She went over the video again, watching her approach the parking space on the fourth floor of the garage. Max pulled the rental car out of the space he'd been holding, and she pulled into it. Max's face wasn't on film, but hers was when she emerged from the car and made the switch. Then Max drove off and the video showed her walking off.

She'd returned the key to the valet stand, the attendants too distracted by her outfit to see her slip the key back on the rack. But none of that appeared in the video. Either they didn't have video of that, or they'd left it out.

That's when it clicked for her.

Someone captured that part on film, but not her coming and going into the parking garage at ground level. And the video was close enough to show her face in profile when she drove the car. She'd scoped out the garage before the job and hadn't spotted any cameras on the upper levels. Everything was filmed at entrance and exit points, stairwells, and elevators. This camera captured the fourth floor, where Sebastian's Mercedes had been parked, from outside the building. She didn't know if it was a drone or a camera mounted across the street, but she was certain that someone had trained that camera on Sebastian Hayes's car.

Someone had been waiting for her to steal that car. Someone knew what she was planning before she ever did the job.

She'd been set up.

10

S tella shut down the computer and put it away. On her way out of the library, she resisted the urge to throw it in the garbage. She wanted it as far away from her as possible. But it was harmless so long as she didn't turn it on in her house.

On her way to her car, Stella heard the popcorn sound from her phone. Her stomach sank. She'd forgotten about Richard.

> Richard: Everything ok? I thought we were
> going to grab a coffee.

Stella answered him with a call. He picked up immediately.

"Get held up at practice?" he asked.

"I'm sorry, I had a work emergency. I lost track of time."

"Anything I can help with?"

"I have a cranky client, and they want some edits done before a deadline tomorrow. I'm going to be working all night."

"I can bring over dinner and a bottle of wine if it would help ease the pain of working late."

Stella appreciated his thoughtfulness, but she didn't have the luxury of time right now. She needed to prioritize figuring out who was pursuing her or get the hell out of town. "That sounds lovely—

truly, it does. But I really want to knock this out. Can I call you tomorrow?"

"Of course. Take care of yourself." They said their goodbyes and hung up.

Stella hoped she had things under control enough to talk to him tomorrow. Right now, she wasn't so confident.

She headed home and shut herself in her office, leaving her phone on the kitchen counter. She wasn't sure how many times this person had tried to reach her, or if they'd sent some other email that had given them access to her phone. If she was going to spend time in her office to figure out what to do, she wanted to make sure no one was spying on her while she worked.

Continuing that thought, Stella thoroughly searched her office for any bugs or cameras that someone might have planted. She couldn't imagine how someone could have planted a camera in here, but she wasn't willing to take any risks. She took the framed photo she'd taken of Caitlin and her mother off the wall and ran her fingers over it, flipping it over and examining the back. It was clean. The overhead light, lamps, and her desk all appeared safe. The computer was the biggest vulnerability, so she took a cue from Mark Zuckerberg and put a sticky note over her camera to make sure no one could use it to spy on her.

Stella grabbed a legal pad out of her office supply closet and made a list of critical things she needed to do for safety. Keeping it all on paper would make it easier to burn. Some items were obvious: new phone numbers for her and her mother and getting Caitlin her own phone. Up to now, Caitlin had to call and text Stella from her tablet, but Stella wanted a way to reach her immediately. She would also grab some additional burner phones. Until she was sure her Wi-Fi network was secure, she would run all their devices on the cell network instead.

She also wanted to add more cameras outside the house to capture the comings and goings of those nearby. It was time to track every blind spot and cover every angle.

Right now, her surveillance system saved activity of anyone near her house for the last year. She even had video analytics software that would run through the information faster than watching it herself. She fired up her laptop and launched the software to run it while she worked on the rest of her list. Thankfully, before she clicked on the program, her training kicked in. If someone had been tracking her for a long time, they might have compromised the system months ago.

Stella fired up her antivirus software. Until it finished scanning her systems, it was back to the legal pad.

This list had been in her back pocket for years. She had several levels of plans to keep her family safe, and this was step one. But did she need to take things further? Someone knew who she was, and the threat against her felt imminent. They obviously had been trying to contact her for a while. She had to assume they knew everything about her.

Stella needed to switch gears and go on the offensive. Years of preparing to break into other people's homes trained her well. Instead of looking at how to keep people out, Stella looked at her house as a target. How would she approach the house to get inside? What would she be looking for? Looking at it from this angle, she saw a thousand different ways someone would gain access to them. She flipped the page on her legal pad and made a new list. Where were they most vulnerable?

As Marcus had said, the low-tech ways to get people were more important than ever. Delivery people, servicemen, mail carriers—there were so many people "expected" to be at a stranger's house, and all of them could easily be faked. Stella jotted down every change needed for immediate protection.

A knock sounded at her door.

Rita entered without waiting for an invitation. "Forget something?" She waved Stella's phone at her. "This thing has been beeping in ten different tones for the last hour. It sounds like some kind of texting symphony." Rita put the phone on the desk, but Stella didn't move to pick it up. "You are never more than six inches from your phone. You'd take it with you in the shower if you could. What's going on?"

Stella didn't have the brainpower to do this dance with her mother. On the other hand, she also didn't want to tip her off that something was wrong. "I needed to get some work done, uninterrupted," Stella said. "Sorry if it bothered you." She stared at the phone for a minute, then picked it up, and powered it down. Problem solved. No more text tones. And no one could spy on them if the phone was off.

Stella saw her mother survey her office space. "You look like a deer caught in the headlights. Tell me what's going on. Now." Rita locked the door behind her and leaned against it. She wasn't going anywhere.

Stella was slow to respond. She didn't want to tell her mother the truth without knowing what was fully going on.

"Is something going on with Richard? Are you two having a fight?" asked Rita.

Stella's mind raced as she answered. Could she blame this on him? "Things are okay there, I think?" Stella asked more than stated. She could blame her current insanity on a fight with him, but that wouldn't help her sell their new security measures tomorrow. "I had some work to do tonight, so I missed a coffee date with him. He didn't seem upset, though, so I think we're good."

"Then tell me what's going on. Are you planning a new job? Something I should be worried about?" Rita crossed her arms over her chest, standing her ground.

Stella saw a way through the mess she had made for herself.

"Actually, I am looking at a new job," Stella said. "I met with someone today who wants to hire me to work for them. It's a security firm." Stella watched her mother's face go from upset to hopeful in an instant.

"Is this a real job? One that won't land you in jail?"

"It is. Max introduced us. We met today and discussed the possibility of me working for them."

Rita dropped her defensive stance and crossed the room to put her hand on Stella's shoulder. She couldn't contain her excitement. "Are you going to do it? Are you really going to quit risking your life and get a real job?" She put her hands over her mouth like she was saying a prayer, begging Stella to take the offer. Stella saw tears glisten in her mother's eyes.

"I'm thinking about it. I'm not making any promises, but I'm considering it."

"Is that why you have the notepad? Making an old school pro-con list? I can help with that." Rita was laughing, excited at the slightest hint that Stella might consider a new profession. Stella wondered how disappointed she'd be to learn she'd still be sneaking into places if she worked for Marcus, although the risk of her being thrown in jail or killed on the job would be low.

"Actually, meeting with him helped me see how exposed we really are. I was making a list of things we could do to be a bit safer around here."

"We're not in danger, are we?" Rita asked.

"Not really. I always thought I had all this technology protecting us, but Marcus—that's his name, Marcus Williams—gave me a peek into his world and it scared me." Stella warmed up to the narrative as she spun her story. "Someone could have compromised our Wi-Fi network, our phones, or our computers without us knowing it. How many phishing notes do you get every day? They look so real. And now with AI? You could get a phone call from someone using Caitlin's voice saying she's in trouble. People are getting scammed every day. No matter what I decide to do about the job, I want us to be more careful."

"Sounds a touch paranoid to me. But if this guy has earned your respect enough to consider his offer, then I'll go along with it."

"Good. I'm getting us new phones tomorrow, as a precaution. I'm going to install a few more cameras around the house, too. Little things like that."

"I don't need a new phone, Stella. I only talk to you and Fiona."

"Humor me, please. I'm also going to surprise Caitlin with her own phone." Rita raised her hands to protest, but Stella didn't give her the chance. "She'll have extremely limited use of it. It's just so we can get in touch with her if we need to. I promise I won't turn her into a zombie. No social media, no gaming—only calling."

"That seems riskier than leaving her without a way to contact you."

"Well, that's what we're doing. I'm happy to discuss what rules we should give her, so we can present a united front. She'll be good about it, I'm sure."

"If you say so." Rita headed to the door but then turned back. "Anything else I should know?"

"Last one. I want us to stop getting deliveries. No more Amazon packages, no DoorDash, or Ubers. I don't want anyone approaching our home that we don't already know."

"It's three weeks before Christmas. How are we going to have a holiday with no deliveries?"

"We go old school. There were lots of Christmases before Amazon came into existence. How about we go on a shopping spree in the city for gifts? We'll make a day of it. I'm also not saying we can't get restaurant food, but we need to pick it up ourselves. We could have Amazon send packages to the address at the post office, too. That's what it's for. We don't need strangers coming to our door. It's not smart."

Rita unlocked the door. "This sounds like overkill to me, but if this has you seriously considering a different profession, I'm all for it." She lowered her voice and stared at Stella. "You will consider this job, right? Really and truly?"

Stella nodded. "I promise."

Rita smiled, pulling the door open. "I know you haven't eaten all day; I'll bring you a plate."

Stella watched her mom leave and felt calm for the first time today. She was handling the situation. She had everything under control. Tomorrow she'll talk to Max about locking down their systems and give him the same story as her mother.

She could see a light at the end of the tunnel. In another day, she'd have her house secure. If someone was gunning for her, Stella was going to make it difficult for them to catch her.

11

Stella spent the morning putting her plans into action. It was amazing how fast things could get done when you were willing to pay top dollar for new equipment.

She got new phones and numbers for the family and picked up four additional burner phones. She also bought herself a new tablet that ran off the cell network so she could monitor her new security systems. Cell networks weren't secure, but they were the best option for now. She could also camp out in a coffee shop and use their Wi-Fi if it came down to it.

Everything was falling into place.

Her last stop was to pick up two more cameras to cover the blind spots in her home security. She made it home in time for lunch and installed the cameras over her garage and in the corner of her backyard, pointed at her shed. Now, her cameras covered every inch of the house outside. She had complete control over what they filmed, so she could shut them down if she needed to sneak out.

Rita balked a bit at the new phone but accepted it.

"Remember not to download any information from the cloud to this new phone. Keep the Wi-Fi off and only use cell data for now. This is a fresh start." Stella opened the contacts and showed her the ones she'd already added. "Me, Caitlin, and Fiona. I'll add Max's once I talk to him. Anyone else you need?"

"How about Richard?" asked Rita. Stella knew her mother was really asking if everything was okay with them. "Of course. You can add him and anyone else you want. Use your old phone as a reference, but don't transfer anything electronically. Got it?"

Rita sighed like a disgruntled teenager but agreed. "Does Max approve of all this? Is he doing this too?" Rita asked.

"He's the one who set up the meeting with Marcus," Stella told her. It wasn't a straight answer, but hopefully her mother didn't notice. "I'm meeting him in the city in a bit to talk about the job offer. I think he'll be thrilled we're updating our security."

Stella headed into her office, closing and locking the door behind her. She opened the supply closet door and reached behind the lenses she stored on the shelf for the express purpose of obscuring the button to her safe. When she pushed the button, a wall of shelving swung open to reveal a five-foot gunmetal gray fireproof safe secured behind the wall. Stella placed her hand on the scanner to open the safe. Instead of protecting rifles and handguns from unintended use, as the installers had presumed, Stella filled her safe with a collection of items she needed to protect her family. New identifications for each of them, credit cards under those assumed names, and cash in a number of different currencies. She added the burner phones she'd purchased today to the safe, holding one back for herself.

She needed a secure way to contact Max.

Stella locked the safe back up, closing the shelves and covering the button again with her lenses. She fired up the burner phone and texted Max their code for red alert.

> Stella: We want to talk to you about your Mercedes' extended warranty.

It was a message people received every day. The only thing that made it stand out to Max was the mention of a Mercedes. He would know it was from her.

STELLA TOOK the train into the city to meet Max at the predetermined location. Washington Square Park provided good cover should someone be following her. To anyone watching, it would look like she was meeting a friend for a walk and chat.

They'd planned for Max to arrive first. The park was closer to his location than hers, giving him ample time to sip tea and read the paper while he looked around for anything unusual. He'd been at the park nearly an hour already. She knew he'd been shifting between walking in circles and sitting on the bench, taking note of every person in the vicinity. She caught his eye when she entered the park, but took the long route to get to him, giving him plenty of time to observe her entrance and see if anyone was following her.

Max gave her a subtle nod when she approached, signaling the all-clear. He rose to meet her. "Lovely of you to join me," Max said, making a show of kissing her cheeks. "Shall we walk, or do you want to sit for a spell?"

"I need some coffee and a quick bite. Let's walk."

They headed to a café up ahead, keeping a steady pace. Stella put a smile on her face and pretended she had all the time in the world. "See anyone?" she asked.

"No," Max said. "I believe you're in the clear."

Stella relaxed a bit. "I haven't seen anyone on my tail, either. I took a crazy route to get here."

Once inside the café, Stella ordered a cup of coffee and got pastries for both of them. They chose a table at the rear of the restaurant, Stella's back to the wall so she could see everyone coming and going. Finally convinced it was safe to speak, Max demanded to be filled in. "Start from the beginning and leave nothing out."

Stella bristled at the command. She hadn't decided how much she was going to share with Max today.

"The red alert was probably overkill," Stella admitted. "I've been getting some messages that concern me. I'm circling the wagons now, tightening our security protocols. I wanted to know if you've gotten any cryptic messages?"

"None that I know of, but I admit I might miss them if they're veiled. Do you have any information about the sender? Have they made any direct threats or demands?"

Stella took a sip of her coffee, buying herself a little time. She was walking a line here. Max was her mentor, her friend. He was the only person in her life who she didn't keep secrets from. Until now. She'd thought about it all the way here. Someone could have compromised Max without his knowledge. She couldn't tell him everything. At least that's what she told herself to justify adding Max to the list of people she moved around the chessboard of her life. She didn't want to hurt him, but she had to control the situation. She couldn't tell him the full truth. Not yet.

"No demands. No direct threats." That was true. Although the video was damning, they hadn't told her what they wanted in exchange for their silence. She presumed it would be blackmail of some sort, maybe even the return of the painting. But she didn't know. "Mostly it's been emails and texts phishing for information. I'm worried I clicked on one of them and didn't know it, so I'm updating all my security information."

Stella went over the list of things she'd done to protect herself and her family. "That's why I contacted you from a burner. I think you should update your phone and systems as well."

"Have you traced the number of the sender?"

"That's the funny part. Every message comes from a different phone number, even when they're sent moments apart."

"Salespeople use those programs to hide their actual location from the unsuspecting souls who answer their calls," he said. "They're likely using something similar."

"That's what I assumed. I think it threw me when they came in so close together but from different numbers."

"No doubt accomplishing what they'd set out to achieve."

Stella took a deep breath while she prepped herself for her next question. "Can I ask how you got the line on the job in April? How did you know it was there?"

"Someone put me on to it. I had a buyer before we had the product. Why?"

She ignored his question and pressed on. "Did you trust them?"

"I did. Why do you ask? Is it connected to the messages you've been getting?"

"I can't be certain. It's the biggest job I've done in a while, so it makes sense to ask."

Max stood and gathered his things, nodding at Stella to follow him. They made their way back onto the street and headed away from the park. Stella remained quiet while he processed everything she'd told him.

Finally, Max asked, "How can I help you?"

"I'd like you to switch out your phone. Maybe run a check on your own security protocols and update them. We need to be alert that someone might be on to us." She kept calm and asked, almost as an aside, "And if you can get me information on who turned you onto that job, or who you sold it to, that might help."

"If you think it's needed," Max relented, raising his eyebrows. "What else are you doing to protect your family?"

Stella cringed; this was the very thing Max had warned about. She walked through her new plans, including no longer letting any delivery or service people come to her home. "We're going back in time, doing our Christmas shopping in person. Eating meals we either cook or pick up from the restaurant ourselves. No more convenience deliveries."

"That's a good idea for many reasons," he said. "What about your systems? Your network? Do you have a way to see if they've been compromised?" Max asked the question, but he already knew the answer.

"I have some software I can use. If they've already breached my network, nothing I do will matter, though. They'll see every new machine I bring online and every password I change."

"Precisely." He appeared to be enjoying this moment. "I know you value your privacy, but there's an obvious solution here. You can speak to Marcus; see what he can do to help you. You've met with him already, it's not inconceivable he could be of service now."

"I told him I knew what I was doing—that I've never been caught." She hated how her ego showed up now when it really shouldn't matter at all. "Besides, are we sure we can trust him?"

Max turned to face Stella. "He deals with far more sensitive data than a home network. He will be discreet. I think you should call him."

"Fine," Stella mumbled. She checked her watch. It was 4:30 p.m. now, nearly the end of the workday. "Maybe he can fit me in tomorrow."

"Dear, I believe they keep odd hours there. I suspect their day is only getting underway. Call him now." Max waited while Stella made the call.

Stella used her new phone and searched the web for Onyx Intelligence Group. When the site came up, she clicked on the embedded phone number and then asked for Marcus Williams. She explained she had met with him that weekend and needed to speak to him about something urgent. In less than a minute, she had Marcus on the line.

"I'm sorry to bother you with something so small," she said. "Max is with me, and he insisted I call you. I'm concerned I might have a virus on my computer or my network. Is there any way you could help me determine if someone is tracking my movements online?"

"Absolutely. We can scan your hardware and get an answer quickly. The network will take longer to review. Do you want to come into the office or have us work remotely?"

"Can we do this remotely? Even if my network is compromised? I don't want to infect your systems."

"We have safeguards for that; don't worry about us," said Marcus.

"Wonderful. Can I call you tomorrow?"

"Whenever you're ready."

Stella clicked off the call. She turned to Max and smiled. "Satisfied?"

"I take no pleasure in watching you betray your principles," said Max.

Her eyes widened at the comment, her mind racing to figure out if she'd been caught. Did he know she was lying to him?

"I know you value your privacy. I appreciate you trusting me and letting Marcus help you."

She relaxed. She hugged her friend goodbye and headed to the subway for the ride home. She didn't love having to let Marcus see her flaws, but if he could put her mind at ease about her computer and network, it was worth it. After all, he still didn't know how she'd managed to break into his house and steal his key fob.

12

S tella hopped on the crowded subway and checked in with her mother. She wanted to make sure Caitlin was home safe and nothing unexpected had happened. Rita texted back a thumbs up.

> Rita: I haven't given Caitlin her phone yet.
> Waiting until you're home.

Everything in her world was fine.

Next, Stella texted Fiona and let her know she had a new number.

> Stella: Don't delete this! It's Stella. I got a new phone number.

Fiona replied immediately. Stella knew her friend had a life and a family and responsibilities, but one of the things she loved most about Fiona was whenever Stella texted her, she responded with lightning speed. It made Stella feel special, even if the truth really was Fiona had a raging case of ADHD and was never far from her phone.

> Fiona: Your mum got a new number, too.
>
> What's up?

Are you going into hiding?

Are you on the lam?

Jesus, she loved and hated this woman in equal measure. How the hell did her guesses get so close to the truth?

Stella: Not going into hiding. I had a beef with my carrier and told them to go screw themselves. They got mad back and wouldn't release our numbers in time, so here we are.

Fiona: That's kind of boring. My ideas were better.

Stella: Thanks for typing two whole sentences in one text.

Stella couldn't resist poking fun at her, but she knew Fiona would make her pay.

Fiona: I

Am

So

Glad

You

Gave

Me

Your

New

Number

So

Now

I

Can

Bug

You!

Stella: Bitch! I'm turning off my phone.

Stella typed as the messages kept coming through. She followed through on her threat and shut the phone off. She could use the rest of the ride to review her protocols and see if there were any holes she'd missed in her plan.

Stella arrived home feeling good about her progress. With the additional help from Marcus to see if her computer and her network were secure, she was gaining some peace of mind.

As she pulled into her driveway, her spirits lifted even more to see Richard's car out front. After such stressful days, the idea of him putting his arms around her calmed her ragged nerves.

She walked inside to find Richard seated at the family table, enjoying a meal with Caitlin and Rita. "You started without me." Stella teased, not mad at all to find them eating dinner together.

"We couldn't get ahold of you," said Rita.

"Probably would have helped if I had my phone on. Sorry," Stella said. "I forgot I'd turned it off."

"Not sure it would have helped me," said Richard. "I've been texting all day, but your mother informed me it was in vain. You've gotten a new phone?" He kept his tone light, but Stella could see he was hurt by her secrecy.

"Sorry, it's been a day. Fiona nagged me for the same reason." Stella put her stuff down and joined them at the table. Her mother had made lasagna with garlic bread and a Caesar salad to accompany it. She smiled at her, knowing Rita was providing comfort in a storm of chaos the only way she knew how.

Stella loaded up her plate and explained the phone switch to Richard. "I had a fight with our carrier and decided to tell them to go stuff themselves." Stella received a reassuring smile from her mother that she hadn't given him a reason for the new numbers. "And I got a surprise for you today, too," she said to Caitlin. Stella nodded at her mother to let her give the big reveal. "A little something ahead of Christmas since you've been such a good little girl this year."

While Stella teased, Rita grabbed the box she'd stashed in the kitchen and gave it to Caitlin. "Please," whispered Caitlin, clutching the package.

"What are you hoping for?" asked Richard.

"I don't want to say in case it's not it. I don't want to seem ungrateful, but I'm hoping this is what I've been wanting forever." She took her time removing the bow from the package.

"Why are you moving like a turtle?" asked Rita. Then, to Richard, she said, "She normally rips right into packages."

"I'm giving the universe plenty of time to turn this into what I want," Caitlin said. She wasn't kidding. She pulled each individual piece of tape off the wrapping paper, then unfolded the paper without messing up any of the seams. Honestly, if she had to re-wrap the gift right then, she could do it using all the same materials and no one would be the wiser.

"Come on, girl," groaned Stella. "It is what it is. Open it already." She was confident the phone was what Caitlin had been wishing for, but a small part of her worried she'd missed the mark.

Caitlin finally pulled the wrapping paper from the box and saw her gift. "Oh, my god." Her scream was loud enough to scare the neighbors. "Thank you, thank you, thank you, thank you!"

"Are you thanking the universe, or me?" asked Stella.

"You." Caitlin jumped up and ran around the table to hug her mother. She planted kisses on her cheek and kept thanking her repeatedly. Then she ran and hugged Rita. "I know you had something to do with this, too, Gram. Thank you." And for good measure, she gave Richard a quick hug. "In case you had something to say in the matter. You know better than anyone I'm the only one in 4th grade who didn't have a phone."

"It was all them," said Richard. "But I can confirm you will no longer be a social outcast."

"This comes with a long list of rules that you will follow to the T, or it won't be in your possession for long," Stella added.

"I know. No problem, I promise. I'll do anything you say." Stella knew she genuinely would follow the rules, but she also knew this opened a whole can of worms.

"You already know the classroom rules. No phones in class," said Richard.

"He collects them all and puts them away every morning," said Caitlin. "He doesn't hand them back out until the last bell rings. He's the only teacher who takes it that seriously."

"And you're the smartest kids in the 4th grade, so you be the judge."

Stella ate while Caitlin set up her new phone. She didn't waste any time getting the backgrounds and tones she wanted to use for all of them. She typed Stella's and Rita's contacts in and made a list of everyone she wanted to tell about her early Christmas gift.

"Not so fast," Stella chimed in. "There are rules with this. We'll go over them later."

As the meal wound down, Caitlin and Rita cleared the dishes and got to cleaning the kitchen. Stella invited Richard to sit on the front porch swing with her, freezing weather be damned. She grabbed a blanket from the hall closet and headed outside. "Sit with me?" she asked, patting the space beside her.

"Won't someone see us?" he teased as he sat down.

Stella pulled the blanket over them and grabbed his hand underneath it, relishing the warmth of his touch. She felt some of her stress ebb. While she stayed bundled up, he kept one foot on the ground to swing them.

"I hope you're not upset that I came over tonight. I tried texting you all day but never heard from you, so I decided to be rude and come over uninvited." He kept his eyes facing forward but squeezed her hand.

Stella was in uncharted territory in every aspect of her life. It wasn't a feeling she relished. "I should have told you about switching my phone when it happened. That was a mess, and then I had some work to do, and the day flew by. Regardless, I'm glad you're here." She meant what she said. She rested her head on his shoulder, letting herself pretend for one moment she was a normal woman, and this was a normal relationship.

Stella loved her double life. She cultivated every aspect of it, kept everything moving in the direction she wanted, and had never once considered a different life for herself. Even Max's job offer seemed like a joke to her. She didn't want to give up the one thing in life that made her feel alive. And as long as things stayed the same, and she kept all the balls in the air, she didn't need to give it up.

But now here she sat, swinging on the front porch in December with her daughter's substitute teacher, finding real comfort in his touch. If someone told her this was in her future six months ago, she'd have called them crazy. Now? She didn't know what to think, but she knew she liked this man.

"You've been distant the last few days. It worries me. I want to be here for you. I want to help take care of you." He tried to make his tone light, but Stella caught the hurt in his voice. "You put up these walls and I don't know what to do."

"I'm not sure I know how to let anyone take care of me." Stella spoke the absolute truth for the first time all night.

"Are you okay? Is there anything I can help with?" Though his tone was casual, Stella knew he was sincerely asking. After all, he'd shown up on her doorstep when she didn't answer his texts.

"Just work," she said.

"I didn't know photographers had so much to worry about."

"Everyone has stress. But . . . I'm not just a photographer."

"No?" he asked, turning to face her and staring at her profile. "What else are you?"

She turned to face him. "I'm also a mom. A friend. A daughter. A human. I'm a lot of things, just like you. Any one of them can cause me stress at times."

A flash of disappointment crossed his face. Before she could even comprehend what it meant, his expression changed to worry. "I hope I'm not causing you stress."

"Not at all. You're the bright spot in my life right now—nothing stressful. I promise." He smiled at her but didn't say anything, which seemed unusual to Stella. She realized in that moment there were two people in this conversation, and she'd been only thinking of herself. "How about you? Am I causing you any stress? Is that why you came over tonight?"

One side of his mouth pulled up in a small smile. Releasing the breath he'd been holding in, he said, "Possibly a small amount." He lifted his hand to put his thumb and index finger together with a tiny bit of space between them.

Stella grabbed his hand. She shook her head, at a loss. "I'm so sorry. I didn't mean to stress you out."

"I'm fine, really. I'm just feeling a bit . . . hung out to dry?"

"In what way?" Stella was legitimately confused by his comment.

"My life changed the moment I saw you, Stella Meyers. I've never felt this way about someone before. I wanted to learn everything about you. Who you are, what you do, what makes you tick. Everything I learn about you makes me want to know more, to go deeper with you. I look at you and I think I've finally met my match. I've finally found someone who can stimulate every part of me and be a real partner in my life."

Stella was blown away by what he was saying. He'd never been so forward with her.

Richard shifted his body, angling it toward her on the bench. "I don't know if you feel the same, but I'd do anything for you, Stella."

The swing stopped moving. She reached for his chin and pulled his head up, forcing him to meet her gaze. "I am so, so sorry. I didn't mean to hurt you in any way." She shook her head at her own stupidity. She'd tailed Marcus, and then this threat had upended her. Richard fell to the back of her mind, and it obviously hurt him. "I really have enjoyed getting close to you."

He laughed softly. "You have a funny way of showing it."

"I've never been in a relationship before." She let that sit for a second. "The last real relationship I had was with Caitlin's father, and look how that turned out."

"I think you did well there," he said.

"Yes, I got Caitlin, and she's the best thing that's ever happened to me. That relationship wasn't real, though. After she was born, I turned all my attention to taking care of her and building a life for us. I haven't allowed myself to get close to any man, or any other person, really. I didn't want anything to disrupt my life with her."

"Is that what I am to you? A disruption?"

Stella nodded, needing to be honest. "Yes, you are." He dropped his head again, and she pushed on. "But you're the best kind of disruption. I didn't expect to find someone like you, and I certainly didn't expect to have fallen for you so hard."

"Is that true? Have you fallen for me?"

Stella locked eyes with him. "I have 100 percent fallen for you, Mr. Medina."

She leaned in, and brushed her lips against his, barely touching him. She felt her body warm at the anticipation of a kiss. She placed her hand on his cheek and rubbed her thumb along his jawline, admiring his chiseled face and bright blue eyes. Then she gave herself over to the warmth spreading through her body, closing her eyes, and pulling him into a deep, sensuous kiss. With the deepening of the kiss, her body came alive.

Eventually the kiss slowed, then stopped altogether. "Ms. Meyers, we are in public," Richard finally whispered to her. "What will the PTA think of this?"

"Fuck the PTA," Stella said. She closed her eyes and kissed him again, hungry for more. More of him. More of feeling connected to someone. More of her nerves being set on fire.

They kissed on her porch in twenty-degree weather in front of anyone who happened to pass by. If Richard hadn't stopped her, she might have taken him right there on the swing.

Richard was clearly more in control of his emotions than Stella. He ended their kiss and pulled back, smiling at her as he broke the connection. "I'm happy I'm a disruption in your life, as long as the disruption is good." He pivoted to face forward again and got the swing moving. Stella rested her head on his shoulder.

"Definitely good," she said.

"Then you will let me in a little bit?" he asked.

"Absolutely. I know I'm bad at relationships, but I really do want to make this work." She shrugged. "I'm new at this."

"I'm new to this as well, you know." Stella picked up her head and stared at him, incredulous. "Yes, I've had relationships with other women, but nothing like this. I've never met anyone like you. I can't get you out of my mind. I want to know everything about you and be with you all the time. That's never happened to me before."

Stella's mind seemed to split in two. Part of her felt overcome with happiness that someone had captured her heart and made her want to have a real relationship for the first time in years. The other part of her mind went on the defensive, noting all the lies that kept piling up. Surely if he ever found out who she really was, he'd head for the hills.

She took a deep breath and tried to banish the negative thoughts. She put her head back on his shoulder and smiled. For this single moment in time, she was sitting on a swing in the dead of winter, cuddled up with a man who knocked her socks off. Whatever mess awaited her when she walked back into her house could wait. She wanted to sear this memory into her brain so she could return to it if everything collapsed around her later.

13

Mercifully, Stella's world didn't collapse. Her protocols were working. She had everything in her life under control.

Marcus had personally scanned her computers and confirmed they were clean. He explained it would take longer to monitor her network and search for any malware to see if someone was spying on her, but with all her computers in good condition, Stella hoped her network would be clear as well.

She ran her new iPad on the cell network to review her security camera footage. The sheer volume of footage she needed to analyze was too big for her to do manually. The Degas came on her radar almost a year ago; there were far too many events for one person to review. Instead, she used facial recognition software to catalog every person that came to the house in the past year. Once it identified everyone, she ran a search for any faces that came up more than once. The list was longer than she expected it to be, but several people were easy to eliminate.

The software picked up Stella, her mother, Caitlin, and Max all at the house multiple times. Fiona, Malcolm, and Levi were added to the list. Richard appeared six weeks ago; she put him on the approved list.

Caitlin had friends caught on camera, both Amelia and Rachel frequently tagged. The next level of people making multiple appearances were delivery drivers, the mail carrier, and trash collectors. Neighbors who walked by with their pets were routinely caught on film.

The remainder of the list were individual events of delivery drivers, people canvassing prior to the election, and salespeople. Stella laughed to see none of them made it on camera a second time. She wasn't her best self when someone tried to sell her something she didn't need. It also tagged Pam Fisher and her besties visiting the house this time last year. Stella had been roped into hosting the annual PTA Board Holiday Social so she could photograph them for the school website. Stella cringed at the memory.

The software alerted Stella if the camera caught anyone outside of the list. While that meant she would get alerts when neighbors or the mail carrier came by, the list of people Stella could trust was finite.

She could breathe a little easier with her systems secure and her security protocols in place. She'd done it. This was the first legitimate threat against her family she'd experienced since Caitlin was born, and she felt good about how she'd handled it.

She'd worked to keep her promise to Richard, too. He'd come over in the evenings to spend time with her and her family. They grew closer by the day.

She appreciated the attention Richard paid to her; he seemed to sense her stress and knew the exact thing she needed to feel calm again. Whether it was a bottle of wine with dinner, a text in the middle of the day, or holding her hand as they watched a movie together, his steady presence kept her blood pressure within normal range.

On Sunday night, one week after Stella met Marcus in the park and received the threatening video, Stella finally felt safe enough to leave home for a few hours. Richard had been patient with her all week, never pushing her out of her comfort zone. When he mentioned a pop-up art exhibition opening tonight, Stella couldn't justify hiding in her house any longer.

Richard pulled out all the stops for the date. It was a high-society evening, and the who's who of the New York social scene would be in attendance. These were people who ran in his mother's circle, but Richard knew them well enough to score an invitation. His cufflinks were much more suitable to the sleek black suit he wore tonight than with the outfits he wore teaching 4th graders.

Fiona lent Stella a form-fitting Prada suit with a top that looked like silk overalls without a shirt underneath. It plunged as far down her front as her back, resting at her naval in front and the base of her spine in the back. Two swaths of red fabric snaked over her shoulders, covering only the barest of essentials. She had to hold herself poised so the fabric didn't slip from her shoulders and leave her standing topless.

Fiona, Caitlin, and Rita cheered them on and took pictures of the stunning couple when Richard arrived in a limousine he'd rented for the evening. Stella was so nervous she couldn't decide if her apprehension was because she was leaving Caitlin and Rita on their own for the first time since setting up the new security systems, or because she was heading out on the fanciest date she had ever been on.

THE ART EXHIBIT WAS EXQUISITE. Richard and Stella strolled through the rooms, taking it all in. Soft music played throughout the gallery, curated as perfectly as the paintings hanging on the walls. Each piece seemed to mirror the emotions the artwork provoked in Stella.

Waiters slipped through the crowds offering champagne and canapés, while guests clustered in groups close to the artists to hear them share the inspiration for their work.

Stella used to assess art based on its black-market value, but the Degas had changed her. Where once she'd have walked into this gallery only to tally potential profits, now she walked the rooms with Richard by her side and paid attention to the emotions each piece evoked from her. Some were neutral and Stella couldn't connect to them, but others made her stop in her tracks.

One painting of a mother and a child made Stella catch her breath. The mother sat on the ground, a blanket wrapped around her shoulders, encompassing the child sitting in her lap. The colors were dark and the lines amorphous; Stella couldn't discern where they were or why they were huddled together. But in the abstract lines and dark tones, one thing was evident: Stella could see fear in the mother's eyes. She stood in front of the painting mesmerized, the sounds of the guests fading from her perception. All she could see was the mother clutching her child, holding on for dear life.

"You're like that," Richard whispered into her ear. "You'd do anything for your daughter."

Stella answered without taking her eyes from the painting. "Any mother would."

"That's not been my experience." He took a sip of champagne.

Stella pulled herself back to the gallery. She turned and looked into his eyes, speaking softly. "You deserve to have someone love you like that. I'm sorry your mother couldn't give that to you." She put her head on his shoulder and let him guide her away from the painting.

The artwork wasn't the only thing that grabbed Stella's attention. Although she could now look at the paintings for their creative value, she found it harder to separate her professional instincts from the patrons in attendance.

This crowd offered artists-in-residence programs, funded endowments, and supported the artistic community with bequests when they passed. If anyone wanted a career in the arts, getting anointed by any of the attendees at this event would set someone up for life. Stella's mind flashed to Sebastian Hayes; he would fit in well with this crowd of benefactors.

This was the definition of a target-rich environment.

Stella listened to the room's chatter as people sipped champagne, gossiped, and talked about their own art collections across their multiple homes. The women sparkled in jewels, and the men boasted about leaving the city after the holiday to spend a month skiing in the

Alps or sunning on the beaches in Brazil. They were comfortable among their own kind, speaking freely about their lives. They had no idea there was a fox in the henhouse.

"I wish I had my camera with me," said Stella as Richard brought her a fresh glass of champagne. "This would be an incredible event to capture on film."

"You're always in work mode, aren't you?" Richard asked. Stella opened her mouth to protest, but he stopped her with a kiss. "Don't apologize. It's one of the things I like most about you. You never stop being who you really are, no matter the environment."

"I like to think I can blend into different crowds." Stella sipped her champagne to stop herself from saying more.

"I bet there are some real potential marks in this group," said Richard, pointing at the guests with his glass. Stella choked on her drink, drawing the ire of people around her as she coughed. Richard pulled a handkerchief from his pocket and gave it to her. "Did I say something wrong?"

"I think you mean clients," said Stella. She wiped her mouth and slipped Richard's handkerchief into her clutch.

"I could get you into these circles. I imagine you could make a killing off them."

"I don't disagree." Stella cleared her throat. "Excuse me, I'm going to get some water." She headed for the bar at the back of the gallery.

A voice sounding an awful lot like Fiona rang in Stella's head, encouraging Stella to let her hair down a little. Meanwhile, Stella's own voice reminded her that she couldn't afford to relax. She ordered a club soda with lime; Fiona's voice be damned. She wasn't comfortable losing focus tonight.

Richard caught her eye from across the room, and a smile spread across his lips. Stella felt like there was a spotlight on her. He had eyes for her and no one else. He tilted his head toward the door and mouthed, "Let's go."

Stella set down her club soda and headed for the exit. She was done with the art crowd tonight.

It didn't take long for Stella to see the genius behind having the limousine. She'd assumed it was because they'd be drinking at the gallery and were too dressed up to take the subway home, but Richard introduced her to the true benefits of the luxury car by raising the privacy screen between them and the driver. He pulled her close and crushed his lips to hers.

His passion matched her own. While Stella ran her hands over his chest, she stopped fighting to keep her straps up. Richard welcomed the view with a gleam in his eye. He laid her on the back seat and traced her body with his lips. Every inch of her wanted more from him. They couldn't get enough of each other, devouring each other with an energy Stella had never experienced.

Stella reached for the button of his pants, but Richard gently moved her hand away. "My god, I want all of you." He groaned in her ear while he ran his hand over her breasts again. Stella tried to nod her head and agree, but she wasn't sure he understood she was his for the taking. "Not yet." He shook his head in her neck, then took a playful bite of her ear. "Not here."

Now it was Stella's turn to groan.

Richard sat up, pulling her with him, but she resisted. She understood why he wanted to wait, but she couldn't turn it off so quickly. She rested her hand in his lap, hopeful he couldn't shut this down, too. With a smile, she distracted him by drawing him into a deep kiss while she shifted in the seat. Only when she was kneeling in front of him did Stella pull away and move her lips down his body. Richard groaned in protest, but didn't stop her. She freed him from his suit and made certain he understood just how much the night had meant to her.

Once the limo dropped them off, Stella and Richard couldn't move fast enough. They left their clothes strewn across the house as they made their way to his bedroom and ripped off the final barriers between themselves.

"Now it's your turn," Richard whispered as he descended on Stella in a flurry of activity, his hands, lips, and tongue moving together like a symphony. He brought her to the brink again and again, forcing her to beg him to push her over the edge.

Richard demanded patience as he worked his magic, but she couldn't control herself any longer. Stella released herself in a wave of energy so intense it left her legs and arms shaking.

They were just getting started.

Richard denied Stella any time she tried to take control. He kept her hands away from him as he moved her into positions that gave him the greatest access to all her pleasure points. He kissed her fervently, their mouths crashing together, unable to get enough of each other, then he'd pull back and kiss her entire body with slow, light kisses, and the barest flicker of his tongue. Stella could barely process what was happening to her; her entire body overwhelmed by each touch.

Throughout it all, Richard curated every sensation. He controlled when he brought her to the edge and controlled when she reached each climax. By the time he finally entered her, she was begging for relief, both wanting more and needing the onslaught of sensations to stop. He unleashed the full force of his emotions on her as he brought them both to climax together, crashing over a wave of sensations unlike anything Stella had ever experienced before.

Once both of them were spent, Richard kept his arms around Stella and maneuvered her frame to curl into his, spooning her from behind. They were as close as two humans could be. He whispered to her softly in his native tongue. She could only imagine what he was saying.

All the voices that normally echoed in Stella's mind fell silent for once. They stayed glued together for some time. Eventually, Richard pulled a blanket from the foot of the bed over them. Stella gave herself over to sleep, feeling safe and warm in Richard's embrace.

STELLA WAS TRAPPED, her body pinned down, her mind jumbled. Her heart beat faster, panic rising in her veins. Her brain tried to figure out where she was while her body fought for release. A picture of Richard flashed in her mind. Then Caitlin.

Caitlin! Her brain locked on that image. She was in trouble. Stella had to help her.

Stella wrestled against her restraints, but they grew tighter, until a sound broke through the darkness.

"I've got you," Richard whispered, his arms secure around her body. "It's okay. I'm here."

Stella's eyes flew open, and she took in the unfamiliar room.

"It's just a bad dream." Richard spoke in hushed tones. "You're okay. Caitlin is okay."

She'd fallen asleep. She relaxed against him as Richard stroked her arms with his fingertips.

"I've got you. It's okay." He continued to soothe her as she came out of her stupor.

"I have to go," said Stella, fully alert now. "I can't stay here." She untangled herself from his embrace and pushed the covers aside, rising to search for her clothes.

He got out of bed and took her arm, spinning her around to face him. "It was just a bad dream. Everything is fine."

Stella shook him off. She didn't even know what the dream had been about. The feeling that her daughter wasn't safe clung to her. Every nerve in her body told her that was real.

"This was a mistake. I shouldn't have stayed this long." Stella spun around the room, putting her clothes on while she talked.

"I don't understand. She's ten years old. She's been away from you plenty of times," Richard protested, but he opened his drawer and pulled on his jeans.

"I just need to go. I have to get back to her."

He grabbed her again, stopping her before she left the room. "Stella. Stop this. Tell me what's going on. You travel for your work. You've been away from her plenty of times. This can't be just about a bad dream."

Stella slowed down for a moment and gathered her thoughts. He was right, she'd been apart from Caitlin countless nights in the past. But she couldn't ignore those threatening texts. That video. Richard had no idea what it cost her to be away from her daughter tonight, and she'd stayed out for too long. She'd fallen asleep, and now her brain was punishing her for the lapse in judgment.

Her choices were to look like a crazy mother who couldn't be away from her daughter, or to tell him she was being threatened. Neither option was good. Stella decided to put the blame on herself. "I trust my instincts, Richard, and my instincts tell me to get home to my daughter right now. I don't know what else to tell you."

She pulled on the straps to her suit and headed downstairs to find her shoes. Richard followed her, pulling on a T-shirt, and grabbing his car keys from the kitchen table. The ride to her house took less than ten minutes, each of them excruciating. Stella had a physical need to get to her daughter, to ensure she was safe. She also knew the man sitting next to her had just given her the best night of her life, and he had no idea why she was acting so insane.

As soon as Richard pulled the car to a stop in her driveway, Stella opened the door to leave. Richard grabbed her arm and held her back for one more moment. "I wish you'd let me in. I thought you'd let your guard down tonight. Was I wrong?"

Stella shook her head, not knowing what to say to him. "I'm sorry, Richard. Really."

She closed the door behind her and hurried into her house, kicking off her shoes as soon as she entered. She took the stairs two at a time until she was outside Caitlin's door, her heart racing. Stella eased the door open. Relief washed over her when she saw her girl curled up with her favorite stuffed animal, sound asleep. She walked quietly into her room and bent to kiss her on her cheek, as she'd done so many nights when she was a little girl. She was safe. Stella didn't know if she had any future with Richard after her behavior tonight, but her daughter was safe. Nothing else mattered.

14

S tella checked her phone for the third time that morning. She felt bad about how she'd acted last night but didn't know how to tell Richard the truth. She'd texted him this morning and said she wanted to talk to him, but he hadn't replied.

"I didn't expect to see you here this morning," Rita teased when she walked into the kitchen. Stella grabbed the tub of Greek yogurt out of the fridge and some strawberries while her mother put the kettle on. It was their morning ritual, and Stella felt she needed it today more than ever.

"Did he turn out to be a dud in bed?" Rita asked.

Stella almost cut herself with the knife. "What?"

"You leave here in a limo headed to the fanciest party you've ever attended, and you wake up in your own bed. It feels like the obvious question." Rita motioned toward the coffeepot, silently asking if Stella needed a second cup. Stella nodded. "Sometimes the best-looking ones turn out to be a real disappointment."

"Definitely not the issue," said Stella.

Rita ground the coffee beans as the kettle came to a boil. She'd developed the perfect system for brewing Stella's coffee. Sometimes

Stella thought the reason she tried to stay out of jail was because the coffee there would be terrible.

"Was it you? Did you not measure up to the European women he's used to?" asked Rita.

"Mother!"

She watched Rita scoop three scoops of freshly ground beans into the French press, then poured in the water. With the timer set for three minutes, Stella wondered if she could speed up the steeping time just this once.

"All I'm saying is you're a bit out of practice. Might want to give it another try."

Stella dropped the yogurt bowl in the sink, heat rising to her cheeks. "I've got work to do." She headed to her office, sacrificing the caffeine for her sanity.

Stella went into her office and turned on her computer, determined to shove the conversation aside, but her mother wouldn't let up. She knocked on the office door a few minutes later, the fresh cup of hot coffee in her hand.

"I come in peace." Rita extended the mug to Stella with a smile. "All joking aside, what happened?"

Stella took a sip of her coffee, debating how she could explain last night to her mother. Even knowing what she did for a living, Rita probably wouldn't understand why Stella ran out of Richard's house after the best sex of her life. And if Rita didn't understand it, there's no way in hell Richard would.

Before she found the right words, her phone pinged. Stella grabbed it, hoping for a note from Richard. She didn't even register that it wasn't his popcorn tone.

She clicked the text message and saw a photo of Caitlin sitting in her classroom looking cute. She was reading her favorite novel, *Safira and the Serpent Queen*, completely engulfed in the story and apparently unaware someone had snapped a picture of her.

Wait. What?

Something clicked in Stella's brain.

She raised her eyes slowly, praying she'd see Fiona's name on the message. Or Richard's. Even Pam's. Let the sender be someone she knew.

The contact image showed a gray circle with a white cutout of a person. The number underneath wasn't one she knew.

She froze.

The entire pause probably lasted two seconds, but to Stella's mind, everything slowed into a frame-by-frame view. As she jumped up to grab her car keys, her mind splintered to run through different scenarios all at once. How did they get her new number? Why were they targeting Caitlin? What the hell did they want from her?

This was not an empty threat.

"Stella, what happened? Where are you going?" Stella heard her mother chasing after her, but she was already sprinting for her car.

"Stay here. Lock the doors," she yelled, pushing the ignition the second her foot hit the brake pedal. Her car screeched out of her driveway, and images of Caitlin being hurt bombarded Stella's mind. She yelled at Siri to call Richard as she drove, hoping he had his phone on.

"Fuck," she said when the call went straight to voicemail. She wanted to scream into the phone asking if Caitlin was okay, but better judgment prevailed. She couldn't let Richard know she was terrified for Caitlin's safety again.

She ditched her policy against attracting attention to herself as she raced to the school. She knew she'd have to fabricate a good reason for breaking all traffic laws if she got pulled over.

If Richard couldn't pick up his phone, there were others who could.

"Good morning, love," sang Fiona as she picked up. "What . . ."

"Are you at the school?" Stella shouted into the empty car before Fiona could finish.

"No, I'm heading back home." Fiona's voice instantly turned serious at Stella's panic, and then someone honked their horn. "I'm turning around."

"Don't. I mean, it's okay. I'm heading there now and need to check on Caitlin. I was hoping you could do it for me if you were there still."

Stella tried to lighten her voice, masking the fear coursing through her veins.

"I know something's wrong; I can hear it in your voice. Is Caitlin okay?" Fiona clearly didn't buy the easier tone Stella had taken. "I'll be there in five minutes. Where is she?" Stella heard Fiona yell at someone to speed up; she was breaking some traffic laws, too.

"I don't know where she is. In her classroom, I think."

"Stella, tell me what's going on."

"I need to know she's safe inside her classroom. I also need to know if you see anyone hanging around outside the school." Stella tried to keep the information brief, not giving away too many details. "I'm sure she's fine. I'm sure this is something stupid."

"Stop it. I've never known you to panic. Let's focus on Caitlin and see what's going on." That was Fiona for you. She was jumping in feet first without a second thought.

They stayed on the line together as they raced toward the same destination. Fiona arrived ahead of Stella, but not by much. She narrated her every move as she jumped from the car and ran to the classroom. "I'm going to stay outside since you're almost here. You can go in the main entrance and see from the inside, while I look for shady fuckers hanging around outside."

"Agreed," confirmed Stella. She pulled up to the school's entrance and raced out of the car, leaving the door wide open and the car running. The second she reached the front doors, she waved at the security camera, motioning to the attendant to let her in. Her heart calmed for a fraction of a second, grateful the school had these safety measures in place. The door buzzed, and she pulled it open, running into the hallway toward the principal's office.

"I need to see Caitlin. Right now," she said to the administrative assistant at the front desk. She tried to slow her pace a bit, so she didn't frighten anyone, but she was on high alert.

While she rushed, Stella swiveled her head back and forth, noting every person she saw and cataloging them as safe or a threat. She saw Mrs. Sullivan, the school librarian, and thought of her as a friend. She also passed two teachers from the lower school as she rounded a corner but knew them both on a first-name basis. The last person she saw out of the corner of her eye was Pam Fisher coming out of the teacher's lounge. Stella bristled. She didn't have time for her bullshit today.

"I've got eyes on her. She's okay," said Fiona, the connection still open on her phone. Stella took a deep breath and allowed herself to slow her pace.

"Do you see anyone outside? Walking the grounds?" Stella asked. "Was anyone pulling out when you drove in?"

"No one. The yard is empty, and no one has left since I pulled into the school. Where are you now?"

Stella didn't need to reply. She came to the classroom door and saw Fiona standing outside. She held up the phone and waved it at Fiona before ending the call. Taking a deep breath, Stella steadied her nerves and opened the door to the classroom. Several students looked up from their work to stare at her. Fortunately, Caitlin was among them.

"Mom?" She cocked her head to the side. "What are you doing here?" Caitlin looked at her mom, who caught the eye of Mr. Medina. They both got up and headed her way.

"Can I help you?" Richard asked as he made his way toward her. "Keep working, class. I'll be back in one minute."

Caitlin reached the door first, and Stella gave her a quick hug and reassured her everything was fine. "I'm sorry to bother you, sweetie. I wanted to let you know that Fiona is going to pick you up today. I've been called to do a job and didn't want you to worry about me."

"You could have just texted me, Mom." She looked around at her friends and tried to hide some of her embarrassment.

"I know, but I happened to be passing the school, so thought I'd pop in. Besides, doesn't Mr. Medina collect your phones during the day?" She smiled at her daughter and put her hand on her shoulder, reassuring herself that Caitlin was, indeed, okay.

"Yeah. Any idea when you'll be home?"

"Probably late." She hugged Caitlin as much as the girl would allow and flashed her the sign for "I Love You." Cait smiled and returned the gesture, making the "I Love You" sign followed by two fingers in the air. "I love you, too," it said.

"Sorry for the interruption," Stella said to Richard.

"No problem. I wouldn't want Caitlin waiting around for you after school." He waved Caitlin back to her seat, then guided Stella into the hallway, closing the door behind them. The students looked up from their work again, and Stella heard snickers, one boy saying, "You're in trouble," before the door finally closed.

"Now tell me for real. Are you okay?" Richard pressed.

"I'm fine. Really," she said, catching her breath. "I just needed to see Caitlin."

"This is exactly what happened last night." He whispered the last two words so softly Stella almost couldn't make them out. "What's going on?"

"I don't really know." Stella glanced at the phone in her hand, then looked around the hallway again. "Did you see anyone outside the classroom earlier? Anyone hanging around?"

"No." His brows furrowed. "And I was out there myself not fifteen minutes ago. Why?"

"Nothing, really. I got a strange note about Caitlin."

"A note? What about?"

"It's nothing, really," she insisted. "Look, I know I'm acting crazy, but I need you to trust me. Can you do me a favor and keep an eye on her? I don't want anyone except Fiona picking her up from school or chatting with her. Not until I'm sure she's safe." Stella looked past him to Caitlin again.

"Of course. But you've got me worried now. Why won't you tell me what's going on? It's hard to protect her when I don't know what I'm looking for." Stella looked up at him and saw the sincerity in his eyes.

"Don't I know it." She agreed. "It's probably nothing, but I'd appreciate the extra attention if you can spare it."

"Without question," he answered. He opened the classroom door and nodded to her as he stepped back inside, offering her a quick, discreet smile. "Thank you for delivering the message, Ms. Meyers."

"Sorry for the interruption," she answered, waving at Caitlin before she turned to head back to the front of school. Her phone buzzed in her hands three seconds after she left the classroom.

"Anything?" she asked Fiona when she picked up.

"No, still clear. Is she really okay?"

"I think she's fine. Can you meet me at the front?"

"Be right there." Stella ended the call and took the down time to connect with Max. She knew she couldn't say anything of importance on this phone since it was compromised, but she couldn't wait until she got home to use a burner. He answered on the third ring.

"Yes?"

"I need you here. Now," Stella said, then ended the call. Why hadn't she told him the truth from the beginning? He might have helped her get out of the country instead of thinking Marcus and his team could shore up her systems. She'd wasted precious time when she could have been thousands of miles away by now.

Stella waved to the office staff as she walked out and returned to her car—door still wide open, car still on. Thankfully, no one had stolen it. Fiona drove up and jumped out of her own car, grabbing Stella in a hug.

"She's okay. She's okay," Fiona murmured in her ear while Stella held onto her for dear life.

"For now, yes." She pulled away and looked her friend in the eye. "But I don't trust she's going to stay that way."

"What's going on?"

Stella inhaled a deep breath and looked around the school grounds. Fiona probably thought she was looking for a sign of the stranger, but Stella needed a moment to think. She hated lying to her best friend, but she needed her help. She had to tell her something, and Stella didn't have the time or inclination to tell her the full truth. Not yet. Hopefully not ever.

"Someone is stalking me." It was the first explanation that came to her mind. "That's the real reason I got a new number. I've been trying to protect us, and I thought it had worked. But today I got this." Stella held up the picture of Caitlin sitting at her desk, clearly taken right outside the classroom window.

"What the fuck?" yelled Fiona. "Stella, we have to call the cops. This is insane!"

Stella kicked herself for not realizing that's what Fiona would say. It was the obvious next step. Fiona peppered her with questions so quickly she couldn't get a word in edgewise. Instead, she let her friend freak out while she scrambled for a way to stop her from going straight to the police.

"Does this have to do with Caitlin's dad?" Fiona asked.

Stella latched onto the idea and went with it. "I think it might," said Stella. "I don't want to involve the police yet. If it's him, he's got connections everywhere, at the highest levels. They'd never believe he was threatening me. He'd just say he wanted to see his daughter."

"Do you think he'd take her away from you?"

"I can't take that risk." She could run with this story. Stella had kept tabs on Caitlin's biological father since they'd broken up. She was nothing more than a blip on his radar, but his family had money and power, and he was their golden child. "Please promise me you won't go to the police. Not yet."

"Okay. But if anything happens to you or that little girl, I'm going to go after him myself."

"You don't even know who he is," Stella said with a laugh. She knew her friend was serious, but it also was the levity Stella needed right now.

"That really doesn't matter. I'll become some kind of Wonder Woman who takes down all the self-righteous rich fuckers who leave their girlfriends in trouble. People will love me."

Stella loved the sound of her laughter. "That's a powerful image."

"No doubt. Fine, we won't go to the cops. Yet." Fiona squeezed Stella's arm in reassurance. "How can I help?"

"Can you get Caitlin after school?"

"That's easy. What else can I do?"

"I've got to think about next steps. Knowing she's safe with you is a huge help already."

"I've got your back, girl. Always. And I know you have mine.

Sometimes it's the only thing that keeps me going in this fucked-up life we live." They hugged again, and Fiona waved goodbye.

Stella climbed into her car, her hands shaking. She closed the door and rested her head on her steering wheel, blinking away tears. She didn't deserve Fiona. All Fiona wanted to do was protect and support Stella and her family, and Stella had lied right to her face.

How did she get here? She'd had everything under control. And now here she was, her daughter in danger and her best friend coming to her rescue thinking she was a victim, not the culprit.

She shook her head, clearing her thoughts. This was no time to fall apart. She'd made every decision in her life with her eyes wide open. She prayed Fiona would still be there when the dust settled, but she couldn't let that worry cloud her thoughts. Not now.

Stella headed home. She wanted to make sure her mom was okay, then connect with Max to tell him what had happened. Maybe the three of them could figure out what she was supposed to do next.

15

S tella arrived home to find her mother pacing the living room. The second she walked through the door, she bombarded Stella with questions. "What's going on? Where did you go? Are you okay?"

Stella wanted to tell her mother what was happening, but there wasn't time. Instead, she answered Rita's questions with a question. "Did anyone come here while I was gone?" Rita shook her head. "Has anyone called or texted you? Even a spam or junk message?" Again, Rita said no.

"Tell me what's happening."

Stella looked down at the phone in her hand, and then around the house. Despite her efforts to protect them, someone had made it through their defenses. Right now, she couldn't trust anyone or anything. Stella didn't want to have any conversations someone could overhear. She switched gears.

"Nothing to worry about, Mom. Caitlin forgot an assignment at school and texted me about it. If I didn't get it to her in fifteen minutes, she'd get a zero." Stella waved her phone at her mother and put her finger over her lips, silently screaming at her not to say a word. "Sorry I scared you by racing out of here."

Stella went into her office and retrieved a new yellow notepad from her supply closet. She carried it into the kitchen and scribbled on the pad, then passed it to her mother.

Someone could be listening.

Her mother picked up the pen and wrote her own message back. *Cops?*

She almost looked hopeful. Rita Meyers had no love for the police, but being arrested was something she could understand. Stella wished she could tell her that the only threat was her daughter going to jail. Stella shook her head. Rita's eyes went wide.

Rita headed into the kitchen, pulling things out of the fridge and making a racket. When she took the blender out of the cabinet, Stella figured out her plan.

"You missed breakfast. Want a smoothie?" Her mother glared at her, but her voice remained neutral.

"That'd be great, thanks." Rita dumped some ice into the blender and added strawberries and protein powder for good measure. She motioned for Stella to come closer. When she hit the blender on high, it sounded like an airplane taking off in the house.

Rita leaned close. "What is going on?" She gritted her teeth and spat out each word.

Stella raised her arms and mouthed her answer. "I don't know."

Rita grimaced and shook her head, looking at Stella like she was crazy. "Stop lying to me."

The blender screeched a high pitch as it finished chopping up the ice and fruit. Stella spoke directly in her mother's ear. "We need to go somewhere we can talk. Max is coming."

Rita looked disgusted but had the answer in a flash. "Laddin's." Laddin's was a rock sanctuary not far from their house that Caitlin loved to play in when she was little. The wooded area spread out over eighteen acres. Practically no one would be there on a Monday morning in December. Even better, Stella hadn't been there in years. If someone knew her routines and hangouts, they wouldn't know to plant themselves there. She gave her mother a thumbs up.

Stella clicked on her watch, indicating they needed to figure out when to meet there. It would take Max at least another hour to get to them. "Eleven thirty?" She whispered to her mom. Her mother nodded, and then turned off the blender.

"Here you go. This should get you through the morning. If that's all you need, I'm going to get ready. I've got errands to run."

"Thank you," Stella said aloud, then took her mother's arm and squeezed it. She mouthed the words, "I'm sorry." Rita just shook her head and dismissed her.

Stella headed into her office and locked the door. Once again, she was a prisoner in her own home, unsure what she could safely use and what someone had tainted trying to break through her defenses.

Stella put on some music, hopefully covering the noise she made as she went into her supply closet and opened her safe. She got out another burner phone and alternate IDs for her, Rita, and Caitlin. She also grabbed $5,000 and another €5,000 and put them in a bag. She'd planned for something like this years ago. She knew she wasn't ready to leave the country yet, but she wasn't taking another step without having emergency identification and cash on her just in case.

Stella texted Max from the burner phone and told him to meet them where Caitlin liked to play pirate as a little girl. Max had loved taking her to the rock sanctuary and spent hours with her pretending to be Blackbeard. She then headed upstairs and packed a bag for herself and Caitlin. She saw her mother in her room packing her own bag. She might be mad, but her mother understood the assignment.

———

MAX, Rita, and Stella met up at the first footbridge at Laddin's Rock Sanctuary. The trees were bare, so there wasn't much coverage from wandering eyes, but that worked for them as much as it did against them. Stella could see anyone watching them as well as they could see her. And as her mother had guessed, they were the only people here. It was forty degrees outside and nine days before Christmas.

Stella handed them each a new burner phone. "Consider the new phones we just got compromised. Keep them, but use these when we need to talk to each other privately."

"What the hell is going on?" Rita didn't mince words. She glared at Max and Stella as she ranted. "And don't tell me it's nothing. You go racing out the door like your hair's on fire. Then you tell me someone might have bugged our house. What have you done?"

She directed this last question at Max, and Stella winced. "He hasn't done anything. He doesn't know what's happening any more than you do." If she had told him the full truth last week when she'd met with him, they might all be safely out of town by now.

She motioned for them to walk. They needed to stay on the move.

"I'm in trouble. And it looks like that trouble is about to spill over into Caitlin's world." Stella braced herself for her mother's response. If something happened to Stella that was ultimately on her, her mother would survive. But something happening to Caitlin was beyond the pale.

"Who did you piss off?"

Stella had asked herself the same question a million times, and it was the one thing she couldn't figure out.

"I don't know."

"Don't lie to me. You've brought Caitlin into something, and I want to know what it is. The full story, Stella. What the hell did you do?" Stella shrunk a bit. She'd never seen her mother this angry before.

"I don't know how this happened, but someone knows who Caitlin is." Stella pulled the new phone from her pocket and opened her messages, turning the screen to show her mother and Max. It was the picture of Caitlin sitting in her classroom, completely oblivious that someone was outside the window taking pictures of her.

Rita's eyes widened. "Oh, my god."

"I know. I ran down to the school and tried to find out who it was, but didn't see anyone. I even asked Richard if he'd seen anyone strange lurking around, but he didn't."

"Now the new phones and crazy rules make sense," Rita said. "When did this start?" Stella knew her mother wasn't blind to the ways of the seedier side of the world. She had kept her husband's secrets and had been his confidant in everything he did. "I need to know the truth."

"Tell us what happened. Leave nothing out," added Max. The 'this time' was implied, but Stella was grateful he didn't say it out loud.

"I've been getting messages for a couple of months. I thought they were spam. But last week, after I met with Marcus—"

"Is this the man about the job? Or is that a lie, too?" Rita asked.

Max replied, "I connected Stella with an individual looking to hire someone with her set of skills. She met him at my request. We were discussing her getting out of this field." Stella was grateful Max phrased it that way, as if she'd been at all interested in quitting. It worked; her mother calmed down enough to let Stella continue her story.

"Anyway, I met with him and got another text message afterward. This one had a video attached to it, and I knew it wasn't spam. This was a threat." Stella thought back to all she'd done since she'd gotten that video. She'd worked so hard and thought she'd been so smart, and for a while, she thought it had worked. "I had no idea they were going to involve Caitlin. I don't even know how someone found out I have a kid."

"Do you really think you can parade around here and live this double life, and no one will be the wiser? Once someone knows you, there's a direct line to Caitlin. It's no secret she's your daughter. There isn't some fortress built to protect her. We live in Connecticut. Anyone can find out who we are." Rita's voice wavered between anger and exasperation.

"What was on the video?" asked Max.

"The last big job we did." Max's eyes widened at her response. "You're not in it. And most of the footage is from the security cameras at the entrance. There's one shot at the end that shows me moving the merchandise from my car to yours. That's the one that disturbs me most. When you see it, you'll understand. Someone had to know we were going to be there to get it on film. We were set up."

"How could you let this happen?" Stella looked up to respond but saw her mother was talking to Max.

"I never intended—"

"I don't give a damn what you intended. You knew the risks, and you encouraged her anyway. You promised me you'd protect her and look at her now. They took Caitlin's picture. In her classroom."

"I would never knowingly let anything happen to any of you. You're like family. I will do anything I can to protect you."

Stella could see Rita wrestling with her emotions, wanting to lash out and hurt Max for putting them in this situation. "God willing, there will be time to blame people later. Right now, we need to focus on keeping Caitlin safe." She looked at Stella with conviction in her eyes. "What's the plan?"

"I have $10,000 and our IDs. I'm ready to go," said Stella.

Max shook his head. "That's 'running from the cops' money, not 'running from the mob.'" He looked around as he spoke, realizing how much danger they might really be in.

"It's something," said Stella. "It'll get us on a plane out of here."

"Where will you go? You have no idea who you're dealing with. Whoever it is has gone to a lot of trouble to find you. You need to disappear for good, not for a weekend."

Rita released a long sigh. "I can't believe it's come to this."

Stella felt her pain. When the papers reported her father had been killed while trying to rob a bank, Stella and Rita's community shunned them, casting them out as pariahs. She didn't want to live through that again.

"We need to get you to a safe location while you make preparations to leave," said Max. "We also need to figure out who is behind these threats."

"That's what I've been trying to do," said Stella.

"This isn't something you can do on your own," said Max. "You need help."

"That's why I'm talking to you."

"Stop being stubborn and listen to the man," Rita snapped. "I might be angry with him, but I'm betting he's been in this position before. It's time to hear him out." Rita glared at Max as she said it, both putting her trust in him and wanting to kill him at the same time.

Max nodded to Rita. "Let's get you and Caitlin to a safe place." He turned to Stella. "Then, you and I will work with Marcus and his team to track the threats against you. In the meantime, you can make an escape plan. Marcus can even help with that. He's got eyes and ears everywhere. He'll know a safe place for you to go."

"I've already talked to Marcus. He scanned my computers and told me they were clean." Stella made her final protest, wanting to keep her mistakes to herself.

"You cannot expect him to help you when you failed to tell him the extent of the threat against you."

He was right, and she knew it.

"Fine. Where do we put Mom and Caitlin?" Stella looked at her mother for any ideas. "A random hotel in the middle of nowhere?"

"I don't think that's a good idea. I'd rather her be close so you can leave the second you are ready," Max said.

"And I'd prefer to be able to call for help if needed," said Rita. They walked a bit down the path, each lost in thought. "How about Fiona's? She's got that house in the Hamptons. It's abandoned this time of year, but only two hours away."

"That'll work. I'll talk to her," said Stella.

"Does Fiona know what's happening?" asked Max.

"About that." Stella half smiled, half grimaced. "Fiona might be under the impression Caitlin's biological father is stalking me." She bit her bottom lip and furrowed her brows together, not ready to hear their comments.

"You told Fiona what?" asked Rita.

"She helped me look for the guy at school. I had to tell her something."

"And you opted for the deadbeat dad?" asked Rita.

"Not at first. I told her someone was stalking me and that they'd taken Caitlin's picture. It was actually the truth." Stella waited for them to argue, but they both stared at her. "Then she said we had to call the cops. I panicked."

"I still don't see how you got there," Rita said.

"Actually, she brought it up, and I ran with it. I told her he was an immensely powerful person and that he could take Caitlin away from me if I caused trouble—all of which is true. So she agreed not to go to the police." Stella rationalized her story. "I know it's not ideal, but there was no time for an extended explanation about this. Please, just go with it when you talk to her."

"Aren't you tired of keeping all these secrets?" Rita asked.

Stella didn't answer.

"You can't keep living this way." Rita shook her head. "All of this is going to go away. You're not perfect, and you damn sure can't do this on your own. Fix this before you lose everyone who matters to you." She left them standing there as she headed for her car.

Stella turned to Max. "I'm sorry I didn't tell you about the video. I thought I could handle it." She gestured to her mother driving away. "Clearly, I was wrong."

"I'm hurt you didn't trust me," he said. "But I know you've done everything you could to protect your family. You can't ask for much more than that."

"Look where that got me." With a sigh, Stella looked at Max and felt the heaviness settle in her body. She felt two inches shorter and twenty pounds heavier. Someone had thrown a grenade into Stella's perfectly constructed life. She had no idea who would be left standing when the dust settled. She prayed she wouldn't lose her mother, daughter, or even her best friend over this. It seemed like a futile prayer, but she had to ask.

16

There were a million things to do all at once. She buried her stress, pushed the threat aside, and drew on her training to keep herself sane. Her mind cataloged everything that needed to happen and prepared to run down any number of scenarios depending on how each domino fell, exactly like how she prepared for a job.

Top priority was to get Caitlin and Rita to safety. Stella texted Fiona from her compromised phone to meet her at CFCF, one of their favorite coffee spots. She had to keep up appearances. Anyone tracking her would think it was a routine coffee date with her best friend. Stella ordered an Americano for herself and a Matcha Latte for Fiona, her current drink of choice.

The moment Fiona stepped into the shop, Stella felt her heart constrict and tears flooded her eyes. She reached out to her like a life raft in a storm. More than Rita, Max, or even Richard, seeing Fiona gave Stella hope that everything would be okay. Even when the deck seemed stacked against her.

"It's okay, love, I'm here," whispered Fiona as she hugged Stella and kissed her cheek.

Stella held onto the hug as long as she could. "Thank you for coming." She wiped her eyes as they broke apart.

"Thanks for the tea, but I think I'd have preferred a shot of tequila." She raised her cup to toast Stella. "Couldn't we have met at a bar instead?"

"I need to keep my wits about me, and I need you to do the same."

"That's true." She gave Stella's hand a reassuring squeeze. "What's the plan?"

"I want to get Caitlin somewhere safe with my mom for the next few days. Somewhere no one can find them."

Fiona took a sip of her drink and asked, "Any ideas?"

"I'm hoping you won't object to them staying at your place in the Hamptons. As long as no one is there right now?" She wanted to be sure she wasn't putting Fiona's family out in any way.

"Easiest yes ever, great idea. I'll get Lucas to open the house and get some food for them." Lucas was the handyman and property manager Malcolm and Fiona used to watch their home when it wasn't in use. Fiona checked her watch and ran some numbers in her head. "He can have it ready to go by dinnertime. Will that work?"

Stella released the breath she hadn't known she'd been holding. "That's fantastic, thank you. Can you do it without telling him who's coming? I'd rather keep this as discreet as humanly possible."

"Of course. Give me a list of foods they like. I want to stock the kitchen with comfort food since they're going through all of this."

"Caitlin doesn't know what's happening," Stella said. "I'm trying to keep her safe without scaring the shit out of her."

"I know, but she's going to know something happened when you pull her out of school the week before Christmas. Dr. Pepper and Oreos will help." Fiona took a sip of her drink before she kept going. "Now, how can we get her there safely? We need a way to transport her without drawing attention, right?"

Stella nodded. "I think I'll have my mom rent a car, but I need to get her from your house to the rental without anyone watching." Rita would rent the car under her false ID, but that didn't matter if someone watched her get in the car with Rita and followed them to Fiona's house. It wasn't a safe house if everyone knew where she was.

"I need sugar. I can't think on this healthy crap." Fiona went to the counter and returned with two chocolate croissants and a giant gingerbread cookie. "'Tis the season," she said, nodding at the gingerbread. "Which gives me an idea."

Fiona grabbed her phone and opened Chrome, searching for something. Stella tried to see what she was looking at, but Fiona was too fast for her. She held up her hand and begged Stella for patience.

"Got it," said Fiona, louder than she should have. Stella touched her arm, quieting her.

"Got it," she whispered when she caught her mistake. "I was going to take Levi to see *The Polar Express* this holiday. Like the book? I know the kids are too old for it, but damn it, I want to go. How about I take them tonight?"

"You mean the movie? Is it showing somewhere?"

"No. Well, yes. You take a train where you watch the movie, have treats, and Santa comes for a visit. They've got the whole car decked out to look like the train in the movie. It's so adorable. Levi would probably be much happier if I dragged Caitlin along with us. Your mum can meet us there, too. We'll do it together, then she can take Caitlin to our house in the rental when it's over. Even if someone follows us there, they're not going to stick around for three hours while we see Santa." Fiona tapped her screen a few more times. "There's one tonight at Port Jefferson Station. It's between here and the Hamptons. It'll be perfect."

Rita would have enough time to finish packing and rent a car while Fiona picked up the kids, then she could meet them there for the night. They'd separate at the end and Rita and Caitlin would head to the Hamptons while Fiona and Levi went home.

"It could work," Stella said.

"Damn right it'll work," exclaimed Fiona. "I thought of it." She took a bite of the gingerbread cookie as her reward, then she leaned in to whisper, "I'll make sure I pull focus from Rita and Cait when we leave so anyone watching us will follow me." She nodded. "I got this."

"I think people follow you even without all the spy moves." As Stella took a bite of her croissant, her burner phone rang. It was Max. "One second, I have to take this." Part of her wanted to walk away from Fiona while she took the call, but she knew that would set off more alarm bells for her friend. She decided to answer in front of her and keep it vague. "Hello?"

"Can you be at the house at 4:30 today? Our friend is sending someone to your place to pick up your equipment and sweep the house."

"Sure. But I hope they're coming under some pretense that won't raise any eyebrows. I have to assume someone is watching us."

"They'll take care of it," Max reassured. "Do you have everything squared away for tonight?" They were being cautious on the call despite Stella having cut these phones out of their cases not three hours ago.

"All set." She hung up and tried to explain what she could to her friend. "That was Max. He has some friends who know a bit about security. They're going to help me make sure my house is safe."

"I always figured there was more to Max than he let on." The comment made Stella laugh, but she also wondered what more her friend suspected. Maybe Stella hadn't been as sly as she thought. "Anything else you want to talk about now?" asked Fiona.

"I think that covers it," said Stella.

"I'm glad we've got the spy shit covered, but I mean about your date last night." Fiona bent over and stage whispered loud enough for the entire restaurant to hear. "Did you and Mr. Hottie finally do the deed?" Stella almost spit out her drink. She coughed and fresh tears filled her eyes, this time from choking instead of crying. Fiona patted her on the back. "I'll take that as a yes."

"Honestly, it's been such a crazy day I almost forgot about that," Stella admitted. "We had a lovely evening. That's all I'm going to say."

"I don't need to hear anything else. Yet." Fiona waggled her eyebrows. "When things calm down, I demand to hear every single detail." She turned serious for a moment and lowered her voice. "Does he know about this guy creeping around?"

"I haven't told him. It's all happening so fast. I don't want to freak him out."

"He might be able to help you. I know I'll feel better knowing he's up to speed and watching your back. Caitlin isn't the only one at risk in all of this."

"She's the only one who matters." Fiona protested, but Stella stopped her with a raised hand. "I know. I appreciate what you're saying, but don't you think he's going to run for the hills if I am losing my mind over some stalker?"

"Men love to play the hero. If you think the sex was good last night, imagine how good it'll be if he thinks he's your protector." Stella laughed at that thought. She didn't think there was a way to top last night, at least before she left the house in a blind panic, but Fiona didn't need to know either of those things. "Give him a chance to be the man and stand up for you. That's all I'm saying. Don't use this as an excuse to push him away."

"Feels like a pretty good excuse to me," said Stella.

"Girl, do not fuck this up."

Fiona didn't realize Stella was planning on leaving the country before Christmas. There wasn't room in that scenario for a new boyfriend, no matter how much she cared for him.

Stella and Fiona gathered their things and headed for their cars. Fiona gave Stella a hug goodbye and promised to keep her posted on their whereabouts.

"As to that," said Stella, "keep your communications with me on my new phone. Try to text as if nothing has happened, but don't say anything that would lead someone to know where you are or what you're doing. Can you do that?" Fiona nodded her agreement. "My mom has a new number for me and can let me know they're okay, but I want to keep up the appearance that I'm not rattled by this, and that Caitlin is still with me. That should give them enough time to get settled at your place."

"You got this shit down." Fiona waved goodbye and set off for her car.

A week ago, Stella would have agreed with her friend. Now she hoped she could stay one step ahead of these assholes long enough to get out of the country.

17

I t was all Stella could do not to text Caitlin every five minutes to make sure she was okay. For her part, Fiona took to the spy game quickly. Stella got a text from her saying she'd picked up Caitlin and they were heading to a coffee shop for some treats, then home for dinner. Stella knew they were really on their way to experience *The Polar Express*, but she loved Fiona's dedication to the ruse. She prayed it would work.

Stella gave Rita her fake identification and some credit cards under the same name. She would head into the city and rent a car, then meet up with Fiona, Levi, and Caitlin at Port Jefferson Station. Stella was glad Caitlin would get to have this night with Levi before she left for the Hamptons. There was no way they were going to have a normal Christmas this year; Stella wasn't even sure what country they would be in when the holiday arrived. She was grateful her daughter could have this last evening with her friend and a taste of holiday magic before it all went away.

As promised, at 4:30 p.m., a van pulled into Stella's driveway with the name O'Neill Plumbing & HVAC painted on the side. Her phone pinged as he walked up the drive—her security system alerting her that an unapproved person was approaching the door. She didn't need the reminder to be cautious but loved that at least this security protocol was working. She hoped there would be some way to confirm this man was who he said he was before she let him inside. He rang the doorbell, and Stella opened it, letting him speak first.

"I'm here about a plumbing problem? Got a leak in your crawl-space?" He handed her a card as he spoke. Stella recognized the black calling card of Onyx Intelligence Group. "Is this the correct house?"

She scanned the card with her burner phone, launching her browser to what looked like a private page on Marcus's website with a note written expressly for her.

> Patrick will sweep your house for bugs and pick up your computers and phone for analysis. Come to our offices in the morning to discuss next steps. Call from a safe location if you need anything else tonight.
>   –M.W.

Stella smiled at the gentleman standing in her doorway. "You've got the right house. Thank you for coming so quickly."

Once inside, he got to work setting up his equipment, Stella relegated to making passable small talk and trying to keep up the ruse of a plumbing issue. It took him three trips back to his van, but he brought in a bunch of equipment that made a considerable amount of noise when he turned it on. That gave him the cover he needed to pull out his scanning equipment and begin his search for bugs.

They signaled to each other when needed, and Stella watched him move methodically through her house. While he worked, she went into her office and put her original computer and the new laptop with the threatening video on it in a bag for him. She also added the cell phone that received most of the threats. She didn't want to give over the phone she'd received Caitlin's picture on in case they tried to contact her again. She hoped Marcus and his team could get enough from her computers and phone to track them down.

As Patrick was finishing his scans upstairs, Stella heard her door-bell ring. Confused, she checked her phone to see who it might be.

She hadn't received an alert that someone new was approaching the house. Patrick slipped down the stairs as she opened her app and saw Richard standing on her doorstep. She turned and pointed Patrick toward her office. He nodded and closed himself inside so Stella could open the door.

"Hey, how are you?" She intentionally shouted her hello, pretending she couldn't hear anything over the noise of the pump. Acting exasperated, she used the sound as an excuse to step outside and talk. "Sorry about that. How are you?"

Last night felt like a million years ago, and Stella didn't know where they stood anymore. She didn't know whether she should kiss him hello or even touch him. Thankfully, Richard took the lead and bent down for a kiss. "I think I'm better than you are," he said. "What's all this?"

"Leak in the crawlspace. I paid a fortune to get a plumber here today. It's noisy as hell in there, but hopefully he'll get the mess cleaned up."

"You can't catch a break, can you?"

Stella's exasperation was genuine. "No shit. Literally. What a mess." She collapsed against the door, letting her real emotions through for a moment.

Richard took her hand and kissed it, then entwined his fingers with hers. "What can I do to help? Do you have dinner plans?" he asked.

"Kind of lost my appetite with a crawlspace full of shit."

"That would do it. Are Caitlin and your mom inside? Do they want to get out of here?"

"Fiona picked Caitlin up from school, as you know." Richard nodded as Stella spoke. "My mom's joining them at Fiona's house for dinner. I think they might even spend the night. It's not fun to be here right now."

"If Caitlin and your mom are at Fiona's, why don't you come stay with me tonight?"

Stella bristled at his question. Her rational mind knew it was a generous offer, and a normal one for a man to invite his girlfriend to his house when she needed a clean place to stay. But after how last night ended, and with the day she'd had, she didn't care what her rational mind told her. He was pushing her, and she didn't like it. She dropped his hand.

"Thank you, but I don't think that's a good idea. I landed a big job in the city and will be working around the clock for the next week or two. I'm probably going to be staying in the city for the foreseeable future." She wanted to buy herself some time away from him without raising his suspicions but hoped it wouldn't take that long. Regardless, her mind was tired, and his was fresh. He caught her mistake before she could spin her tale another way.

"Last night you ran out of my house after our night together because you couldn't stand to be away from your daughter for a full night." The more he spoke, the more his voice rose. "And now you tell me you're going to stay in the city for the 'foreseeable future.' What does that even mean, Stella? What's going on with you?"

She didn't know if her training kicked in or if she was genuinely fed up with every aspect of her life right now, but she unleashed on him. "What do you want me to do, Richard? I have a life. A kid. A job I need to pay the bills. The holidays are coming up, and now my crawlspace is filled with shit. I am doing everything I can to keep all these balls in the air, and I don't need you or anyone else asking any more from me."

She saw a flash of anger in his eyes before hurt settled on his face. "I wanted to be part of your life. A good distraction. Isn't that what you called it? I'm not trying to be a burden, but this is what relationships are. They're about trusting someone else. Letting someone else carry part of the burden. That's what I want us to be."

"I don't know how to do that." For the first time in years, Stella spoke the absolute truth. "Not right now. I still have a messy life and a kid I love more than anything. I have to provide for my family, and I have to keep them safe. It's all on me. It's always been all on me. There's never been anyone else in my life to share a burden with. I can't turn all of that off so quickly. I'm trying, Richard. I'm really trying. But I'm not there. I don't know how to be who you want me to be."

"I can't wait forever, Stella." He put his hands in his pockets. "Call me if you're ready to let me in." He shook his head, then turned and walked back to his car.

Stella watched him leave, willing him to turn around. One glance back and she would have run into his arms and let him come to her rescue, exactly like Fiona said. She wanted to be rescued.

Only, he didn't glance back. He got in his car and drove away, leaving Stella on her doorstep to handle her life by herself, just as she'd asked him to do.

Stella stood outside on her porch, the temperature dropping as the last rays of the December sun disappeared on the horizon. She'd been wrong to think she could have it all. She chased off the first man who mattered to her in a decade, while a stranger searched her home for listening devices. This wasn't the life Stella wanted for herself or her family. Not at all.

She inhaled a deep breath and went back inside to learn what, if anything, Patrick had found.

18

P atrick had found one listening device in her kitchen and a tracker on her car. It shook her to her core. She hadn't seen anyone unfamiliar when she'd analyzed twelve months of security footage. That must mean this went back even farther. The bug in her house and the footage capturing exactly where she moved the merchandise for the heist made her feel like a marionette dancing at the end of a puppet master's strings.

She changed her plans and called Marcus, requesting a meeting with him tonight. She'd bring her equipment and see if there was anything he could do to help track the person who was sending these threats. With Caitlin and Rita on their way to the Hamptons and Richard no longer asking to spend the evening with her, Stella was free to go to the city and be on the offensive.

Max agreed to meet her at Marcus's office at 8:00 p.m. Twenty-four hours ago, she'd been driving into the city in a limousine, dressed to the nines, and feeling great about the night ahead. Now she took an Uber to the train station to hide her movements from whoever was tracking her car and listening to her every word in her home.

Stella arrived at 30 Rockefeller Plaza and hit the button for the twentieth floor. Last time she was here, only a skeleton crew was working. She'd assumed most of his employees worked from home— surely hackers could work anywhere. As she stepped out of the elevator and approached the offices of Onyx Intelligence Group now, she saw she'd been mistaken. Instead of an office barren of people, the place was positively buzzing.

Stella opened the door to the office and was immediately greeted again by the young man who'd helped her sort out her pizza issues. He shook her hand, welcoming her. "I'm Raf, nice to see you again." He smiled at her. "I heard you pulled one over on the boss. I've been wanting to meet you again to congratulate you."

"I'm not sure congratulations are in order, but I'm Stella." She looked down after shaking his hand.

"I know some shit's going on, but no one gets the best of Marcus Williams. You really should be proud of that." Stella mumbled her thanks and wished again she were visiting under better circumstances. "I'll tell him you're here. Do you want anything while I get him? A drink? A snack?"

"Nothing for now, thank you."

"Got it." He motioned to the conference room off to her left. "Your friend is already here. If you want to wait with him, I'll tell Marcus you're both here."

Stella walked into the conference room, happy to see Max sitting at the table. He stood when she entered. "Is she safe?" he asked after pulling her into a hug.

"They're on their way," Stella confirmed. Fiona had checked in with another innocuous message, and Stella discerned Rita and Caitlin had left for the Hamptons. She expected her mother to check in with her any minute that they'd arrived safely.

Stella set her bag in a chair and looked around the room, taking in her surroundings. Like the rest of the office, the conference room seemed uniquely designed to create a very specific experience for its occupants. Instead of being a bland, cold room full of equipment, the environment was warm and welcoming.

The conference table was the centerpiece of the room, not only because it seated twenty people comfortably around its perimeter, but because it demanded to be seen. Stella ran her fingers over the stunning wooden tabletop, a single slab of Cocobolo, rich with vibrant red hues that deepened into saturated black accents. She looked for outlets or places people could plug in their tech, but thankfully the table was uncut.

Behind her a bench wide enough to lie down on ran the length of the room. It had plush leather seat cushions and several throw pillows, inviting people to either sit or sleep, Stella didn't know which. Tight-weave carpet on the floor and acoustical tiles on the ceiling suppressed any noise from the busy office outside their door. Faint scents of lavender and sandalwood danced in the air.

The entire room calmed her nerves and put her at ease.

"I've never seen a conference room like this," said Stella, taking her seat and motioning for Max to do the same. "He's created an oasis of peace and calm in the place he meets with clients to deliver upsetting news."

"He certainly thinks of everything," Max agreed. "You're in good hands here."

As they settled in, Marcus joined them. He nodded at Max, then crossed the room and extended a hand to Stella. "Good to see you again, Stella. Welcome to the office."

"It's a lot busier here than the last time I came," she said, glancing at her watch again to confirm the time. "I hope you're not keeping everyone here late for me."

"No, this is pretty normal for this crew." Marcus nodded at her seat, and they sat down. "Last time you were here, most of these people weren't out of bed yet, much less at work. This place gets hopping around two and goes all night sometimes."

"I assumed most people were working from home, but clearly, that's not the case today."

"Our office is the most secure place for any of us to work, and I think we enjoy the camaraderie of being around each other most of the time. We don't have big social lives outside of work, so being together at the office counts as our social time," he said. "I make sure safety protocols are in place on everyone's private networks and homes to allow them to work from home when they want."

Stella glanced at him and smiled, thinking of how secure his own home was. Marcus picked up the blunder immediately. "Clearly we have some work to do there. I still want to know how you did that."

"Another time. I'll be giving away enough of my trade secrets today, I'm afraid."

Marcus nodded. "Patrick relayed what he found in your house. He said you were bringing your equipment over." Stella nodded to the bag she'd set in the chair next to her. "What's going on? How can I help?"

Stella glanced at Max, and he encouraged her to proceed. "I thought it best to come from you. I didn't want to misrepresent something or make any assumptions about what's happened up to now."

Stella recounted the story from the moment she received the first threatening message. Embarrassment colored her cheeks when she had to admit how she'd handled opening the link, but she explained her reason for buying a new computer and not exposing her own equipment to a potential virus. Marcus pushed back a little on why she didn't contact him immediately but seemed to understand she didn't know enough about anything—about Marcus or the text message—to bother him at the time.

"After you saw the incriminating video, what happened exactly?" Marcus asked.

"I tried to figure out who might have sent it," said Stella. "I didn't have a way to trace the message or anything like that, but I watched the video over and over, trying to figure out what details it revealed."

"What else did you do?"

"My main focus was making sure I increased my security protocols. You helped verify my computers weren't infected and monitored the network."

"We haven't seen any suspicious activity on that, by the way," said Marcus. "We'll continue to monitor it, but I suspect it's clean."

"That was my thought as well."

"Did you get any follow-up messages?"

"None. I continued to monitor my old phone and new one and tried to figure out who might have sent that video. No more messages came from the sender, though. At least none that I could tell."

"Your protocols were working," Max said.

"That's what I thought," Stella said. "Now I realize I was mistaken."

Stella filled in the rest of the story. After being lulled into a false sense of security and letting her guard down a tiny fraction, she got a picture of Caitlin texted to her new phone. Stella explained the frantic race she'd made to get to school and confirm her daughter was safe.

Marcus absorbed the entire story, interrupting only to clarify information. Then he cut to the chase. "How can we best help you now?" he asked.

Stella reached in her bag and pulled out both computers, placing them and her original phone in front of her on the desk. "I really want to know who sent these messages to me. Where they are, what they want—anything you can do to track these people down so I can figure out what to do."

Max interrupted, "Our top priority is to keep Caitlin safe. Stella and Rita as well. We must know who we're dealing with to accurately assess the threat."

"We can definitely do that." Marcus turned to Stella and asked, "Can I bring in a couple of team members to discuss this? I'll try to keep the information to a minimum, but I want their input as to how we should proceed."

Stella closed her eyes for a moment and took a deep breath. She'd come this far, and she was almost completely out of options. She couldn't be picky now. She gave her permission.

Marcus summoned Aidan and Celina and brought them up to speed on the situation. He was kind enough not to explain what had been on the video Stella received, but she knew they'd see it soon enough when they opened the file. The three of them discussed the best ways to get the information off the phone without risking a virus. The team ultimately agreed on a course of action that would give them the most access to the perpetrators moving forward.

"We want to clone your machine," said Aidan. "I can set up a virtual computer that looks like yours and open the file there. If there's a bug in the link, which we assume there is, that would likely grant someone access to this virtual machine."

"They'd be able to see everything on my computer?" Stella asked. She could have done that herself.

"They'll see what we allow them to see," said Celina. "We can clone your entire system and then sit down with you and get rid of anything you don't want them to see."

"I don't want them to see any of it."

"I understand," Marcus said, "but this gives us a way to play with them a little bit. We can manipulate things on our end and leak information to them as we need to, as well as trace any additional messages they send to you. It's the best way to bait them."

"What about my original phone? I didn't click on the link from the phone, but there could have been other messages from them. I identified a few of them myself. I switched to a new one, but they sent me the picture of Caitlin on it today. I've got a burner phone now but am still using this for communicating with my daughter and anything I want to do publicly."

"We'll do the same thing with your phone. We'll isolate it and make them think they can see you, and then we can fuck with them," said Aidan, clearing his throat. "Sorry, mess with them."

Stella laughed. "Don't hold back on my account. I definitely want to fuck with them." She passed her equipment over to Aidan. "I think we have a plan. How long will this take? When do you think you'll have a line on who is sending these notes?" Stella glanced at her watch. They'd been talking for almost an hour now.

"I think we can get the machine cloned and cleaned within forty-eight hours. Then we'll open the message and see what happens from there. Even sophisticated viruses will take a bit to run, but we'll know more then. Probably three or four days to get everything set up," said Celina.

"Three or four days? Just to get it set up?" asked Stella.

Marcus jumped in. "It's the best we can do. We'll try to go faster, but this isn't something we want to mess up. We're way behind the people who are orchestrating all of this. If we do it wrong, we risk total exposure. You, your family—it's too big of a risk. We have to be careful."

"I appreciate that. I was holding out hope this would be faster." Stella looked around the luxury offices, all the sophisticated equipment in this opulent office. It felt like it should be faster.

"Everyone thinks it's instant gratification," said Aidan. "It's not like that in real life."

Marcus gave him a cutting look, but he didn't disagree. "Tech gets a bad reputation from television. People assume you can summon anything from a satellite and deliver a map of a nuclear site to Tom Cruise while he crawls through a heating duct and direct him to the exact location he needs to find. But that's not the way it really works." He looked at Stella. "We need time."

Stella looked at Max, and he nodded. "Let's get started."

Max waited for Aidan and Celina to take the equipment out of the room before he spoke. "While you begin your forensic analysis," said Max, "Stella and I will work on getting her to a secure location. With the breaches we've seen today, I'd prefer she have completely new identifications for herself, her mother, and daughter before she leaves the country. The sooner we get those, the sooner we can open new bank accounts and move the money she'll need to survive."

Marcus nodded. He wasn't new to this side of the game, either. "Where are you going?" he asked. "I want to make sure your IDs are welcome where you decide to go. I don't think using an American passport is a good idea."

"I concur," said Max. "We have yet to pick a location. Can you assist with that as well? Do you know a place that might be easier to hide all three of them?"

Stella turned to him. She didn't realize until this moment that leaving could mean leaving Max, as well. "Aren't you coming? You're on that video, too. I don't want anything to happen to you, either."

"I'll get to you one way or another once it's safe. I want to be here monitoring the investigation and doing everything I can to shut down who is threatening you." He reached for her hand and squeezed it. "I want to get you back to your life if that's at all possible."

Stella nodded, too strung out to argue anymore tonight.

"I'll look at some options and get back to you in the morning," Marcus said. "We'll find a secure place your daughter will love."

"Thank you." Stella highly doubted Caitlin was going to love being uprooted from the only home she'd ever known, but she appreciated the effort.

Marcus set things in motion. Tonight, they'd begin cloning her laptop and isolating her phone on a private system, ensuring nothing this person had sent her would pass beyond the virtual cells they put them in. They didn't need Stella tonight, but she could return in the morning to begin eliminating anything she didn't want them to see.

"Think about what information we can show them," Marcus said. "What contacts you have that they'd expect to see, what things on your calendar that are safe to share—we want them to think they're in your actual system. If you know that information, it'll help us move faster once we get everything set up."

Stella thanked him and agreed to work on that list.

She would move the chess pieces of her life around the board, bolstering her defenses to ensure she was ready for any attack her opponent would launch. As she left the office, Stella was grateful to have Marcus and his crew of professional hackers stepping in to help her trace the scumbag threatening her. As hard as it was to expose her mistakes to them, she relished the idea of finally going on the offensive.

19

F or three days, Stella worked around the clock to get ready to disappear. It was difficult enough to plan her own retreat. It was exponentially more complicated to take her mother and daughter with her. For now, Stella told Caitlin they were taking a surprise trip for the holiday. Once they were safely out of the country, Stella would figure out how to tell her they might not return.

Fiona did not leave Stella's side all week. Stella fed her what information she could to explain what was happening but continued to lean into the lie that this involved Caitlin's biological father. She told herself she was protecting her friend, but deep down, she knew she was really protecting herself. Stella couldn't dump her life story on Fiona's doorstep and risk alienating her best friend. Right now, losing Fiona would be her undoing.

While Fiona stood by Stella, Richard had all but disappeared. He called Stella the morning after their fight but only asked why Caitlin wasn't in school that day. Stella had neglected to call the office. She explained she'd gotten sick at Fiona's house and didn't know when she'd be back, hoping Richard might show some empathy for everything Stella was going through.

"Hope she feels better soon. Enjoy your holiday." Stella's heart sank when Richard didn't say more and abruptly ended the call. It seemed any chance she'd had with Richard Medina was well and truly over.

While Stella worked to plan her getaway, Marcus and his team stepped up to help make their departure as smooth as possible. They'd completed setting up her computer in a secure environment and had opened the incriminating video, analyzing both the embedded virus and the contents of the video. She'd spent Thursday afternoon reviewing the footage with them, narrating what was happening on and off the screen while the video played. Aidan agreed with Stella's assessment of the video; she had definitely been set up. Marcus's team impressed Stella, giving her a sliver of hope they'd be able to identify the perpetrator before she had to tell Caitlin the truth.

That same night, she packed their bags and made final preparations to leave. She'd gotten used to maneuvering around the house with the bug eavesdropping on her, playing loud movies on the television or blasting music to drown out her movements in the house. Rita had even secretly recorded her and Caitlin chatting at Fiona's, and Stella played the recordings so whoever was listening might believe they were still at home. She needed to keep the ruse up for one more night.

Stella went to sleep in her own bed for the last time. She'd bought this house when Caitlin was two years old. Shortly afterward, Rita came to live with them. It was the only home Caitlin ever knew, and Stella regretted she didn't have the chance to say her goodbyes as well.

Stella planned to meet Rita and Caitlin at East Hampton Airport tomorrow and sneak out of the country. No matter what happened now, their lives would never be the same again.

STELLA WOKE up at 6:00 a.m. Friday morning to the sound of her burner phone trilling in her ear. She hadn't set it up properly, so it took her a bit to recognize what was making that noise and how to make it stop. Stella fumbled to find the device and answer it before she missed the call.

The second she connected the call, her mother yelled, "Caitlin is gone."

"What?" Stella shook her head, trying to process the words coming at her.

"She's gone. Caitlin's gone!"

The words slammed into Stella's chest. For a second, she couldn't breathe. Then her body lurched into motion while her mind lagged. She clawed at the sheets, her legs tangling as she fought to get out of bed.

"What do you mean gone?" Her voice cracked, raw. "Gone where?" She freed herself from the bed and frantically searched for her clothes. Her hands shook as she put her phone on speaker and threw on jeans and a sweater.

"Someone took her. They had to have." Rita's voice cracked.

"Tell me exactly what happened," said Stella. She took the phone into the bathroom and pulled her hair up while she listened to her mom.

"I don't know. I came down for my coffee, there was a mess." Rita sobbed, barely able to catch her breath. "I went to the living room... I shouted... I went to her room. She's gone."

"Did you look anywhere else?" asked Stella. She stared at the toothbrush in her hand, not sure what to do with it.

"I looked everywhere. She's not here!"

Stella finally recognized what the toothbrush was for. She dropped it on the counter and picked up her phone again.

"When was the last time you saw her?"

"When I went to bed. Just before nine."

Stella ran downstairs and pulled on her boots. "Her phone. We can track her phone. This is exactly..." Rita didn't let her finish her thought.

"Her phone is here. Right next to her video game she paused. She doesn't even have her phone, Stella." Rita wept.

Stella paced while she tried to make sense of what her mother was telling her. "Mom, look at her phone. Did someone call or text her?"

"It's locked. I don't know her password," said Rita.

"12-13-89. It's Taylor Swift's birthday." Stella's eyes filled with tears over this simple fact. Her little girl set her phone password to her favorite singer's birthday. She was so innocent. She didn't deserve this. "I'm in."

"Check the phone icon. Did she have any recent calls?"

"The last call she had was from you early yesterday morning."

"That's right; I called her then. Now check the text messages. What do you see?"

"The most recent text message doesn't have a name. It looks a lot like your phone number, but it's off by one digit."

"What does the message say?" Rita lost all composure, sobbing into the phone. "I need you to get control of yourself, Mom. Take a deep breath. I need to know what that message says."

"It says it's you. That you were coming to surprise us. They asked her to come outside and help carry stuff into the house. Stella, that's how they got her—they pretended to be you."

"What time did that text come in?"

"Eleven forty-seven. Why did Caitlin think you'd be coming in the middle of the night?"

Stella moaned. "It wasn't the middle of the night for her." Stella could see exactly how it all played out. Caitlin had had no reason to doubt it was her mom; showing up like that was exactly something Stella would have done. "She was probably absorbed in the game, got a text she thought was from me, and responded automatically. I bet she put on her shoes and went right outside."

Panic threatened to overwhelm her, making her lose her ability to think. She shook her head; she had to focus. "Mom, sit tight while I figure out what to do. Someone will call you with next steps."

"Should I call the police?"

"I need to think. I don't know that contacting the cops right now would do anything but make them hurt her."

In an instant, she heard a ping go off on her personal phone. Default tone.

Stella pulled the phone out of her pocket and read the message.

> Unknown: Do not contact the authorities. If you do, she will be killed.

Stella read the text to her mom.

Rita gasped. "They're listening to you? Right now?"

"I gotta go. Sit tight," Stella commanded. "Do not answer the door for anyone or go outside for any reason. Wait for me to contact you before you do anything."

Stella clicked the phone off and stared at the other cell in her hand.

The phone pinged. A new number, but the same person on the other end.

> Unknown: We have a job for you to do. Do this and your daughter will be returned to you unharmed.

Another ping. Another number.

> Unknown: There is an event in the Grand Ballroom at The Pierre Hotel tomorrow night. Use any means necessary to gain admission to that event.

"What the fuck?" Stella whispered to herself.

Another ping. Another number.

> Unknown: Additional instructions will follow.

The tone went off again.

A picture of Caitlin lying on a cot with only a green blanket to keep her warm popped up. There was a brick wall behind the cot. Nothing else was visible in the picture. The picture blurred, her tears making it impossible to see. She screamed. "*NO!*"

Stella didn't bother texting back. She knew they were listening. She ran to the kitchen and ran her fingers under the breakfast bar where Patrick had located the bug. She ripped it out from under the counter and screamed into the mic.

"Listen to me, you motherfuckers! You touch one hair on her head, and I will hunt you down and kill you." She was on fire now, rage coursing through her. "Keep your fucking hands off her!"

She dropped the mic onto the floor and stomped on it, smashing it to pieces. She went to smash her phone against the wall but stopped herself. There was potential evidence they could use to locate Caitlin.

Finally, she went to her car and yanked out the tracking device. She grabbed a hammer from the workbench and beat it until there was nothing, metal pieces scattered around the bench and the floor.

Satisfied they couldn't hear her or track her movements anymore, Stella leaned against the garage wall and slid to the floor, burying her head in her hands. "My baby. My baby," she muttered over and over. "They took my baby."

She stared at the picture on her phone, willing it to move, wanting to see some sign of life from her daughter. The pain she felt completely overwhelmed her. She wanted to die. She couldn't imagine one day on this earth without her daughter. Caitlin was everything to her, and now she was gone.

She'd brought this on herself. She had no idea who these people were or why they had targeted her, but if Stella had been a normal mom—a good mom—none of this would have happened. This was her fault. This was her punishment for thinking she was better than her father—that she could control her life better than he controlled his.

Stella had always blamed her dad for ruining her life by getting killed. But this was far worse. He'd left Stella and Rita behind, but that was all. He was the one who died. Now here she was, but her life wasn't at risk. It was Caitlin's life that hung in the balance.

She pulled her knees to her chest and pressed her head to her knees, her muscles straining to hold her together. "How did I let this happen?" A sob escaped her throat, and the dam broke. She wept uncontrollably.

The world fell away as she huddled on the floor, drowning in grief. She didn't know how long she'd been sitting there when the sound of tires squealing outside broke through her stupor. Images of people coming to kill her flashed in her mind. Stella jumped up—to protect herself or to hand herself over to them, she didn't know which.

"Stella! Stella, where are you?" Fiona yelled from the living room, her voice frantic.

"Out here," Stella yelled back. "In the garage."

Fiona ran into the room, engulfing Stella in a hug the moment she could reach her. Stella broke down crying again. "I know, sweetie. I know. Your mum called me." She held her tight while Stella wept on her shoulder.

They stayed like that a few minutes, Fiona soothing Stella as best she could, whispering how much she loved her in her ear, saying Caitlin was going to be okay. Over and over, she whispered to her friend.

As the crying subsided and Stella could finally pull away a fraction, Fiona changed her tone. She locked eyes with Stella and echoed the same thing Stella had told the kidnappers eavesdropping on her. "We're gonna kill this asshole."

20

Something inside Stella clicked into gear. She wiped her tears on her sleeves and curled her fingers into fists, digging her nails into her palms. There was no time to fall apart. She would spend a lifetime blaming herself and trying to make this up to Caitlin, but right now, she needed to focus on getting her daughter back. Nothing mattered until Caitlin was home safe.

"Have you called the police?" Fiona's question cut through the noise in Stella's head.

"No." Stella grabbed Fiona's wrist and held it tight.

Fiona shouted in her face. "You have to call the police."

Stella shook her head, her eyes widening as she insisted, "No, no, no. We cannot call the cops. They'll kill her. Do you understand? They will *kill* her!" Stella handed Fiona her phone with the picture of Caitlin they'd sent.

Fiona gasped, putting her hand over her mouth. "Oh, my god. What the fuck? What is going on?" Her eyes pleaded with Stella to make it all make sense.

Fiona went silent, staring at the picture. It was the scariest sound Stella had ever heard. Stella watched Fiona's mind connect the dots.

"Why would Caitlin's father hurt her?" Fiona stared at Stella while she worked through everything her friend had told her. "Why would he send you a picture like this?"

Stella's eyes widened, but she kept her mouth closed. She was in too deep already.

"What the hell is going on, Stella?"

Stella closed her eyes and confessed, "I don't think it's Caitlin's father who's been stalking me."

"No shit. When did you figure that out?"

Stella didn't answer.

"I'm sorry, I can't do this right now." Stella pushed past Fiona and went back into the house to grab her coat.

"Do you know who's behind this? Do you know who has her?" Fiona chased after her, peppering her with questions.

She'd never acted this way around Fiona before, never even hinted she had something shady going on in her life. Now, someone had suddenly kidnapped her daughter, and she forbade Fiona from calling the police.

"I don't know who has her," Stella admitted. "That's the truth. But you're right; it's not her father. It would have been better if that were true, because he wouldn't hurt her."

"So, it's not about her."

"It is now. Someone is using Caitlin to get to me. If I do what they want, I'll get her back."

Fiona threw her arms in the air in exasperation. "Then why haven't you called the police? The FBI? Someone's blackmailing you. How do you know they'll return her after whatever this is? How do you know they won't hurt her?"

"I don't know that." Stella pressed her hands to her face, blocking out the world, shaking her head back and forth. All at once, her emotions and her thoughts overwhelmed her. She dropped her hands and screamed in her best friend's face. "I don't know anything!"

Fiona recoiled as if someone had slapped her.

Stella wanted to give in and tell her everything. If there had been more time, she might have laid it all on her doorstep.

Only . . . she wasn't ready for her worlds to collide yet.

Stella took a deep breath and held it in. Her hands clenched into fists, fingernails pressing into their familiar grooves in her palms. She squeezed her eyes shut and counted to ten, keeping her body locked. Then she slowly pushed the air from her lungs, released her fingers, and let the tension drain from her body. She opened her eyes and pleaded with her friend.

"I need you to promise me you won't go to the cops. These people will absolutely know if we do that. They've been three steps ahead of me this whole time. I cannot take that risk."

"Okay," said Fiona. "I hear you. I won't call the cops. For now." Stella let her shoulders drop, relieved. "Do you know who's doing this? Tell me the truth."

Stella raised her hand like she was taking an oath. "Swear to God I don't know."

"What do they want? Is it money? I can help with that." Stella wished it were as simple as that. She had no idea what the demand was going to be, but it wasn't cash.

"All I know so far is I'm supposed to attend some fundraiser at The Pierre tomorrow night." Stella found the message on her phone and showed it to Fiona. "They said they'd tell me the rest later."

"Are you supposed to take pictures there? That doesn't make any sense."

Stella knew Fiona was trying to sort through all the lies she'd told her, but she'd actually hit on a good idea. "That might work," said Stella. She ignored the puzzled look on Fiona's face and took a moment to think. She picked up her phone to call Max. Before she could click on his number, she realized her mistake. "Max. I haven't talked to Max." Her eyes filled with tears again. "This is gonna kill him."

"Do you want me to tell him?" asked Fiona. "I want to help, Stella. I don't know what the fuck is going on, but I want to help."

Stella smiled at her friend. Fiona knew she'd lied to her, that she was still leaving her in the dark, but she still wanted to help.

"Is there any way you can go be with my mom? She's going crazy.

And I'm sure she blames herself. I'd feel better knowing someone is with her."

"I can do that." Fiona glanced at her watch. "I need to check in with Malcolm. He took Levi to school for me. I'll go home and talk to him, then pack a bag and head to your mum."

"Thank you," said Stella.

"You want me to stay while you call Max? Do you need support?"

"No. It won't be fun, but he'll keep it together. He might have some ideas to help me."

Fiona hugged Stella, lending her strength. When the embrace ended, Fiona rested her hands on Stella's shoulders and looked her in the eye. "I need you to tell me the truth about all of this." Stella protested, but Fiona held up her hand and kept talking. "Not now. I get it. That's not the priority." Stella relaxed a beat while Fiona finished. "When this is all over, I want to know what's really going on with you. Stop shutting me out. I don't deserve that, and you know it."

Stella nodded. There was nothing left to say. Fiona kissed her on the cheek and headed home. Stella stared at the phone in her hand. It was time to call Max and let him know he'd been right all along. Stella had taken too many risks, and now the only innocent person in their lives was paying the price.

21

Stella called Max from the car instead of wasting any more time in her house. She was almost manic with the need to move, to make progress of any kind. She wanted to be closer to the action and figure out how to get the event at The Pierre tomorrow night. She threw her luggage into her car and headed into town.

Stella also thought if she called Max from the car she wouldn't break down when she told him about Caitlin. The chaos of rush hour on I-95 would keep her too busy to think, too distracted to feel.

She was wrong about that.

"Someone's kidnapped Caitlin. They got her from Fiona's house last night." She told him in steps, knowing he'd need time to process everything she was saying. The prim and proper British thief filled her car with curse words she'd never heard him utter before. She worried he might drop dead of a heart attack right then.

"I know, I know," she said. "They texted her a bit before midnight last night, pretending to be me—said I needed help getting stuff out of the car. She must have jumped up to help without ever questioning it. She left her phone on the couch and her video game paused."

Max was silent on the line, and Stella wondered if the call had dropped. Then a soft sniffle and a ragged intake of breath came from the other end. Max was crying.

With tears streaming down her own face, she let him process the news, not rushing to fill the silence. After a few minutes, Max shifted from despair to being ready to act. "How did they find her there?"

"I have no idea. I'm killing myself trying to figure that out."

"Have they made any demands?"

"I'm supposed to go to an event tomorrow night in the grand ballroom of The Pierre. That's all I know right now. They said they'd send me additional details later."

"What did they say exactly?" He waited while she fumbled with the phone, trying to pull up the messages while she maneuvered through traffic.

She clicked on the messages and read them to Max. Tears flooded her eyes again. "They also sent a picture of Caitlin on a cot. I can't even tell if she's alive."

"Bastards! Why involve a child in this? What could you possibly steal at that event that justifies kidnapping a young girl? This is insane." Stella wondered the same thing. She let him rant while she tried to focus on driving. "We need to call Marcus. He can help."

He spoke with a conviction Stella didn't share.

"I don't see what he can do. For all we know, he's the one who leaked Caitlin's location." She lowered her voice when she said it, either to keep from upsetting Max or because she didn't want to consider that a real possibility.

"That is preposterous. He's done nothing but help us, and he has resources we need right now."

"I have to get into a ballroom tomorrow night. I don't need his help for that."

"Stop being so stubborn," said Max. "We cannot call the authorities, but we can use the resources Marcus and his team have available. They can tap into phone lines, trace calls, hack into security systems—they access information for a living. Information that most governments can't obtain. And they're willing to operate outside the law. That's exactly what we need right now."

Stella squeezed the steering wheel. She'd already exposed herself enough by giving Marcus her computer. He'd seen the video of her breaking into the Hayes house; he knew what she did for a living. Part of her wanted to throw her hands up, admit defeat, and hand this problem over to him. Another part of her recoiled at the mention of his name. She didn't want to let anyone else into her life. Vulnerability had cost her too much. She wanted her old life back, her old self that kept her worlds firmly separated into black and white. How did everything spiral out of control so goddamn fast?

Max broke through the debate in her mind. "You can't fight this. Getting Caitlin back is the only concern. Marcus and his team give us the edge we need."

"You're right. Let's do it," Stella said. Max put Stella on hold while he contacted Marcus and merged their calls. She was grateful he took on the burden of bringing Marcus up to speed; Stella didn't know how many more times she could survive explaining what had happened.

Marcus asked a couple of clarifying questions, then jumped into action. "I've got an investigator I can send to your friend's house to talk to your mother. He can grab the security footage from her house, and might be able to pull some from the neighbors as well. Will that work?"

Already Stella could see why Max insisted they call him. "Yes, thank you." Her phone pinged with a text. "I can't look at that right now; I'm driving. Can you send it to Max to relay to my mom and Fiona?"

Marcus sounded confused. "Happy to, but I didn't send it yet."

The realization hit all three of them at once. It was another text from the kidnappers.

"Be careful, Stella. Pull over before you read it."

It was all Stella could do to comply. Images flashed through her mind, more pictures of Caitlin, maybe a video of her? She needed to know what was in the message. Her phone pinged two more times. This asshole texted like Fiona.

She spotted an exit ahead and jerked the steering wheel, horns blaring at her.

"I'm exiting now," she said. Marcus and Max stayed silent. Stella turned at the bottom of the exit and pulled her car to the side of the road. She reached for her phone and read the first message aloud. "'You will pick up a suitcase here using the attached QR code tomorrow before five o'clock.' It's got a link to a storage locker on 7th Avenue."

She switched to the second one that had come in, scanning it before she read it aloud. "What the fuck? They can't possibly want me to do that."

"Do what, Stella? Tell us what it says," Max demanded.

"No, no. This can't be." Stella stammered, shaking her head. She forced herself to read them the note. "'You will attend the Freedom for America Gala and plant the device inside that suitcase beneath Table Three.'" Tears welled in Stella's eyes; the screen blurred.

"Are there any more messages?" asked Marcus.

Stella clicked the last message they sent. Her voice broke as she read it. "'Do not contact the authorities. If you attempt to locate your daughter or deviate from these instructions, she will be killed. We are watching you.'" She closed her eyes and inhaled a deep breath, trying to stave off a wave of nausea threatening her.

She failed.

Stella dropped her phone and jumped out of the car. She ran to the sidewalk and heaved. She hadn't eaten breakfast or even had a cup of coffee this morning; she'd been going on pure adrenaline. Now her body wanted to expel anything it could find from her system. She coughed up some bile and almost relished the burn against the back of her throat that kept her from passing out.

Why did they think she would be capable of something like this? She stole jewelry and paintings for a living; she never caused any real harm. The people she stole from had money to burn, and their pieces were insured. It was white-collar crime all the way. This was different. This was murder.

She let tears stream down her face as she climbed back into her car. Max and Marcus were both yelling her name, not knowing where she'd gone.

"I'm here," said Stella. She grabbed a tissue from her console and wiped her mouth, then blew her runny nose. "I am fucked. I'm a thief, not a killer. Why is this happening?"

"That's what we need to find out," answered Marcus. "Will you let me help you?"

Stella let her head fall against the headrest and closed her eyes. Images of Caitlin on the cot came to her mind, alongside pictures of a bomb going off in a hotel ballroom. "I can't do this. I'm gonna need all the help you can give me."

"Let's meet at Marcus's office," said Max.

Stella checked her map. "I'm forty-five minutes out. Get your investigator on the job, Marcus. If there is any way to get my daughter home without me having to hurt someone, let's find it."

22

W hile Stella drove to the city and tried to come to terms with her new reality, Marcus rallied his troops. By 8:30 a.m., Stella walked into an office overflowing with people, only a few hours after some of them had gone home.

Coffee beans were grinding, kettles boiling, and every imaginable way someone could get caffeine into their system was on display. Stella was running on enough adrenaline to power an entire city, but she accepted a fresh cup from Raf when she entered. She knew she would crash soon without it. When she reached the conference room with the steaming mug, the room was full.

Celina rose as Stella crossed the room and hugged her. Stella tried not to let the kind gesture break her.

"I'm so sorry," Celina whispered. "We'll get her back." Stella raised a hand to acknowledge Aidan. He stood from the table and offered her his chair, but she was too anxious to sit.

"Thanks for coming in, everyone," Marcus said, gesturing to the remaining people who were stepping into the conference room at the last second. "We have an emergency that requires our collective expertise. We're in uncharted territory as a firm, and we won't be conducting business as usual until we get this resolved."

Stella watched a few pairs of eyes go wide; apparently not everyone knew why Marcus had summoned them to the office this morning.

"Before we begin, is anyone working on a critical issue that cannot be paused for the next thirty-six hours? This is time sensitive, and we need our full crew working this if possible."

One woman stepped forward. "We have a red-level threat on Dubois we discovered last night. We've been patching it most of the night. Once that's done, their systems should hold."

Marcus nodded. "Let me know when it's fixed. You can write up an incident report and I'll review it, then your team can pivot."

No one else raised any concerns.

"Even if you're continuing on your current jobs," Marcus went on, "I want you in the room for this briefing. We need everyone's brain-power on this. Please listen to this update, complete your tasks, and report back to your team lead immediately when you're available for reassignment. And if something—anything—strikes you before you're reassigned, speak up immediately. Lives are on the line."

Marcus made eye contact with every person in the room. He had their attention, and their full focus. She marveled at how quickly everyone locked in. She only knew a handful of people's names and had no idea what skills each of them had, but she was grateful for this group of people who might be able to help her solve the biggest problem of her life.

"As a reminder, everything you learn here or from working on this project remains under strictest confidence. Stella Meyers, Max Tabor, and their associates are to be treated as priority clients for this firm, with all the rights, responsibilities, and security that status entails. You are not to repeat anything you learn outside of this company. Understood?" Again, he waited for each person to acknowledge him before continuing.

Satisfied everyone understood the parameters, Marcus hit a button on his laptop and an image of Caitlin appeared on the giant screen behind him. It was a picture of her outside the Eras Tour concert they'd attended last summer. Someone must have pulled it from her computer. Stella's eyes filled with tears at the special memory that seemed so distant now.

"Last night, sometime close to midnight, someone abducted Stella's daughter from her friend's home in the Hamptons."

Instantly, the mood in the room shifted from curiosity to concern. Stella heard one person gasp and saw several people shake their heads at the news. Marcus pointed to the screen as he continued. "Caitlin Meyers is ten years old, lives in Riverside and is in the 4th grade at Northbrook Academy. She and her grandmother were holing up after Stella received a threat against Caitlin at school on Monday. We believe the same people who have been threatening Stella are the ones who took her."

"We were set to leave the country today," Stella added. Stella felt Max's hand on her shoulder, offering support. "They'd bugged my house, and someone was listening when my mother called to tell me the news. I got a text message telling me not to contact the authorities or they'd kill her." Stella heard the tremble in her own voice, and her vision blurred with unshed tears. She took a breath to steel herself; she had to stay focused.

"Have they made any demands yet?" asked someone at the back.

Marcus nodded and relayed the details of the messages Stella had received to the group. "It's reasonable to assume the device she is being asked to place under that table is a bomb."

The tension in the room broke free, several people talking at once as they realized the full extent of the task they were being asked to work on. After the initial torrent of reactions, Marcus's voice rose above the noise, quieting the chatter. "Which brings me to my next point. A young girl's life is on the line. So are the lives of the people attending that party, the staff working it, and even guests in the hotel." He watched his words hit their mark.

"My goal in taking on this job is to protect the lives of the people at The Pierre, and bring Caitlin home. I firmly believe our resources and expertise can bring a swift resolution to this, but I know you didn't sign up for this when you joined this firm. If you're at all uncomfortable working on this, I will reassign you. No questions asked."

No one objected. Stella exhaled slowly, her breath unsteady.

Marcus gave them a minute to take it all in, then got to work. "Let's get organized, people. Divide into two teams—one working on getting Caitlin home, the other on the job at The Pierre."

Stella pulled Marcus's arm and objected, "I can't ask for their help with the event. I won't do that."

She turned and addressed the group. "I can't ask anyone to do this with me. This isn't an art theft or cybercrime; this is cold-blooded murder."

"None of us want it to come to that," said Marcus.

"Let me handle the job at The Pierre. Please do everything you can to find Caitlin."

Some people looked down, avoiding eye contact, but others nodded their understanding. This was beyond anything they'd ever done. Stella wouldn't taint them with that. At least a few people appeared to understand the burden she now carried.

Marcus nodded at Stella. "I think we have some people here who can make your job a little easier. We need a couple of people to gather information. Building designs for The Pierre, learning more about the event. Pure tech support."

Stella felt the room collectively exhale, no one wanting to be an accessory to this kind of slaughter.

"Let's see how we're sorting ourselves and then go from there," said Marcus. "Everyone wanting to work on Team Caitlin, please stand on the far wall. Everyone believing they can assist Team Pierre, move toward the doorway." The group sorted itself, with a few stragglers who seemed to weigh the decision like Sophie's Choice. Risk losing a child to some monster on one side, or plan a job intended to kill a room full of strangers on the other. There was no good choice.

Eventually, people found themselves in a group. Most of the office chose Team Caitlin, which relieved Stella. At least twenty-five people would work to find her. Four people joined Team Pierre. To her surprise, Celina was one of them.

"We have a lot of good tech people who can trace the calls and the messages they're sending you," Celina said. "I have a little sister. I won't be able to focus if I'm thinking about her instead of the job."

Someone on Caitlin's team heard her and spoke up. "I do, too, but that's why I'm on this side. I'd kill anyone who touched a hair on my brother's head."

Stella understood they would perform best on the team that aligned with their values, not undermined them. Marcus knew his crew and how to motivate them.

"Looks good. Now that you're sorted, I want team leads chosen for each group. Each lead must stay informed on inquiries or tasks assigned to their group, as well as to make updates to a shared server for us all to review." Marcus radiated confidence, setting up the job like a standard operation in the firm. Stella enjoyed the bird's eye view of how Marcus ran his company of tech wizards. "Even though you're on different teams, I want all eyes on hourly updates from each. As I've said, we're in a new world now, and information may come to light that you can assist with, even if you're on the other team. We're on the clock here, people. Let's bring Caitlin home as fast as we can."

There was a collective "Yes, sir" that sounded like a military call and response. Not mocking, but it reminded Stella that Marcus had learned his skills keeping soldiers safe in the field. He knew how to run a high-stakes operation with a million moving parts.

Her shoulders relaxed a fraction. For the first time this morning, Stella thought there might be a pinprick of light at the end of this very long, very dark tunnel.

They needed Stella on Team Caitlin at the outset to help formulate a plan and get moving. Max could take charge of the Pierre team and gather the necessary information to secure resources on her behalf.

Caitlin's group quickly chose a woman named Annie as team lead. Stella liked environments where women weren't afraid to take charge. As they looked at the scope of the assignment, someone spoke up. "Let's ask the obvious question," said a guy in a Superman

T-shirt. "Should we call the cops? The feds deal with this stuff all the time."

"I don't think we can take that risk," Raf said. "Especially not while they're still tracking everything Stella says and does."

"What's our timeline for securing her equipment? You killed the bugs, right?" Marcus asked Stella.

"I did, but there could be more. I don't know how anyone got into my home. It makes me worry there are more things out there letting them track me."

"I'd prefer to know more about what is happening before we call in the feds and get them looking too closely at Stella, and frankly, at us." Several others nodded in agreement. "And as we know, we aren't bound by any laws that could potentially slow our response time. We might find her well before they could." He looked at Stella again. "Is that okay with you?" She nodded.

Stella watched everyone process this, wondering if there was enough collective brainpower in this room to solve this problem without involving the authorities. Marcus seemed to have read her mind. "If it comes to it, we won't hesitate to call in the cops to save her life. Period. But we're going to do our best to learn who's behind all of this before we do that. The goal is to keep everyone alive."

"Last thing on my end before I let you go," Marcus announced. "I did some cursory research into the event tomorrow night while everyone was coming to the office. It appears Blake Cameron will be the guest speaker. This fundraiser is a $50,000 per plate dinner to raise money for the upcoming Presidential Inauguration. It's an A-list event for sure, so we can't be 100 percent sure Blake Cameron is the target, but it does make sense."

Blake Cameron was a private sector businessman and one of the wealthiest people in the world. He'd tossed his hat into the political ring this election, not by running for office himself, but by donating a small fortune to ensure his candidates won their slots. From local elections to the presidential race, Blake's money almost single-handedly financed a victory for his party.

"As we dive into the data, be on the lookout for any connection

Stella or Max might have to someone who wants Blake Cameron to go away." He shook his head. "That list is growing by the minute; he's pissed off a lot of people. If there's someone in Stella's background with the means and motive to take him out, let's look at it."

Stella spent the next half hour answering questions and giving the team access to all her information. They'd already cloned her phone and computer, so she filled in the gaps about her history, in particular the heist she'd committed in Spain that ended up on film.

Stella had to remind herself why she was letting these strangers hear how she worked. Even with so many lives on the line, speaking about her real job put every cell in her body on alert.

They reviewed the video as a group, and Stella explained what she and Aidan had concluded about the job being a setup. This was the most damaging piece of information Stella received before the picture of Caitlin was sent to her; it had to be an important piece of the puzzle.

Stella watched the team sort themselves into subgroups. Two people wanted to follow the painting's trail. They asked to see Max's records of who he sold the painting to. Aidan led another group analyzing the virus that had been on the original video sent to Stella to see if they could determine who created it. A third subgroup contacted the investigator Marcus had already put in play and began gathering intel about the moment the kidnappers had taken Caitlin from Fiona's house. Stella put them in touch with her mother and Fiona and cleared them to tell her anything they could to help locate her daughter.

Another group dove into researching Blake Cameron and anyone who might want him dead. Marcus was right; it was a long list.

Stella marveled at how quickly they all identified their lines of inquiry and began gathering data. This group had access to information and was laser-focused on finding Caitlin. It was incredible to watch.

As Stella watched them dive into their tasks, her cell phone rang. She saw Fiona's number and excused herself to take the call. "Everything okay?"

"All good here. I'm almost at the house. I remembered something from the message they sent. I know about the event tomorrow night. I can get you into it." Fiona's husband was well connected, and Stella didn't doubt he was on the short list for any and all exclusive events in the city. But his politics didn't run to tyranny.

"Were you going to go?" asked Stella.

"Fuck no! I didn't want to give a penny to pay for that jerk's inauguration. But we got the invite. I can go if that's what you need. I'll put you down as my plus-one. We'll go together." Stella was kicking herself for keeping Fiona in the dark. If she'd told her the truth, she'd understand why it was impossible for Stella to let Fiona anywhere near The Pierre tomorrow night. She had to convince her to stay away.

"Absolutely not," Stella protested. "You cannot go to this thing. I'll get in another way. Promise me, Fiona."

"Why not? These assholes told you to get into the event. I can get you in. I don't understand what's wrong."

Fiona would call the cops immediately if she knew about the bomb. And Stella couldn't blame her. No one deserved to die because of their politics. Stella had to make sure Fiona stayed away from the fundraiser and didn't contact the police. It was getting more and more difficult to control her friend.

Stella's gift for telling the truth—but not the whole truth—kicked in. "This is already a nightmare. I'm in my own personal hell, Fiona, and I don't know what's going on. I don't want to risk something happening to you, too. The only thing that matters to me is getting Caitlin back. I need you fully focused on helping us find out who took her."

"I don't know how you're going to get into this thing without me," said Fiona. "I guess you could ask Pam Fisher for an invitation. Unless you're worried about her, too?"

Stella struggled to figure out what Fiona was saying. "Wait. What? Pam Fisher is going?"

"She's running it. She's the one who invited Malcolm and me. I think she has an entire table there she's trying to fill as the hostess."

"You told her you weren't going, right?"

"Of course. I can get back on the list, though. She wants this event to be a real feather in her cap. I'm sure she'll let me come, and bring you, too."

Fiona kept coming back to that. "No, I don't want that. You brought up the idea of me photographing the event. Do you think you could drop a hint to Pam that I'm available to be the photographer?"

"Sure, but I'm sure they've already got a photographer. They've been working on this since election night." Stella's mind raced as she considered this angle. If she could attend the event as the official photographer, she'd have an excuse to get in early. That might give her a window to set the device under the table, if she had to go through with this.

She couldn't bring herself to call it a bomb.

"This could work," said Stella. "I've got some work to do. Let me call you back."

"Sure. Let me know how I can help."

"Last thing. A friend of Max's knows a private investigator who is going to look at your security footage and see if he can get some from other neighbors in your area. They want to see if they can figure out who took Caitlin. Can you help him when he gets to your house?"

"Absolutely. I'm on it." Stella could hear how excited Fiona was to have a job to do. It would help take her mind off the fundraiser.

"Thank you. I'll be in touch. I love you."

"Love you, too."

She clicked off the call and nodded to herself. She felt like she was beginning to regain control. *Focus on the task right in front of you. Let everything else fall to the back of your mind.*

23

S tella made her way to the small group gathering information about the "Freedom for America Gala" at The Pierre, happy Max had already put them to work. She knew there was more than one exploit in his past that involved getting into an event like this. Until the Degas job, Stella's expertise lay in slipping into houses after dark and taking what she wanted from walls and safes left unguarded. It took a unique skill set to commit a crime in front of a room full of people.

"I've asked them to get as much information about the gala as they can. The guest list, vendors, room layout—everything they can find about the plans," said Max.

Stella laughed, skeptical. "That would be amazing, but how can anyone get those details this quickly? Do we have someone on the inside?"

"No need," said Celina. "We hacked into the PAC's network. They're sponsoring the event." Celina motioned to the chair next to her.

Stella took the offered seat, and Celina gestured to the screen behind her, projecting her computer onto the larger screen so everyone could see it. "As we suspected, it was a weak point for them."

"Naïve of them to be so lax, considering the people who fund the organization, don't you think?" asked Stella.

"It's that ignorance that helps Onyx thrive. We're pulling up the files for everyone attending the gala now. Because this is an A-list event, the organizers want everything personalized as much as possible. It looks like the invitations are requesting the names of every guest in attendance, not a generic plus-one. That'll help us. I've also got to look at the seating charts, the program for the night, and the list of which vendors are doing what for the event."

"This is perfect. Can you tell me who the photographer is for the evening?" asked Stella. "Fiona told me Pam Fisher is running the event. She's a mother at our school."

"Her name's all over this thing," a guy on the team confirmed. He waved to Stella. "I'm Min." Stella nodded at him with a smile, appreciating his manners in a situation like this.

"Fiona thinks she can direct Pam to hire me for the event. All I need to do is get the photographer to back out at the last minute. I'm hoping a nice bribe will do it."

Celina hit a few buttons on her computer and sifted through the files on her screen. Stella marveled at how fast she absorbed and understood the data in front of her. She flew through the files as if she used them every day. You'd never know she broke into the system less than half an hour ago.

"Here we go. Luca Bonetti." Stella cursed under her breath. "Do you know him?"

Stella scowled. "Yeah, I know him." Luca and Stella ran in different circles, and she liked it that way. Luca was a first-rate snob, a photographer to the stars, and all-around prick. It didn't surprise her at all that he'd agreed to photograph an event supporting the new president. "He'd deliver the bomb himself if it meant getting him into this gala. No way will he take a bribe."

Stella paced for a moment, considering her options. "He's so full of shit," she mumbled. As she said it, an idea flashed in her mind. If he got sick, he might pull himself from the gala voluntarily.

"How about a stomach bug?" Max raised his eyebrows at her suggestion. Stella explained, "Mix some laxatives into his coffee, and he might think twice about going out tomorrow night."

Max smiled, and Stella asked Celina, "Is there a number for Luca in the system? Preferably his cell phone?" Celina had the number in under ten seconds. "Perfect. He doesn't share this with just anyone. If I fake a call from a celebrity and schedule to meet him for coffee, I think he'll take the bait."

Stella checked her watch. It was 12:15 p.m. now, lunch already underway. She didn't have time to go to her storage unit and come up with a disguise. Instead, she'd rely on her wits and luck.

Stella was happy to have a job in front of her. It was a hell of a lot better than sitting around waiting for news about Caitlin. Before she left, she gave the team some additional instructions. "I want as much information about everyone in that venue as possible. Who's sitting at the table where I'm supposed to plant the device? What servers are scheduled to work the event? Even the cleaning crew. I want to see if any names ring any bells for me."

She also wanted to know the people at risk of being hurt if she ended up going through with this. Stella couldn't accept that as a possibility, but somewhere in the darkest part of her mind she understood it might come down to her having to choose between Caitlin's life and the lives of people in that room. She wanted to humanize them as much as possible, see their names and learn a bit about them; anything to remind her there was more at stake than Caitlin in this nightmare.

She left the small conference room but held back. "Do you have a quiet place where I can make this call? I don't want any background noise."

One guy pointed to a glass box near the back of the room. "That's a soundproof phone booth. It has power connections and a space for your computer, too, if you need it." Stella smiled at him. This place had a lot of bells and whistles.

Stella went to the phone booth and shut herself inside. The light came on when she turned the handle to lock the door, and every single sound from the office disappeared. This would be a great place to sit and think when you needed to concentrate.

She typed out a quick script on her phone, second-guessing whether it was too much. But Luca seemed like the type who'd love a cheesy note from a big-time celebrity, so she ran through it a few times before dialing.

Luca answered on the third ring. "Ciao. Who has the pleasure of speaking with me? I don't know this number."

Stella rolled her eyes. She was going to enjoy this.

"You can call me Aspen."

"Like the tree?"

She didn't answer that. "I represent a well-known celebrity who might tie the knot soon. She wants to capture her *love story* with the perfect photographer." Stella paused to see if he was connecting the dots. She couldn't be more obvious if she tried. "My client knows *all too well* what happens if the news gets out. Your discretion is critical."

"Are you talking about—"

"Do not say her name. This is very, very hush-hush. She will meet you for coffee at Petite Maman on 55th & Madison at one o'clock. If you can make it, they might select you to photograph the big event. Tell no one. And come alone. Are you . . . *ready for it*?" Luca would search the address now and would surely know Taylor Swift's Tribeca compound was right around the corner.

Stella heard Luca try to contain an actual squeal of delight. "I will be there." She hung up the phone. Tree Paine didn't have time to say goodbye to lowly photographers.

Stella had given herself plenty of time to prepare. She bid farewell to the crew and headed to the drugstore in the concourse of Rocke-feller Center. She grabbed some laxatives and eyedrops for good measure. The Internet swore adding eyedrops to a drink would induce vomiting in a matter of hours. Some claimed flight attendants would give it to bothersome passengers, wanting them to throw up after their flight, not on it.

She also went on a quick shopping spree at Michael Kors on 5th Ave. She didn't need to look like Taylor Swift, but she needed to look like someone who would know her. That meant the jeans, sweater, and Uggs she'd thrown on this morning would not cut it. She grabbed a camel coat and a red scarf that would cover most of her outfit. She traded her Uggs for some calf-length black leather boots and grabbed a pair of sunglasses. Sunglasses were ridiculous for this time of year, but that's what would sell the whole thing. Finally, she threw on a leopard beanie to cover her hair. She'd look like someone trying to hide who she was. Which was exactly what she was doing.

Stella arrived at the shop ten minutes before their scheduled secret meeting. She ordered a large caramel brûlée latte and pistachio chocolate croissant for Luca, and picked up a ham and cheese baguette and an Americano for herself to go. She hadn't eaten all day, and although stress and adrenaline were still pumping through her system, she couldn't afford to let her body crash.

By the time Luca walked through the door at 1:00 p.m., Stella had dissolved half the box of laxatives and squeezed eyedrops into the disgustingly sweet drink. She saw him search the café for his celebrity and check his watch when he didn't see her. Stella didn't want him to order his own drink, so she made eye contact with him. "Luca? Luca Bonetti?" He spun around when he heard his name, looking for the source. He saw Stella sitting at a table, motioning him over. As he approached, she lowered her sunglasses a bit and asked, "Are you Luca Bonetti? The photographer?"

"I'm sorry, I'm meeting someone here today and I shouldn't be talking to anyone else."

Stella struggled not to roll her eyes at him.

"I know." Stella looked around the room and then whispered to him, "Is she your *wildest dream*?" She saw him recognize the amended song title. Stella gestured for him to sit. "Our mutual friend apologizes, but she had to leave early and won't be able to meet you." Luca deflated instantly. Stella rushed to get him to take his drink. "She asked you to forgive her for your trouble. She personally ordered you her favorite drink and pastry from the shop."

This had the intended effect. Luca perked up and accepted the thoughtful gifts. "What do you think? Don't you just love it?" He took a gulp and smiled. Either he couldn't taste what she'd put in it past all that sugar, or he didn't want to upset someone close enough to Taylor Swift to be delivering drinks for her.

"It's wonderful," he said. "I regret I couldn't meet our friend today. Do you know when she might be able to reschedule?" Stella took a sip of her drink and watched him do the same. She'd sit here the entire time if she needed to.

"Please keep it in the strictest confidence." Stella leaned in and looked around the room as if someone was watching her. "If word gets out that she's planning a wedding . . . it would be a complete circus." She raised her coffee cup to his and toasted, forcing him to have yet another drink. "Have you had this pastry before? It's her favorite. Mine too."

Luca ate and drank the proffered gifts; it would have been rude not to. As he finished his drink, Stella's phone pinged. Her heart stuttered at the sound. This was no time to hear from the kidnappers. She tried to keep her expression neutral as she checked her phone.

Relief flooded through her when she saw it was from Max. She'd never assigned him a tone on her new phone.

Max: We have updates.

"I'm sorry, I have to run." She picked up her coffee and to-go bag. "Our friend will call when she's back in town. Thank you for your understanding and discretion."

She bid him farewell and headed back to Marcus's office, quietly singing "Who's Afraid of Little Old Me?" to herself. Taylor has a song for every emotion. It was one of the reasons Caitlin and Stella loved her so much.

24

Stella didn't bother to text Max on her way back, unwilling to hear any more bad news. Instead, she ate her sandwich on the subway and wondered how long it would take for the laxatives to kick in. She also considered some alternatives in case Luca Bonetti turned out to have an iron stomach. By the time she returned to 30 Rock, Stella had her first bites of food in her stomach, and a few alternate plans to get Luca out of the way if he didn't succumb to his stomach pains.

As Stella pulled open the door to Marcus's office, she hit a wall of energy. The entire room was alive. It wasn't noisy, but each person in the office was emitting energy as they chased down a lead or gathered information. She could feel their collective power working to find her daughter. It was palpable and powerful. Stella put her hand over her heart and closed her eyes, muttering, "please let them find her," under her breath.

Max broke the spell when he spotted her in the doorway. "How did it go?"

"I think it went well. I stayed while he drank the entire drink. Now we have to hope I got the dosage right. We need him to drop out of the event voluntarily, but I don't want him to end up in the hospital."

Honestly, the only reason Stella would feel guilty is if he blamed Taylor for his illness. "You said there was news?" Stella asked.

"There is. We were waiting for you to give the full company briefing." Max motioned for Stella to head into the large conference room again and went to alert Marcus that she was back. Stella watched as everyone paused their tasks and gathered for an update.

Marcus nodded at Stella as he entered and settled everyone down. "Annie, what's the update from Team Caitlin?" He gave her the floor.

Annie turned to the wall monitor and pulled up some videos. "Our team successfully gathered footage from the neighbors and even some from local security firms. We analyzed cars entering and leaving the area when Caitlin was taken." She clicked on a remote, and a scene came on with a car driving down the street to Fiona's house. "We believe this was the vehicle they used to take her."

"It's my car," Stella said. "Looks almost exactly the same."

"That's why it was easy to grab her. The license plate is different, but it's the same state, and it was dark when she went outside. She had every reason to believe it was your car." Annie skipped the video ahead a few seconds. "This is a compilation video from what we've pieced together. They're good at hiding from the visible cameras, but we picked up some images from the ones they didn't see. We can see there are two people sitting in the front seat. We can't determine if there were more in the backseat or potentially hiding in the trunk, though we must assume there was room for them to place Caitlin back there once they knocked her out."

Stella sucked in her breath. Just thinking about someone cramming her daughter into the back of an SUV made her irate. She clenched her jaw and squeezed her hands tight, but didn't interrupt.

"You can see we got at least one good shot of the driver from a neighbor's camera." Annie zoomed in on the image of the man on the screen. Dark hair, a close-cut beard, no identifying marks or tattoos that Stella could see. "We're running this through the databases to see if we can get a match."

"Local or international?" Marcus asked.

"Local," said Annie.

"Push them to the Interpol sources. Let's cover all our bases." Marcus turned his attention to Stella to explain his rationale. "We don't know how this person found you, but the original video was of the job in Spain. I don't want to leave any source untapped by assuming he's American."

Stella nodded. "Totally agree."

"We're also running a search on the vehicle. It was a rental, but they haven't returned it yet. We tracked the vehicle through traffic cameras for quite a bit of time. It was heading south out of New Jersey. They stayed off the toll roads for most of the trip, but they popped up on the Pennsylvania expressway just north of Philly. They took Exit 333, and we lost them from there. We're pushing the systems to continue to look for the car, but so far, they haven't picked it up again."

A guy from Team Pierre jumped in. "How about we look at the list of attendees and see if anyone is from the area around Philadelphia? It's a safe bet they put her somewhere they're familiar with to keep an eye on her."

"Great idea," said Marcus. "Now we're getting somewhere. With a fundraiser this big, I imagine a lot of people from the area are scheduled to attend, but let's see."

"We've also been doing a deep dive on every threat you were sent, and every text and email that contained a virus, even if it didn't look like a threat." Annie explained what information the team had gathered to that point. "We've been operating under the assumption that the threats were tied to your heist in April." She paused, looking at Max and Stella to confirm. All signs pointed to this being about the Degas.

Annie continued, "We don't see any activity on your machine for phishing prior to October 2024. You get junk email every day, and yes, some of those certainly are phishing, but nothing like the sophistication we see in the messages beginning in early November. Although we haven't identified the exact signature left behind in these messages yet, the coding is advanced enough to help us eliminate a lot of earlier messages. Whoever did this didn't contact you until long after you'd finished that job and sold the painting."

"By that time, we'd already moved the money and considered it safe," Stella said. She turned to Max. "Is there any way someone would have known about this on your end? Do we need to check your devices too?"

Max sighed. "I'm afraid I have a confession to make. Someone tipped me off to this job. Sometimes people request my services for something specific they want to attain, but in this case a connection explained the painting was sitting there for the taking. Because Paraíso is so secure, no one had attempted to break into any residence in the community. But if someone could find their way in, it was a treasure trove of art, jewelry, and even cash for the taking in some estates."

"Did you trust the person that tipped you off?" asked Marcus.

"I did," Max confirmed. "But we also did our own reconnaissance. Stella went in months before to see what security was really like, and to ascertain whether she could even get inside."

"Do you have records of who bought the painting? How difficult was it to move after Stella took it?"

Stella noticed Annie and her team were comfortable asking technical questions, but they left the ins and outs of Stella and Max's criminal activity for Marcus to sleuth out. She was fine with that; whatever distance they needed from Stella would probably help them focus their attention on finding Caitlin. Still, Stella felt them scrutinizing her choices as a mother with every new piece of the puzzle she and Max revealed.

"I had a buyer before the job was executed," explained Max. "I received a wire transfer of funds immediately after a mutually agreed upon source authenticated the painting. The painting was only in my possession for twenty hours from the time Stella put it in the trunk of our car to the time I received payment."

"Who bought it?" asked Stella.

"It was sold to a holding company. That's often the case with stolen goods, especially ones that have a profile as high as this one.

Since no one had reported the theft yet, it went for a premium. We'd managed to get it out and sold long before anyone knew it was missing, giving the new owners ample time to cover their tracks."

"Let's get the name of the buyer," Marcus said.

"I've got my encrypted ledger put away for safekeeping. I'll find the name of the holding company that purchased the painting and get it to you at once."

Everyone nodded.

Annie wrapped up her briefing. "That's where we are now. We're analyzing data as it comes in, and will keep you updated."

"Thank you. Pierre Team, you're up," said Marcus.

Celina stood to present her assessment. "We accessed the organization's systems and have everything they've got about this fundraiser. As you know, we identified the primary target as Blake Cameron. He is scheduled to speak at the event, and seems to be a lightning rod for upsetting half the country right now. The podium is also close enough to Table Three that we can expect the blast to kill him."

Stella took over from Celina. "Thanks to Celina and her team, I now have information about the vendors they're using that night, as well as which security details are on duty. It's been helpful. I'm also going to sort through bios of the guests and staff likely to be at the event. I want to know as much about the people in that room as possible."

Stella watched some people nod their heads, somber expressions on their faces. When they were deep into the tech side of this, it seemed easy to chase leads, gather information, and feel like they were working toward something. But the reality was they weren't just chasing money or reputation this time. Lives were on the line. For all the jobs they'd pulled, none had ever carried stakes like this.

"I'm trying to get invited as the photographer for the event." Stella checked her watch. "We should know in a few hours if my plan worked. Security is tight. Celina got me the schedule for the day's setup, and it includes a final sweep of the ballroom one hour before the event. Anything I plant must be put in after that sweep, but before any guests arrive. There is zero guarantee I'll get into the room with it empty."

"What are you going to do?" asked Max.

Stella shrugged. "I'll figure something out."

Max smiled at her, proud even in the middle of this nightmare. "You always do."

No one had questions for her, so Marcus dismissed the group. "Good job, everyone. Keep the updates coming." Marcus nodded to Stella and Max to follow him into his office. "Let's talk."

"I wish we had more for you," said Marcus.

"Honestly, this is more than I'd expected. I'm grateful for the help," said Stella.

"How do you feel about the progress?" Max asked Marcus. "Do you think it's a good idea to keep looking for Caitlin alone? Or should we call in the authorities?"

"We're walking a line with that already. We have a lot of contacts across the agencies, and people who can do favors for us when we need them. That's who's been running the searches on the car they used to kidnap her and the abductors' faces."

"Have they made it an official investigation?" Stella questioned.

"Not yet. Our friends know the basics—that a kid has gone missing and we're looking for her. They don't know anything about the bomb threat yet. If we can find her in time, we might be able to alert them and clear out the fundraiser completely. That's my goal."

"And if we can't?" She hated to even think about what options lay ahead for her.

"I have some ideas about that," said Max. "I'm calling in a favor. I have a friend who knows everything there is to know about munitions. If there is any way to disarm this bomb or deceive these people into believing someone planted a bomb, he will know how to do it."

The idea that they would gamble with Caitlin's life bothered her, but she understood the goal. She would do anything not to have to choose between her daughter's life and a room full of people. But that's exactly what someone wanted to force her to do.

25

S tella and Max parted ways after the briefings. Max went back to his house to get information on the Degas buyer, and any information he could share about who put them onto the heist. He also brought back his computer for the team to analyze as a precaution.

Stella grabbed her computer from the team so she could sift through the files they sent her about the gala. They'd cleared it for bugs and Marcus's team had cloned it, so they could see any new messages that came through.

She also took the opportunity to get a suite at The Pierre and begin doing some in-depth research on tomorrow night's event. It was important for her to get a feel for the hotel, how it ran, and what preparations they were making. She checked in under a false ID and spent the next few hours alternating between learning about the people set to attend, and learning more about The Pierre.

Before her rendezvous with Max and his colleague, Stella called Fiona and gave her an update. "They found the vehicle used to take Caitlin and are tracking it now. There's some hope they'll be able to find her soon."

"Does that mean they called the cops?" asked Fiona.

"Max's friend has a firm that works in cybersecurity. They have connections across law enforcement agencies and are working with them to get information about Caitlin as fast as they can. It's really the best of both worlds. They're not tied up waiting for a judge to approve a wiretap or something like that, but they also have a direct line to the police if they need it." Stella was happy to know they were crossing that line.

"I'm glad to hear it," said Fiona. "Someday you're going to have to tell me about how you and Max know people like this."

Doubtless she wanted to know more, but she wasn't fishing for information right now. There would be a reckoning coming, and Stella worried her friendship might not survive it. "Also, I got a line on the photographer for the gala. They hired Luca Bonetti for it." Stella heard her friend groan. "I think he might not be able to make it. Not sure when he'll give up the gig, but could you please make sure you're in contact with Pam enough that you get word the second he drops? I need you to get her to give me the job."

"Are you sure I can't just pay these people ten million dollars?" asked Fiona. "I'd rather do that than cozy up to Pam Fisher."

"I hear you. If that were humanly possible, we'd do it. I think you're going to have to bite the bullet, my friend."

"Fine. But you owe me," said Fiona.

"More than you'll ever know," said Stella. She hung up, certain she'd get a call about working the fundraiser soon. Fiona didn't like Pam and her crew, but when she wanted to turn on the charm and get her way, nothing would stop her.

As the sun set and the day wound down, Stella and Max made their way to the Bronx. It was a quiet evening; the area around Fordham's campus was mostly bare since students were heading home for winter break. Stella wished everyone would find a reason to leave the city right now. *Please go,* thought Stella. She wanted to protect every person she passed on the street, worried they might be one of the golden ticket holders planning to attend the gala. Even as far away as Fordham was from the upscale world of The Pierre, Stella worried every person she saw could have a target on their back.

Instead, she knew the opposite was happening. People were likely traveling here to celebrate the holiday or even coming solely for a chance to attend this fundraiser for the inauguration. Nothing could keep them away. Stella couldn't let anyone get hurt because of her.

Max directed them to a pawnshop off Webster. They entered to the harsh buzz of a door alarm alerting the shopkeeper to their presence. Stella thought she'd go mad if she had to hear that buzzing every time someone came in or out of the shop. Looking around the small space crammed with everything from decorative collector plates hanging on the walls to an array of guns and knives on display in the glass counters, Stella realized the buzzing had a purpose. It wouldn't do for a stranger to walk in here unannounced.

Max approached a young woman at the counter and said they were here to see Evan. She looked scarcely out of high school, but as Max made the request Stella saw her stand straight and pull her shoulders back, ready to block the stranger's entrance to see her boss. "Who are you?" she asked.

Max smiled and turned on his full British charm. "Maximilian Tabor, at your service, madam. My associate is Stella Meyers. I believe Mr. Collias is expecting us."

He all but bowed to her. Stella stood stunned as the girl's shoulders relaxed, a smile on her face. She turned and headed into the back room, glancing behind her for a final check before she disappeared. The store was empty save for them.

She returned not thirty seconds later, taking in the shop one last time to ensure nothing had changed in her absence. "He'll be with you in a moment. Please let me know if there's anything you want to see," she said.

Stella noticed her language was a bit more formal now, probably Max's influence. She smiled, thinking of the difference between the demeanor he carried in the world and the life he actually led. Few people saw beyond the veneer of his formal British accent and fine clothes. Max had his own way of hiding in plain sight; it was one of the things Stella loved most about him.

"Max. Good to see you." A man Stella presumed was Evan emerged from the back room, his exuberant energy hitting Stella like a bolt of lightning. He stood only a couple of inches taller than Stella, but his presence made him seem like a giant. He wore a black T-shirt and faded jeans. His close-cut curly dark hair looked on the verge of exploding off his head, full of the same energy he radiated. His eyes, however, were what caught and held Stella's attention. They were hazel, shifting between olive-green and a deep blue even as he walked toward them. In this small, dark, dusty pawn shop in the heart of the Bronx, this man's eyes made Stella forget what brought them to his doorstep for a fraction of a second. They were here to talk to someone about the bomb.

Stella silently prayed this man would rescue her from the train that seemed to be bearing down on her. She did not want to kill anyone.

He crossed the small room and extended his hand to Max, then pulled him into a hug, and patted him on the back. "It's been too long."

"Too long, indeed," answered Max. His smile broadened at the charming man hugging him. When Max pulled back, he introduced her. "This is my dear friend, Stella Meyers. We have some things we need to discuss with you."

"Any friend of Max's is a friend of mine," said Evan, extending his hand to her. The worn-out expression didn't sound trite coming from him, it sounded genuine. Stella shook his hand and thanked him for meeting with her. Evan turned back to Max and got them on track. "Where would you like to talk? Here in my office? Or somewhere else?"

"I think we'd prefer to take a stroll," said Max. Evan's eyes grew wide as he took in this news. A meeting in the office meant it would be on the books—his assistant possibly able to overhear them, customers who might interrupt them. A meeting taken while walking meant the utmost discretion was required.

Evan nodded his understanding. "Let me grab my coat and we'll be off." He walked back to his office and returned with a sheepskin-lined leather coat.

They set off on their walk, Evan leading the way. He nodded in the direction to take, his hands shoved into his coat pockets for warmth. "Let's head to the park," he said. "We can walk around there for a bit."

"We won't take up much of your time tonight," Max offered. "We want to give you the lay of the land this evening."

They'd chosen their time well; most park visitors were on their way home to prep for their evening plans. They could talk without fear of being overheard.

"What brings you here?" Evan asked. "I would love to catch up, but if we're out here strolling in December, you're not here to shoot the shit."

Max nodded. "Thank you for meeting with us. Stella and I have a problem. It's a bit more out of my expertise, and more with yours . . . Stella's daughter has been taken from her. The kidnappers have threatened to kill her if she doesn't go through with their demands."

Evan stopped short. Stella was grateful the weight of the situation seemed to hit him. "Fuck. How the hell . . ." He didn't need to finish his sentence. He shook his head, and they walked on.

"That's not germane to our discussion at the moment. We're here because you know more about explosives than any other person on the East Coast. Specifically, high-end explosives."

"Only the East Coast?" he teased, lightening the mood ever so slightly.

"Touché," Max said. "They asked Stella to place a device in a public place tomorrow evening."

"A holiday event?"

"No, we believe the target is political. We need options. We don't want any harm to come to Stella's daughter, but we also don't relish the idea of going through with their demands." They passed by a coffee shop, and Max signaled they should stop for a drink. Stella thought they could all use something to warm up.

Once back on the walking path, they sipped their drinks which both kept them warm and covered their lips during the most vulnerable parts of their conversation. Evan spoke first. "I haven't heard anything about this."

"Does that surprise you?" Stella asked.

"Yeah, it does. I can ask around, but the fact that I don't know this already makes me think it's not local." He took a sip of his coffee and kept the cup still at his lips as he asked, "Any chance you've pissed off some international folks?"

Stella nodded.

"I'd hoped you'd already know something," said Max. "But barring that, what will our options be going forward? Is there anything you can do to help us?"

"You want to throw them off?" Evan asked. "Make them think it detonated but really keep everyone safe?"

"Everyone, including my daughter," said Stella.

"I might be able to do that . . . It depends on the device, though. There are so many ways to build them, to set them off. I may be able to tell who built it just by looking at it. Let me get a look at the device. I'll know more then. One possibility is to plant a fake—I mockup something that looks real but isn't, buying you time to get your daughter to safety."

"And if we still don't know where she is by the time it's supposed to go off?" asked Stella. She finished her coffee and threw the cup into a garbage can. "What happens to her?"

"I'm a munitions guy. I don't know shit about search and rescue. If they want you to plant that thing in advance, and they're looking to see it's there, a decoy will buy you some time." He ran his hand through his hair, still thinking. "When will you have it?"

"In the morning. I'm going to pick it up at nine-thirty," said Stella.

Evan turned to Max. "Keep me posted. If they allow it, I'd like to be there when she picks it up. The safest thing is to have someone who knows what they're doing take it into possession."

"They may not allow us to do that," said Max.

"I figured that, but let's try." He turned to Stella and put his hand on her shoulder. "However it goes down, I'll connect with you as fast as I can. We'll figure this out. I will not let them hurt your little girl if I can help it."

"And I will not kill a room full of people if I can help it," said Stella. "Thanks for your time, Mr. Collias."

"Please call me Evan." He gave her a hug and whispered in her ear, "I'll help you; I swear."

Stella's eyes teared up at the glimmer of hope Evan offered. She held onto it for all it was worth.

26

S tella called Marcus and updated him on their meeting with Evan, happy he might be able to help them when the time came. Marcus didn't have any major updates on his side, so she headed directly to the hotel. With just twenty-three hours until the gala, the hotel should already be deep in preparations for the event. The weekend crew had arrived—maid services, catering, and hotel staff all switched from the weekday crew to the ones who would be on duty for the weekend festivities. These were the people Stella needed to observe.

An explosion going off in this hotel tomorrow night could kill them. Stella shuddered and pushed the thought away. She didn't want to face the decision that loomed closer to her with each passing hour.

Max met her for dinner, both dressed to the nines to fit into the crowd at the lavish hotel. Each excused themselves at different times to go to the restroom, giving them a chance to wander a bit, reporting back anything interesting they'd seen or heard while they were away.

Stella sipped her wine and let her mind wander to the great heist pulled off at this very hotel over fifty years ago. Known as the kindest robbery of all time, no one was hurt beyond the millions of dollars' worth of jewels and cash the robbers took from the safe deposit boxes.

If she had to go through with this, the hotel would never be the same.

After dinner, Stella bid Max goodnight and headed to her suite to scrub off her makeup and dig through more of the files Celina and her team had put together on the people expected at the event. She managed to get her shoes off and pants unbuttoned before a knock sounded at her door.

She quickly buttoned her pants again and tiptoed toward the door. She squinted through the peephole, and her breath caught. Stella fumbled with the lock, trying her best to get the door open and her visitor inside.

"Oh, my god." Fiona's voice seemed to echo off the walls of the twenty-first floor. Stella grabbed her and pulled her into the room before anyone reported someone screaming in the hallway. "What the fuck have you done to yourself?" She practically yelled the question, still not getting the hint to shut up.

"Shhhhh," Stella hissed. She poked her head out of the room quickly to confirm no one was watching them, then shut the door and bolted it again. "What are you doing here?" she asked. "Is my mom okay?"

"Oh, hon, she's fine." Fiona pulled Stella into her arms. Stella held on for dear life. "I had to come." The two women stayed connected for a while, Stella releasing more of her tension with each passing second that Fiona held her.

When they finally separated, Stella's heart had steadied. Fiona always had the magic touch. "How are you standing in front of me right now?" Stella asked again.

"It's not magic, Stella. I fucking drove here." Fiona picked up the bag she'd dropped and stepped into the living room. "Holy cow, this is stunning. You've been holding out on me." Fiona found the bedroom and put her stuff on one of the empty beds. "Looks like you've got plenty of room. I'm staying the night."

"Is it safe?" Stella asked.

"It's fine. I'll head back in the morning, but Rita and I were both worried about you. She's already asleep. It's better for me to see if I can help with any of this mess than sit around worrying about you all night. I needed to see you," she said, hugging her again. "But what have you done with my best friend?" She gestured to the makeup and clothes Stella was wearing.

Stella laughed. "I have to look like I belong here." She undressed again, getting out of the costume, as she thought of it, and back into her comfortable clothes.

"I thought you hated dressing up," said Fiona. "You look like you know what you're doing, though."

Stella didn't comment, simply padded into the bathroom to wash the makeup from her face. Why had Fiona come? Was she forcing the confrontation she knew they should have? Stella closed her eyes and scrubbed her face with a towelette, rubbing at the foundation, mascara, and eyeshadow she'd caked on. Try as she might, she couldn't erase herself from the reflection staring back at her.

Stella opened the bathroom door and leaned against the frame. She watched her friend settling into the suite, making herself comfortable. Stella almost told her to stop putting her things away. If they got into this conversation, she might want to make a quick exit.

Then again, maybe Stella should be happy, Fiona wouldn't be able to run out the door screaming.

Exhaustion flooded through her. This had been the longest day of her life, and it wouldn't end until Caitlin was home safe. Or until Stella was dead. Because if something happened to Caitlin, she wouldn't sleep until she got the bastards who took her. This didn't feel like the time to have a conversation where Stella scrutinized every word she said to spin a believable story. Which was probably why Fiona was getting settled on the leather sofa right now. She might suspect Stella was too strung out tonight to lie.

"Have you eaten?" Stella asked.

"I have. No need to worry about me," said Fiona. Next to Caitlin, Stella worried more about Fiona than anything else. She wasn't ready for their friendship to end. But she couldn't put this off any longer.

"Were you able to get anything out of my mother today?" Stella knew Fiona would try to weasel information any way she could get it.

"That woman is a fucking vault. I know where you get it now. Someone could torture that woman and she wouldn't give up a thing."

Stella nodded and smiled; grateful her mom had protected her interests. "Is that why you drove all this way? Because you couldn't break her?"

"She told me she couldn't betray your confidence, even though she thought I deserved to know what's really happening. So, in a way, you could say she sent me here."

Stella reached for a bottle of wine at the bar but thought better of it. She'd already had drinks at dinner, and although no amount of caffeine could sharpen her brain enough to outwit Fiona, she felt like a hit of sugar and caffeine could at least help her stay coherent. She grabbed a Dr. Pepper from the fridge and offered Fiona a Diet Coke. "Unless you want something stronger?" Fiona declined.

"Where do I start?" said Stella.

"How about you stop stalling and tell me the truth?" said Fiona. "I'm not going anywhere."

Stella sighed. She wished that were true. A tightness gripped her chest as she sat on the couch across from Fiona and gathered her thoughts. She was bone-tired, her mind fuzzy from stress and alcohol. And she had never had this conversation with another human being.

"You know my job as a photographer?" Stella finally asked. Fiona nodded but seemed to sense that if she interrupted, Stella would retreat to her fortress of lies again. "That's not my real job."

Fiona didn't take the bait. For the first time since they met, Fiona sat completely still; totally silent. She didn't even raise an eyebrow. It was like they were wild animals sizing each other up, and Fiona was not going to give any ground. Stella closed her eyes and shook her head. She knew she'd been beaten.

Stella looked her friend in the eye and said, "My photography career is a cover. I make my money stealing art and jewelry from wealthy people." There were a million things she could say to justify it, to soften the blow, but Fiona deserved to be treated with more respect than that. The time for bullshit was over. "I'm a thief."

Fiona's mouth fell open, but she didn't immediately throw the Diet Coke across the room and storm out. Stella sat back and looked around the luxury suite, resigned to the fact that this could be the last conversation she ever had with her best friend. She wanted to imprint it in her mind—the stylish furniture, the fully stocked wall of books beside her, Central Park outside the window. The park mirrored Stella's feelings with a depth of blackness so complete no light could penetrate.

"Is that why I can't reach you some nights? Because you're breaking into people's houses?" Stella hadn't realized Fiona had noticed her disappearances. What other mistakes had she made that brought her to this moment? When had her facade collapsed? Fiona shook her head. "Here I thought you ran an escort service."

"What?" Stella choked out a laugh.

"Don't laugh, I'm not too far off." Fiona scoffed at her. "I'm not stupid; you're a good photographer, but few artists can afford to live in your house and send their kids to Northbrook. Your mother doesn't work, and I haven't heard you mention inheriting any money. Since you seemed evasive and I couldn't always get hold of you, I thought you might be selling your goods to the highest bidder." Stella's eyes went wide.

"Add that to the fact you never have a boyfriend, and somehow you hooked up with Max, who loves you like a father. And now you have some asshole stalking you? Give me some credit, Stella—I almost nailed it." Fiona took a breath and finished her thought. "And frankly, I'd rather I was right."

Stella picked a piece of invisible lint off her pants, averting Fiona's eyes. "Right now, I kind of wish you were right, too," Stella said. "If that was something you could accept in a friend."

"Don't put words in my mouth. I'm sitting right fucking here. I haven't run out the door. You've told me what you do; now tell me why. I want to know all of it, Stella. No more lies."

"How much time do you have?" Stella asked.

"All fucking night."

Stella rose and stared out the window, trying to figure out where to begin. "The reason my mom didn't tell you anything—"

"Does she know? Does Max know?" This was the Fiona Stella knew and loved. She was done being quiet and cagey, ready to pepper Stella with questions and wear her down.

Stella nodded. "You've got to let me get this out. I've never told anyone this before, and we don't have time for a lot of questions. The reason my mom didn't tell you is because she knows from her own experience how to keep this secret. My father was a thief; she knew it before she married him." Fiona gasped.

"I think she was attracted to the life he led, the smooth-talking conman who could talk his way into fancy restaurants and always had money to throw around. At least at first."

"I had no idea your mum was such a rebel."

"She calmed down a bit later in life, but back then—before me— she liked the fast life."

"So, you came along and ruined all that? Did your dad go straight?"

Stella shook her head. "Far from it. He kept up the life, and honestly, it worked for us. He didn't have a nine-to-five job that kept him away from the house; he and my mother both raised me. It was a pretty good childhood, being the center of attention to two doting parents. Until it wasn't."

"Did he get caught?" Fiona asked.

"Not exactly. He was robbing a bank—something he'd never done before—working with a group of people he didn't know, and they got caught. A cop shot and killed him. I was ten years old." Stella sat back down, her eyes brimming with tears. "Same age Caitlin is now."

"Oh, Stella, I'm so sorry. That's awful. I can't imagine how hard that was for you."

Stella collapsed on to the back of the couch and looked at her beautiful friend. Two minutes ago, she'd learned Stella was a thief and a liar, and she still could muster sympathy for the little girl who lost her father. Tears welled in Stella's eyes. "It was terrible to lose him. But we didn't just lose him, we lost everyone. The story hit the papers, and we were shunned. I went from being a normal kid in school with a best friend, to that same girl mocking me and treating me like an outcast. He ruined our lives."

"You're going to have to connect some dots for me. How can you do this if that's what happened to him?"

Stella reached for her drink and took a sip to buy herself some time. She'd never tried to justify or explain her life to anyone else. There were years of stories and injustices to sort through, a million ways Stella thought about her life and the choices she'd made. She waited for the words to come, settling on the truth she didn't want to admit even to herself.

"I thought I was better than him. I thought I was smart enough to not get caught."

"But the risk? What's happened to Caitlin . . ." Fiona couldn't finish the thought.

"I never would have done this if I'd known this could happen. This isn't my life; I don't know how I got here. I never stole anything that mattered."

"Clearly you're wrong about that," said Fiona.

Stella nodded, her mind going to the Degas. So much seemed to center around that painting. "I have built my life around people not seeing me. I'm a woman, a photographer, a mother. I disappear in crowds. I'm excellent at hiding in plain sight."

"That's not been my experience as a woman."

"I don't look like you." Stella laughed. "It used to piss me off that people dismissed me because I was a woman, or because I was quiet. Never mind what people thought when I got pregnant with Caitlin so young. Stealing became a way for me to use that prejudice to my advantage. I never hurt anyone. It's all been fairly innocent."

"Stealing isn't innocent. You must know that."

"But it's not murder!" Stella realized her mistake the second she said it.

"Who said anything about murder?" Fiona waited for an answer, but Stella quietly cursed herself. "No more lies, Stella. What else are you not telling me?"

"I got a demand from the kidnapper." Stella closed her eyes and shook her head. She didn't want to say it. She didn't want this to be her life. "Blake Cameron is speaking at the gala tomorrow night. They want me to plant a bomb under a table. I think they want me to kill Blake Cameron."

27

Fiona jumped up from the couch as if someone had shocked her. "We have to call the cops, Stella. Lives are on the line."

Fiona reached for her phone, and Stella grabbed her arm to stop her. "They'll kill Caitlin."

"You can't kill a room full of innocent people," Fiona protested. "I may not have known how you made your money, but I know your heart. You're not a terrorist."

"You're right. I have no intention of letting anyone die. Including Caitlin." As she said it, she knew she meant it. Stella couldn't let other people be harmed to save her daughter. But she also couldn't let her daughter be killed because of the choices she'd made in life. She had to find a way out of this.

Stella felt Fiona's energy shift. "Max and I have a plan to switch out the bomb for a fake. We met with one of his contacts tonight. I'm trying to buy us as much time as possible to locate Caitlin before any of this goes down."

"What is Max's role in all this? Now that I know he's not your pimp."

They both laughed at the thought.

"Same role, different profession," Stella said. "He finds the jobs for me and fences the goods."

Stella always thought of Max as her mentor, her savior. He taught her everything he knew and kept her safe. But she realized now that other people might not see it that way; they might blame him for her choices in life. In truth, Max had wanted her to quit from the moment he met her, and he worked hard to give her options outside of stealing to support her life. But she'd been too angry at the world for not taking notice of her, too drawn to the thrill, and pushed him to mentor her.

The mess Stella faced now hurt Max almost as much as it did her.

Fiona sat back down on the couch. "You've gotta be fucking kidding me. Him, too?" She didn't wait for an answer. "I'm friends with an entire family of hoodlums."

Stella had to laugh. "We're much classier than that. Look at this suite."

"Dress it up however you like, darling." She was right. They were a unique family, to be sure. "You feel good about this guy? Max's friend?"

"Evan. Yes, I do. At the end of this, I'm the one who makes the call. I want to give Marcus and his team as much time as possible to trace these threats and track down Caitlin. If they can't do it, I'll call the police myself. I'm the one who has to plant the bomb. If we can't make a good enough fake or something goes wrong, I won't let those people get hurt."

Fiona sat in silence, absorbing everything they'd discussed. Stella gave her time to process, but she couldn't contain her energy. She shifted in her seat and crossed and uncrossed her legs. Her eyes jumped from Fiona to the front door of the suite and back again, wondering if her friend would leave and never come back.

"I don't know what to make of all this. I really don't." Stella opened her mouth to speak, but Fiona held up her hand. "You've had your say. Let me get this out." Stella nodded.

"Honestly, I can't sit here in this fucking hotel suite and make some kind of judgment call on what happens to us after this. This isn't normal, Stella. None of this shit is normal."

Stella broke eye contact and whispered to the floor. "I know."

"But I love you. And I love Caitlin." Stella raised her eyes back to Fiona's, a tiny smile suppressed on her lips. "I'd do anything to help Caitlin. She's family to me."

Stella nodded but kept quiet. She didn't want to break the spell.

"How about we table all this and figure us out later? Let's focus on getting your girl home safely. And keeping the people at that gala safe? How does that sound?"

Fiona hugged Stella. "Fuck, Stella. This is too fucking much. No wonder you're a basket case. Now, put me to work." Stella wasn't sure what Fiona could help with, but Fiona pressed. "Tell me everything you know so far, and what you planned on doing tonight. I'll tell you how I can help."

Not only would telling Fiona give Stella fresh eyes on the entire situation, but it also gave her a chance to say it all out loud.

Fiona produced a notebook and pen from her bag. "Can I write some shit down? I don't want the FBI to find this, but it helps me think." She was half laughing, half serious when she said it, and Stella was grateful she seemed to understand what she was up against.

"Go ahead, but the notebook stays with me."

For the next thirty minutes, Stella walked Fiona through every-thing that had happened so far: what evidence they'd gathered, what they were still trying to get, what each team had found out about their targets so far. She even showed her the video of her breaking into the Hayes house. Fiona kept her mouth shut through most of it but threw questions at Stella if she needed more clarification.

Once she had the full picture of both lines of investigation, Fiona offered her insights. "You've tracked the car as far as Philly, so you're looking into who at the gala might live in that area? Because you think they're hiding her somewhere close by?"

"That's the idea," said Stella.

"And you're analyzing the list of attendees for the event?" asked Fiona. "You think these people would be stupid enough to show up?"

"What do you mean? They'll want to know if I did what I'm supposed to do. And someone has to detonate the device."

"Look for cancellations." Fiona stood and walked around the room. "You're overthinking this. Let's get in their heads. You might be a criminal mastermind, but these people aren't. Their target seems obvious. Taking Caitlin seems like a last-minute move; maybe they believed they could manage the hit on their own. Most likely, planning to slip in a gun and take the shot when the moment came. But at some point, they realized they couldn't. Security is tight. Every time Blake Cameron opens his mouth, more people want to kill him. They might feel like they're forced to do this."

"That tracks," said Stella.

"And somehow, they know about you—have even wanted to work with you. That's what you said about those first threats you got. So, they take Cait and force you to do this."

"Why a bomb? Why not shoot him?"

"Shooting's hard. There's room for error," said Fiona. "You don't know how to shoot anyone. Do you?" She paused long enough to make sure Stella shook her head. "Right. But you can get into places without people noticing. All they need you to do is plant the damn thing and they'll do the rest."

Fiona stopped pacing to look Stella in the eyes. "You haven't killed anyone, Stella. This isn't on you."

"Like hell it isn't," Stella said. Her fingers trembled as she reached for her Dr. Pepper like it was a lifeline, letting the sweet taste wash down her throat while she blinked back tears.

Fiona sat back down and reached for Stella's hand. She squeezed it tight and whispered, "I know, love. I know."

They sat together for a bit, letting Fiona's idea sink in. Stella went to her computer and sent a note to Celina, asking for a list of anyone who had canceled their seat.

"Add the staff to that group," said Fiona. "We can't assume it's an attendee. Someone has to look into the people who are working the event, too."

"I'd pulled the staff list already, but didn't think about people who've called out sick. I've posed as staff lots of times. Why didn't I think of that?" She messaged Celina again, who was already responding to the first request. They had a lot of information to absorb tonight.

"Aren't you glad I came?" asked Fiona.

"More than you'll ever know," said Stella. "Now find me a kidnapper in all of this, please."

28

After pouring over lists of attendees, workers, and property owners outside of Philly, Stella and Fiona were fading. It was a long list of people, and no one stood out as an obvious suspect. They felt frustrated, tired, and cranky.

Fiona got up and stretched, doing a comedic version of Sun Salutation on the hotel room floor. She beckoned Stella to do it with her, saying they had to keep their bodies fresh. They'd had a long day, and there was still more ahead of them. Stella decided she needed the stretch and the laugh; she joined her friend on the floor.

"Is it too late for room service? I need snacks." Fiona declared when she finished stretching. "I'm thinking French fries, maybe some mozzarella sticks, and more sodas. What do you want?"

"What happened to taking care of our bodies?" Stella asked.

"I did some yoga; now I want food. I need to think."

"I think you can have whatever you want whenever you want it at this hotel." Stella placed the order, adding some chips and salsa for herself. Twenty minutes later, their food was delivered, and they were back on the case.

"Let's switch directions. We have to figure out who is pulling the strings here," said Fiona, dripping ranch dressing on her top before she could take the bite. "Shit," she mumbled, wiping at it. "That's gonna stain."

Stella laughed. "I've been trying to figure that out for the last two weeks."

"Well, now I'm here. Let's map this shit out." Stella could see the delight Fiona took in puzzling all this out, and she wondered how she'd ever made it through any of this without her friend. If she'd brought Fiona into her inner circle sooner, all of this might have been avoided.

"Grab your calendar and get me the list of all those threats," Fiona directed. "I'm gonna go get ice. My Diet Coke is getting warm. Where's your room key? I want to get back in without waking everyone up," she asked as she rifled through Stella's wallet. She held up a sleek black card. "This it?"

"No, the key is on the dresser," said Stella. "That's a business card."

"Who has a blank business card?" Fiona flipped it over, inspecting it.

"It's Marcus's. You tap it on your phone like a credit card, and it adds his information to your phone. Pretty slick."

Fiona nodded and set the card down. "Good thing he's on our side." She walked three steps across the room before both of them froze in their tracks. "Oh, shit, Stella. Is it possible?"

Stella shook her head. "No way. Max trusts him completely. There's no way . . ."

Fiona dropped the ice bucket and headed back to the table to look at the information Stella was pulling off her computer. "When did you get your first note?" she asked.

"The first one I noticed was in December, right after I met with Marcus about working for him."

"What were you going to do for these guys? You're not a techie."

"I'm not really at liberty to say."

Fiona shook her head. "But that wasn't the first message. There were ones before that?"

Stella pulled up the sequence of threats Aidan had sent her. He'd accessed her messages through her provider and cataloged all of them. "Looks like the first one came on November sixth."

"What did you do that day? Check your calendar." Stella went through her phone as Fiona read the message aloud. "'I have an opportunity for you.'"

"I thought it was a job offer."

"Sounds about right. What were you doing when you got it?"

Stella glanced at her calendar to check her memory. "I had lunch with Max at Nonna Vita's. I'd been paid for my last job, and I thought he was going to offer me a new target, something similar to the last. But instead, he brought up Marcus's company—tried to get me to go to work for them." Stella could still feel the sting of that conversation, hearing that Max wanted her to quit instead of praising her for a job well done. Stella shook her head.

"When did you get the note?" asked Fiona.

"As I was leaving."

"So Max surprises you by asking you to go to work for this guy; he hands you a blank business card that you have to tap on your phone to see . . ." Stella nodded but let Fiona keep talking. "This is important, Stella. Did you tap that card on your phone before or after you got the message?"

"Definitely before. Max and I were laughing about it. It took me a couple of tries to get it right. Once I did it properly, it launched the company website on my phone's browser. I was impressed."

"And then you get this text?"

"A few minutes later. Yeah."

"Let's not jump to any conclusions yet," Fiona said. She looked at the list of messages Marcus's team had identified as threats. "You got all of these—any calls?" Stella shook her head. "All these come in, all of them have some kind of virus or whatever attached to them, but you ignore them. Then the big one comes. When? A month later?"

"December eighth, almost exactly a month later." Stella pointed to the one that had gotten her attention. "'I don't like being ignored.' That came after I met with Marcus about the job."

Fiona made Stella tell her everything about the meeting. Stella explained every detail, how she'd initially rejected the idea of working with Marcus, but after things were going so well with Richard, she considered it. She'd set up the meeting with him at a safe location and had done her homework in advance.

"You broke into his house?" asked Fiona.

"I only took his key fob." Stella smiled. "He had no idea it was me. I don't think he ever considered someone had stolen it; he thought he'd misplaced it."

"That's badass." Fiona laughed. "So, you stalk the man a bit, learn about his business, and even break into his apartment—then what?"

"We met at Sherman Park to discuss things. It was virtually empty."

"Virtually?"

"I took photos of the entire place in case there was someone watching me. There were some people on the marina and others sitting farther away, but no one stuck out to me."

"Okay, how'd the meeting go?"

"A little contentious at first. He pulled up a video, and it showed me in his office, pretending to be a pizza delivery person who had the wrong place. He acted as if I wasn't as good as Max had told him. He needed someone better than that."

"And then you insulted him, didn't you?"

"No, I took his feedback, and when I shook his hand to leave, I gave him his key fob back." She smiled when she thought back to the look on Marcus's face. "I don't think he's used to people getting one over on him."

"And then you get the message."

"While I was driving home, yes. That one got my attention. It was the video I told you about. It came with a threat."

"Then you went all spy shit on them—locked down your security, got new phones, did all that, right? Did I miss anything?"

"I asked Marcus and his team to scan my computer for a virus; he didn't find one. I also asked him to check my network to see if someone had hacked it." Stella worked through the timeline in her head. "Then I got the picture of Caitlin on my phone. That changed everything."

Fiona paced the room again. "The message after meeting with Marcus came really quickly, right? Like maybe he teed it up before you met with him? He goes to this meeting and thinks he's not going to hire you, but you show your stuff. You prove to him how good you are but then reject him."

"I didn't outright reject him, but I wasn't hurrying to sign the dotted line, either."

"I think it's staring us in the face. These geeks want to hire you. You get your first text after you tap his card on your phone like some kind of fucking wizard. All the messages sound like someone wanting to partner with you. Maybe they're watching you, observing who you are and how you operate. Then you meet this guy and show him up. You pissed him off."

"Why would they be helping me then? Why would they offer to help me find her if they're the ones who have her?" As Stella said it, it clicked for her.

Fiona narrated Stella's thoughts. "How do we know they're actually helping? Stella, you've got thirty-six hours to figure out a way into this place, plant a bomb, and find your kid. These people are the only people helping you, and they keep advising you not to go to the authorities. How do we know they've really traced the car to Pennsylvania? How fast did they come up with these plans for the event? They could have hacked into the site weeks ago."

Stella thought about how quickly Celina moved through the PAC's files. She thought the woman was a data ninja; it looked like she'd been using the files every day for weeks.

Stella felt her stomach churn; a small bit of bile traveled to the back of her throat. She swallowed it back, then reached for some water to wash it down. She grabbed her burner phone and texted Max, praying he hadn't given it to Marcus at any point in the last two days. To be on the safe side, she texted him their Code Black emergency phrase.

> Stella: We want to talk to you about your Mercedes' extended warranty.

She didn't know if he'd get the message tonight or in the morning, but she felt certain he'd know to contact her directly whenever he saw it. She turned to Fiona as tears welled in her eyes. "What are we supposed to do now?"

29

The sharp ping of the default text tone jolted Stella awake. Her eyes shot open, and her heart was already jumping out of her chest. If she made it out of this weekend alive, she vowed to keep her phone on silent for the rest of her life.

She and Fiona crashed around 4:00 a.m., after spending the night waiting for Max to get her message and debating their options. If Marcus's team was pulling the strings here, it seemed an impossible situation for her to get out of. Calling the authorities might work, but his team seemed to have them in their pockets. And any cop or agent they told about this would focus on protecting Blake Cameron and the people at the event, potentially leaving Caitlin hanging in the wind.

Stella rejected that idea immediately.

She convinced herself Evan might be her best bet for getting out of this. If he could switch the bomb, she could plant a dummy and turn her attention to getting Caitlin back alive. That meant Marcus's team would need to believe the bomb was real. It wasn't a solid plan, but it had been enough to help her get some sleep in the early dawn.

She groped for the phone and checked the time as she looked at the message. It was 6:00 a.m.

The second chime of the text notification told her everything she didn't want to know. It wasn't Max. The tone was wrong. The sound was coming from her personal cell, not her burner.

She tried to make sense of the words. "NO!" She yelled, a guttural, primal cry from the depths of her throat.

Her hands shook as she squeezed the phone hard enough to crush it. It was all she could do not to throw it at the wall.

Fiona jumped up, frantically looking around to decipher what was happening.

"No, no, no, no." Stella dropped the phone and fell back on her bed.

"What's happening, Stella? Is it Caitlin? Is she okay?"

Stella couldn't respond—could barely breathe. Fiona picked up the phone and tried to read the message, but the phone was locked. "I can't read the text, Stella. Tell me what it said."

Fiona shook Stella's shoulders, trying to keep her from having a breakdown.

"There are two bombs," Stella said, covering her eyes with the palms of her hands, plunging her vision into darkness. "They sent pictures of two different bombs. One I'm supposed to plant, and the other is under Caitlin's bed." She barely got the words out between sobs. She pulled her hands away and opened her eyes, staring up at Fiona. "It said if the bomb doesn't go off at the gala, they'll detonate the second one. The only way Caitlin gets out of this alive is if that bomb goes off and kills all those people."

"Holy fuck. They know about the plan to switch the bomb out." Stella nodded as Fiona put the pieces together. She'd told Marcus about the conversation with Evan. She'd fed the kidnapper the method she planned to use to stop the carnage.

She didn't realize how much she'd been holding onto the illusion that she could somehow get out of doing this. But with two bombs in place and time running out, she didn't see a way out of it. If she did anything to interrupt that bomb going off, they would kill her daughter. Her only hope was to track Caitlin down before she planted the bomb. Otherwise, she was going to have to choose between saving her daughter and saving the people at the gala.

30

Fiona forced Stella to get up and take a shower while she ordered room service for a hearty breakfast. Stella felt sick to her stomach, but Fiona insisted she couldn't plan her next move on an empty stomach and almost zero sleep.

Standing underneath the showerhead, Stella let the water pour over her, grateful for the endless supply of hot water that ran through The Pierre's pipes. At home, it would have been cold within ten minutes. She let the tears flow in the privacy of the steamy shower, indistinguishable on her face from the scalding water that ran over her cheeks. Surely, this was rock bottom.

Stella tried to imagine living in a world without her daughter. She hadn't let her mind go there before, but now she let it run free. She knew what it felt like to lose her father. As bad as that was, she had her mother with her, and her whole life ahead of her. She picked up the pieces and put her heart back together—if not perfectly, then at least into something resembling a heart again.

But this? Her daughter? The one person on earth she loved more than anyone else? She wouldn't survive it.

She didn't want to survive it.

If something happened to Caitlin, Stella didn't want to live in this world anymore. No amount of time or glue could mend her heart—it would shatter into a million tiny specks, each no bigger than a grain of sand, far too small to be assembled again. Her daughter was everything. She'd do whatever it took to bring her home, without hurting anyone if she could help it. But if she failed, she'd go down tonight with the rest of them.

Stella emerged from the bathroom wearing the plush hotel robe tight around her frame, her arms wrapped around herself. She laid eyes on the spread of food Fiona had ordered, and her stomach rumbled loud enough for Fiona to hear.

"I told you food would be good," Fiona chided.

The only thing Stella felt good about was the decision she'd made in the shower. It freed her from a lot of worry and allowed her to clearly see the steps in front of her.

As they finished breakfast, Fiona took her turn in the shower and Stella pinged Max again. He should be awake by now. Why the hell hadn't he answered her back yet? She sent the code again, hoping nothing had happened to keep him from answering.

At 7:25 a.m. Stella heard a knock and went to see who was there. She threw open the door and walked into Max's arms, the tears flowing freely again. Max held her for a bit and consoled her as he eased her back into the room and closed the door. Stella relaxed her hold on him and peppered him with questions. "Why are you here? Why didn't you answer my text? I thought something had happened to you."

"She sounds like me," said Fiona. She pulled Stella off Max and guided him to the table. "Let the man get all the way inside, sweetie. We have a lot to talk about."

"I left the phone on last night, but my hearing is not what it once was. I woke up this morning to see your message and thought the safest thing was for me to come to you. To our knowledge, no one knows you're staying here. I felt this would be a safe place to talk."

Stella and Fiona glanced at each other. Stella realized in all the revelations they'd had last night, they didn't stop to think Marcus's team knew where she was staying. It's highly possible they'd bugged the room they were in while Stella was meeting with Evan last night.

"Screw it," said Fiona, clearly thinking along the same lines. "If they're listening, then they already know everything we do. Might as well bring him up to speed."

"What on earth? Were you compromised?" Max asked Stella, then switched his gaze to Fiona.

"Not me. But you might have," she said.

"I'm not following. Please explain what's going on." He directed this at Stella, and Fiona took the cue to quiet down. They showed him the timeline of the threats Stella had received beside her calendar. Then they brought out Marcus's black card.

Stella showed Max the message she'd received from the kidnapper this morning. She explained she'd called Marcus after meeting with Evan last night and handed him the ammunition he needed to change the plan.

Max kept quiet through most of it, only asking for clarification when it was absolutely critical. He sat back, taking it all in, processing it as she laid the evidence in front of him. "This is remarkable work. You two make a brilliant team."

"Hard to take a congratulations on this one," said Fiona.

"The only problem is you've reached the wrong conclusion." His voice was solid, not wavering at all. Nothing they'd shown him had affected him at all.

"What do you mean? Caitlin is in trouble," said Stella.

"Yes, she is. And you've done solid work. You could be a detective. But you have drawn the wrong conclusion. Marcus is not your man."

"What makes you so sure?" asked Fiona. Stella was grateful her friend spoke for both of them; her tongue was tied at the moment.

"I know Marcus Williams. I've known him all his life. He is as dear to me as you are, Stella, and as Caitlin is. Marcus Williams would never harm someone I love, and especially not a child. It's simply not possible."

"But look at the evidence." Stella picked up the notebook she and Fiona had been using to record their findings. "Look at when I got my first threat—after I'd used his card. And when the video came through—after I said I wasn't going to work for him. It's all there."

"I don't deny any of that. But I am certain it cannot be him. There is something else going on here, someone else lurking in this calendar and these messages we cannot yet see," said Max. He put a hand on Stella's shoulder to steady her, getting her full attention. "You know he lost a child. That was public information. The papers only reported the accident, not what caused it. It's not my story to tell, but someone took his wife and daughter from him. It was no accident."

Max spoke with conviction, and Stella held his gaze, taking in every word. "Marcus Williams is a genius at technology, and at running a company full of people smarter than he is. He would never hurt another human being, let alone threaten one. He's not a killer."

"So that's it? All of this was for nothing? You're sure?" Stella pressed. "Do you really trust this man with my life? With Caitlin's?" She searched his eyes for any sign of hesitation and found none.

"Unquestionably," he said. "Your work is not for nothing. It's brilliant, and I, for one, am thrilled your conclusions are incorrect." He looked at them and smiled brightly enough for it to reach his eyes. "It would be devastating if people of Marcus's caliber had orchestrated this. But it's not him, and it's not his team. There is still a chance to get Caitlin home safely and keep the people at this event safe."

"What about the bombs? How did they know Stella was going to swap it out for a fake one?" Fiona questioned.

"Someone is watching you, Stella. They have devoted themselves to infiltrating your life in a number of insidious ways. From what you've shown me here, you thwarted them, put them off their game, and probably ruined their plans. Your lack of interaction drove them to such extreme action. I have no doubt someone observed us with Evan yesterday evening and put two and two together. He's the best explosives man on the East Coast."

"In the whole country, according to him," said Stella.

"Precisely. It wouldn't take more than seeing you with him to understand your intention to disrupt their plans."

"We're back to square one," said Fiona. "Someone is pulling the strings, and we have no idea who it is."

"I think we're much closer now than we were last evening. And we have you to thank for that, my dear," Max said to Fiona. "You really do have a brilliant mind."

"This is what I've been saying." While Fiona laughed, her phone buzzed in her pocket. She shushed both of them and answered the call, moving to the bedroom to speak in private.

"Let's finish getting cleaned up and head over to Marcus's office." He looked around the room as he spoke. "I'd prefer any further conversations to happen there, under his security."

Stella stood to gather her things when she heard Fiona holler from the bedroom. "You're in," she declared as she came back into the suite's living room. "That was Pam. Looks like your trick worked, and Luca backed out of the event tonight. She's scrambling and was thrilled to learn you're still in town and willing to step in."

"Is it official?" asked Stella.

"She'll call with the details in a few minutes, but yeah, you're good to go."

Stella hugged and kissed her friend's cheeks, knowing how painful it was for her to have to grovel to their PTA nemesis.

"Have some breakfast, Grandpa," Fiona ordered Max. "I'm guessing you didn't eat before you rode your scooter over here first thing this morning." She kissed him on the forehead and then went to finish getting ready.

"You can head back to be with my mom," Stella said to Fiona. She turned to Max. "And I'll meet you at Marcus's in a bit. I have a package to pick up."

Fiona looked at Max and back at Stella. "I'd prefer to stay here, if that's all right with you. Your mum is fine, and I worked with you on all this last night. I can help the team at Marcus's go over all our thoughts. You'll be busy enough today."

Stella shook her head. "I want you out of harm's way, not in it."

"No way. I'm perfectly fine here, and I want to go over those files to keep digging until we find the bastard who's doing this to you."

Max nodded his agreement. There was no way Stella was going to win an argument against both of them.

"Fine. Both of you head to Marcus's. Let Mom know you're going to stay in town, okay? I'll go get the package." They both tried to protest, but Stella held up her hand to stop them. "I'll call in our friend for help, but I'm getting it now before it accidentally goes off and hurts anyone. Evan will know how to handle the device safely."

Stella set off for the storage locker Every step forward seemed to come with a step back, and Stella knew they were running out of time for the dance to continue. In ten hours, she'd have to be in the Grand Ballroom downstairs setting up a bomb or trying to fake out a terrorist.

31

I t took Stella over an hour to retrieve the package and get back to Marcus's office with Evan in tow. He was reluctant to leave the Bronx and meet the team at the office—especially considering the bomb they were carrying—but Stella convinced him it was safe. At least she could vouch for the privacy that would be afforded to them in the office. It was up to him to see if the bomb was stable enough to travel.

"It's not armed," he assured her. "They'll have it set to arm after you place it at the venue. For now, this is as dangerous as a big fluffy kitten." Stella rolled her eyes at him. "Maybe not a kitten. It's fine. Just make sure we can get into the building without setting off any alarms."

Marcus had assured them he could get the device into his office. He routinely brought in electronic equipment on the weekends and knew the guards on duty. He met them in the parking garage and packed the suitcase in a series of boxes, then slipped into the service elevator while Stella and Evan took the main entrance, passing through security without incident.

Once in the office, Marcus led them into a large conference room at the back of the office. "Just in case," he said. They had the advantage of it being the weekend, and Marcus's company was the only one working today. "I checked the other offices above and below us for several floors, and we're in the clear. I want to be sure no one gets hurt if this thing goes off early."

Marcus left Evan and Stella to study the device on their own. Stella didn't know what she was looking at, but Evan seemed to discern the entire history of the explosive simply by looking at it. "As I told ya, every person has their own special signature for work like this. This isn't a local guy. The parts are from here, but this is European. Has to be."

"Someone got this here on a plane?" Stella asked.

"No, the person came over on a plane, but they assembled the bomb here. Probably sent over a shopping list and had a local guy get everything they needed. Then assembled it here."

"Any idea who it is?" asked Stella. "Could we run a check on someone, see when they came into the country and who they are associated with?" She checked her watch. 10:00 a.m. Only seven hours until she had to plant the bomb at the hotel.

"That'll take time and probably come to nothing. The man who built this—"

"The man?" Stella repeated, raising her eyebrows at him.

He nodded. "Fair enough. The *person* who built this will be in the wind by now. Best to keep working on the problem from this end." Stella understood. "But I have good news. Let's call in your friends."

Marcus, Max, Fiona, and Stella all gathered in the room while Evan explained what he had noticed about the device. Before he spoke, Fiona whispered in Stella's ear. "I need to talk to you." She had a file in her hand and waved it at Stella. "I've got something to show you."

Stella nodded but held up her finger. She wanted to hear what Evan had to say.

Evan explained the bomb to the group. "This is a cellular trigger. Stella will plant the device while it's still inactive, so she shouldn't be at risk. At some point, someone will call this phone"—he lifted some wires and showed them the cell phone on the back of the device—"and activate the bomb. It'll then connect to a satellite signal and communicate with what we think is the second explosive." Stella felt her heart constrict at the thought of the bomb under Caitlin's bed.

"Let me see the picture of the one under your girl's bed," Evan said to Stella. She pulled out her phone to show it to him. Marcus quickly took it, projecting the image onto a screen on the back wall. "Right. See here? That's the same type of trigger. Another cell phone. If the devices are in series, they'll set off one after the other. What did the kidnapper tell you? If the first one doesn't go off, it'll trigger the second?"

"Correct. They didn't say how much time there would be before hers would detonate."

"I bet these guys can figure that out," said Evan. "This is all high-tech shit. Not your average pipe bomb, that's for sure."

Stella's body tensed.

"If they're running off cell signals, we can absolutely intercept them," Marcus offered.

Stella felt her body relax a fraction.

Marcus called in three more people to the back room and explained the situation. They bombarded Evan with questions. He wasn't a hacker, but he knew enough to tell them how the electronics connected to the explosive. It was everything they needed to devise a plan.

"Like I said—knew you'd be happy," said Evan. "Problem is, if you turn any of this on in advance to get into the programming, you'll trigger it. You can't touch this device until it's activated. And I don't think they're going to activate it until it's planted."

"We can handle that," said a young man wearing a Sponge Bob T-shirt. "I'll put an interceptor on it that will give me access to the signal when it goes live." His cohorts nodded their agreement. "Can we stick something beside the device? Right about here?" He pointed to a small space on the side of the device, near the phone.

"Should be fine. As long as you don't interfere with this wiring." Evan showed them exactly what they needed to avoid touching.

"Can you stay and supervise us?" asked Marcus. "I'd prefer you to have eyes on what they're doing."

"I'll go one further. They build whatever they want to add to it, and I'll put it on the device. No one wants this going off before it's intended." He caught what he said and turned to Stella. "Or ever, if we do this right."

Stella thanked him, then turned her attention to Fiona and pointed at the folder she was holding. "You needed me?"

Fiona glanced at Max, then pulled Stella away from the group to speak to her. "I don't know how to say this . . ." She glanced at Max, who nodded for her to continue. "I think Richard is going to be at the gala." She opened the folder she was holding and handed Stella a picture of a man who was unmistakably Richard Medina. It looked like it was a relatively recent photo. But the name on the page was Juan Castillo.

"I don't understand." Stella's knees buckled. Before she lost her footing entirely, Max pulled her into a chair. "What?" She squinted her eyes and slowly shook her head, struggling to get her mind to process the information.

Max stepped away while Fiona pulled up another chair next to her and tried to fill in the gaps for her. "I asked Celina to put together pictures of the attendees. I can't deal with these damn spreadsheets. Swear to God, these people wrote a program to grab images of these people off the Internet and match them with names on the list. I have an entire stack of these things, with pictures of every guest and hotel worker we know will be there."

Max returned with a bottle of water for Stella. "Drink this."

She did as he told her, but her mind still slogged through a thick fog instead of processing things normally.

"I was going through those pages when I saw his face," said Fiona. She put her hand on Stella's shoulder. "Did he tell you anything about being at this thing?"

"He didn't . . . I haven't spoken to him since . . ." Stella shook her head as she tried to get out a full sentence. She took another sip of water. "We had an argument Monday night." She tilted her head and squinted at Fiona. "This isn't even his name. Their program must be wrong."

"The program is correct," said Max. "We're pulling more information now, but it looks like Juan Castillo is his given name."

"How can that be?" Stella shook her head, trying to get some clarity.

Max's words from this morning ran through her mind. This was personal. Someone was trying to hurt her. They'd threatened her daughter, and now Richard—or whatever his name was—was caught in the mix.

Stella glanced around the room, trying to find something to focus on. Marcus and two others were animated, talking about cell signals and satellites. She looked at Evan and saw him examining the bomb, turning it carefully. He looked as confused as she felt. She pointed at him and asked, "What?" Nothing else came out.

Stella sighed and shook her head. She stood up and walked over to talk to Evan. "What's going on?" she asked. Her mind was clearing now. Moving seemed to help.

"Who did you say they're trying to kill with this? That asshole Cameron?"

Stella nodded. "He's the guest of honor. He'll be speaking at the event."

Fiona joined them, putting her arm around Stella's shoulders for support.

"Can I see the floor plan for this thing? Where is she supposed to plant this? And where is he speaking?" Evan caught everyone's attention. Marcus asked Celina to put the seating chart for the night up on the screen.

Evan walked to the screen and pointed at the table. "You're planting the bomb here, right?" he asked. "Did they tell you where exactly?"

Stella shook her head. "They said under the table. I think anywhere in the vicinity is close enough."

"It's not though."

"What do you mean?"

"I mean, there's something else about this bomb. We've got it all wrong."

Stella's voice hit an octave she didn't know she had. She almost screeched at him. "What do you mean we've got it *wrong?*"

You could hear a pin drop in the conference room now. They'd been working on this problem nonstop for the last twenty-four hours. Barely sleeping, throwing every resource they had at it. What the hell could they have gotten wrong?

"This bomb will not kill a room full of people. It won't even reach the bloke at the podium." Evan turned the device over, knowing it wasn't armed. "See this here? This is the explosive. From the way you were talking, I assumed this was going to go off and blow the whole hotel down, but this doesn't have that kind of firepower."

"How much does it have?" asked Marcus.

"This is a controlled explosive. It'll kill anyone within a ten-foot radius, but not much beyond that." He looked at the plans on the wall again. "That table is too far away from the speaker for him to be the target. The person who made this bomb knows what they're doing. They made a small bomb and set a sophisticated way to detonate it. This isn't a terror event; this is murder." He traced his finger to where the bomb would likely have the most impact. "People sitting here? They're goners. But everyone else . . . some will get hit by some shrapnel, everyone will be running and screaming. But this is only going to kill six to eight people."

Stella was numb. She wanted to be happy the bomb was so small, but everything felt wrong to her. First her daughter, then Richard. She didn't know how to react to anything anymore.

Evan broke through the haze of her thinking. "This is a very personal device. It's controlled, calculated . . . Someone went to a great deal of trouble to get it, to make sure you deployed it." He turned and looked at Stella. "This is precise and intentional; it'll kill exactly who the person wants and not much else. I doubt it's a political statement. This seems too personal."

"I agree," Max said. "And taking Caitlin, threatening to kill her in the same manner? You've been set up to take the fall. Caitlin is a means to an end, but this is intended to hurt you as much as the person they're targeting to kill."

Silence engulfed the room. They'd been working under a false set of assumptions. They stared at the device, the layout of the room on the wall, and Stella.

Then, as if someone flipped a switch, the room erupted, everyone talking at once.

32

Marcus reassigned resources and mapped out the rest of the day. "Hourly updates will continue," he said. "Top priority on the tech side is getting an interceptor placed on the device and making damn sure it's going to work." He pointed to one of his guys.

"Who do we know in Philly?" Marcus asked. "We need assets in place before Stella places this bomb, and we need them ready to move once we know exactly where Caitlin's being kept." It was still a gamble—there wasn't a guarantee they'd find Caitlin in the Philadelphia area when the signal went live.

"I know some people," Evan announced. "They'd lay down their lives to protect an innocent kid." He looked at Stella and placed his hand on her back. "If you'll let me, I'd like to go. I can help with the bomb if needed, and my friends will work with me."

Marcus waited for Stella to speak before he confirmed anything.

"Are you sure?" she asked. She wanted to protest. Too many people were putting themselves in harm's way for her. Though when she imagined Caitlin sitting in that room with the bomb under her cot, her stomach cinched. She nodded. "Thank you."

"Great. Evan, call your guys and we'll set up a place to meet. I want to figure out the best place to park ourselves that gets us to

Caitlin the quickest way possible. Map out a twenty-mile radius around the center of the city. Look at traffic cams, construction—all of it. I want us to be able to move when we get that signal.

"We are six and a half hours from Stella needing to plant this bomb. We have a lot of ground to cover and not much time. Let's go, people." Upon Marcus's dismissal, the room emptied, people rushing to their stations to get their respective jobs done.

Stella remembered the picture she'd found of Marcus and his buddies in Afghanistan, arms around each other, smiles on their faces but their eyes bloodshot from the stress and lack of sleep. He was in his element. A glimmer of hope seeped into her heart as she watched him work. He'd give everything to this mission, she knew. They all would.

Celina poked her head in the room and said, "I think you're going to want to see this." She motioned for Fiona, Max, and Stella to follow her into the main office. Min, Raf, Aidan, and Annie were already gathered, looking at a computer screen. Celina spoke first. "Fiona told you we discovered your boyfriend will be at the event?" It was a rhetorical question, but Stella nodded anyway. "She asked us to run whatever information we could on him."

"The name thing threw me. I thought they could find information faster than anyone," said Fiona. Stella agreed.

"We did a cursory search at first, but ended up going a lot deeper," said Min. "It kind of cascaded on us."

"What'd you find out?" Stella asked.

Celina hit the highlights. "The name thing isn't that strange. His full name is Juan Ricardo Medina Castillo. I think he goes by Richard Medina here?" Stella nodded and leaned against Fiona. "That's not uncommon. Spanish culture combines surnames for kids. His mother is Melina Castillo, and his father was Antonio Medina."

"You said his father 'was,'" asked Fiona. "Did you know he was dead, Stella?"

"Yeah, he told me. His father ran a big finance company or something? Pretty affluent. He stepped away from that life."

"More like a multinational empire. Castillo Enterprises. They own half of Europe and are well-placed in South America and the US as well. They own just about everything," said Raf. "He didn't exactly step away, either."

"What do you mean?" Stella protested. Her body felt heavy; her thoughts sluggish. "He teaches my daughter's class now. That's not his life anymore."

"His father died three years ago of a heart attack. Age seventy-two," Raf explained. "Juan Ricardo—that's what he seems to go by most—was in line to take over his father's empire. But his mother stepped in to run the company instead of him. There was an ugly legal battle for a bit, which she won. Seems like his dad screwed him over in the will and left it up to his mother to decide when the time was right for him to take the lead. She didn't think he was ready."

Stella shook her head. "I didn't know those details, but it's not totally out of bounds from what he's told me. I mean, he's teaching now. Something must have clicked with him to make him leave that life behind," said Stella.

"That's the thing," said Annie. "He didn't leave it behind." She hit some keys on the computer and showed her the search for his name. "The gossip columns are all over this guy. He's a playboy, with no family of his own, likes to screw around and not much else. Since he lost the court battle for control of his father's company, he's been seen hanging out with some questionable folks." She clicked on one article from a Spanish gossip blog, then hit the translate button. Before Stella could focus enough to read it, they summarized it for her.

"This says he's been seen with an international arms dealer named Ivan Federov. I think Juan Ricardo is pissed he's not running the company and enjoys embarrassing his mother," said Aidan.

"What? Why are you showing me this?" Stella asked. "How can any of this be true? The man I know has been teaching in my daughter's classroom for two months." She looked to Fiona for support. Fiona took her hand and squeezed it tight.

"We know he's been here," said Raf. "With all of this going on, we didn't want to leave anything to doubt. So, we've been digging. We found out a lot about this guy. He is not who he claims to be."

Min chimed in. "I've been tracking down the person who bought the painting from Max; the one from the video?" He looked at Max as he said it, confirming he was following orders.

"I gave him the name of the company I sold it to and asked him to see what he could find out," Max said.

"Right." Min went on. "The buyer is buried pretty deep, so it took me a while to find it." Annie made a circling motion with her finger to speed him along. "Max sold it to a holding company named Kruger Enterprises. It's owned by Mando, LLC. Three more layers deep, and the company is owned by Juan Castillo. Richard bought your painting."

Stella tried to disconnect, but Celina wouldn't let her. "There's more," she said. She hit some buttons on the computer and pulled up the files Min had on Juan Ricardo Castillo. "His family owns a villa in El Paraíso. He knows Sebastian Hayes. They run in the same circles."

"Did he set this up?" Max asked, eyes widening. He turned to Stella. "The intel on this heist came through a source I trusted, but he admitted he didn't know if it was possible to get in. He said he had a buyer if I ever figured out a way to get it."

"I think he did," said Annie. "I got a reply from Interpol this morning on the picture we sent them of Caitlin's kidnapper. His name is Lev Morozov."

Stella threw up her hands. "Just say it. Does he work for Richard?"

"No. He works for this guy." She clicked the screen back to the image of Richard on a yacht with Ivan Federov.

"We're still digging," Celina added. "But once we saw that, we had to bring it to you."

Stella froze, her brain shutting down completely. Everyone around her was silent, watching to see how she'd react.

Fiona broke through the silence first. "Max was right; this is personal. We were smart to line up the threats and your timeline. We just had the wrong idea."

"Who did you think it was?" asked Aidan.

"Doesn't matter now." Fiona turned to Stella. "Richard is a pissed off, spoiled rich guy who can't get what he wants. He set up this sale for God knows what reason. Maybe he hates this Hayes guy and wants to piss him off, but he also wanted to catch whoever did it. Maybe he thought he'd use you for future jobs. Either way, I bet he had no fucking idea you'd be a woman. And to look like you? You blew him away."

Max, knowing where Fiona was going, picked up the thread. "There were several months between when you took the Degas, and he joined the school. He could have spent that time researching other heists that looked like your signature. He got some right, some wrong, but eventually, he must have pieced together who you were. As Rita said, you live in Connecticut. You're not hiding. Once he found you, it's not impossible to match your face to the video. To confirm he had the right person."

Fiona smacked her hand to her forehead. "The glasses. I gave him the glasses. They were the same ones you were wearing on your heist. If he ever had any doubt, that erased it. I handed you to him."

"It's not your fault," said Stella.

"Like hell it isn't. I pushed you to date him; tried to get you to open up to him. Shit, Stella. I did this." Fiona shook with anger, at herself or Richard, Stella didn't know which.

"Not you, dear," said Max, touching Fiona's arm to calm her down. "He targeted her. The glasses and cajoling were simply icing on the cake. Nothing would stop him from pursuing her."

"All the early messages are almost friendly," said Aidan.

Fiona picked up the thread. "I think he wanted to pimp you out. Maybe replace Max." She turned to Stella. "But you never took the bait. Not in dating him, and not with the threats. You never admitted what you really do."

"Whatever escalated him, he must have seen you wouldn't work for him, or with him. I don't know if he had this bomb in his plans all along or pivoted at the last minute, but either way, he wants to hurt you now," said Max.

Stella's mind flashed through images as everyone gave their theory of how her life spiraled out of control. She saw Richard showing up on her doorstep and sitting at her breakfast bar, probably planting the bug then. She felt like he saw her clearly, knew more about her than anyone. Skydiving on their first date because he knew she liked adventure. Romancing her at home and on their date at the art gallery. He'd said then he could get her into these circles. She thought he meant as a photographer, but he meant as a thief. She'd missed it all; fallen for the idea that there could be someone out there worth letting into her heart.

"We have to know everything there is to know about this guy," Fiona said, giving instructions to those around them. "Dig deeper. Let's find out when he decided to attend tonight's event. Was he always supposed to go, or is this recent? Who is going with him? And for fuck's sake, does the man own any property in this country? See if he owns anything in Philadelphia or New York. Caitlin could be right here in the city."

Stella's stomach tightened. She ran out of the office, racing for the women's restroom. She yanked the door open and dove into the closest stall, falling to her knees just in time to empty the contents of her stomach. Tears streamed down her face as she retched.

The images kept coming to her. All the ways he'd inserted himself into her life. All the ways he'd demanded her attention. Their perfect night together; him acting like a generous lover, then pretending she was crazy for being nervous about Caitlin's safety.

The text messages increasing in urgency from friendly to threats. Interrupting her shot at the school carnival. Pretending to be the perfect teacher.

Mrs. Beaker. Did he run her off the road? He could have killed her. It was a miracle she'd survived. Her hands shook as she retched again and again, expelling any trace of affection she'd once held for the man.

She didn't hear Fiona come in, just felt her pull her hair away from her face and rub her back. When the vomiting finally stopped, Fiona flushed the toilet for her, then went to the sink. Stella heard her pulling paper towels from the rack and running water over them. She delivered the makeshift rag to Stella and sat down on the floor with her.

"I did this. I let that bastard in, and he did this to me."

"Oh, love." Fiona pulled Stella's head to her shoulder. "You did nothing wrong. He's a rat bastard is all." Normally, Fiona was animated and amped up, but her voice was quiet now, soothing Stella's frayed nerves. "Anyone would have fallen for those blue eyes. You're only human."

"My little girl. He's got my little girl." Fiona held her close as memories surged. Caitlin as a baby in her arms, the two of them shouting at basketball games on TV, the stubborn little girl who refused to leave a bookstore, the beaming student with new friends, the teenager blasting Taylor Swift and singing along at the Eras concert last summer. Every moment pulsed through Stella like a heartbeat she could no longer feel. Her daughter, her whole world.

Stella pulled back from Fiona and wiped her eyes, blowing her nose on the wet mass of paper towels.

"I need your help," said Stella.

"Anything."

Stella pulled herself up and offered Fiona her hand. The women walked to the sink, where Stella washed her face again, then leaned on the counter and stared at Fiona in the mirror. "If anything happens to me, I need you to take care of Caitlin and my mom. I'm not sure my mom will survive this on her own."

"Nothing is going to happen to you. You and Caitlin are going to be fine." Fiona turned her to face her, keeping her hands on her shoulders. "Do you hear me? You're both going to be okay."

Stella slowly nodded, but her eyes were vacant. "I have a job to do, and I need to know they'll be okay if something goes wrong. Promise me."

Fiona pulled her into a fierce hug. "I promise I'll take care of them. They're family to me." She pulled back and stared at Stella again. "But hear me, Stella Meyers: nothing is going to happen to either of you tonight. We're going to find Caitlin before anything happens. I swear it."

Stella didn't share Fiona's conviction that she would come home tonight. She took a deep breath and centered herself. The most important thing was rescuing Caitlin. Stella visualized them finding her, rescuing her in time. She planted the image in her mind, just like when she did a job.

Stella's heart rate picked up speed, anger rising through her body. She clenched her fists together, her nails digging into her palms at the thought of all the ways Richard had inserted himself into her life.

"I'm gonna kill him," Stella ground out. She was done leaving this up to anyone else. She was in control again.

"Not if I get there first," said Fiona.

33

Stella headed back to her house to make final preparations for tonight. It'd only been a day since she left the house after finding out Caitlin had been kidnapped, but it felt like an eternity. The clock was ticking, but she needed her equipment to get into the event tonight.

Stella gathered her cameras, lighting boxes, and lenses. She was packing far more than she needed, but she had to carry the bomb into the venue without anyone seeing her. The best way she could think to do that was to have it buried under all her equipment. Evan assured her that whoever built the bomb knew what they were doing —it was sophisticated enough to bypass most security systems. The drug dogs would be the only problem, a wildcard that she could not predict or control. Their noses could unravel everything if they caught even the faintest trace.

Stella knew from her research at the hotel and through the PAC's event information online that the drug dogs would do a sweep of the entire venue two hours ahead of the event. No one wanted the bomb squad there when guests were arriving and potentially scaring them from opening their wallets. After they gave the all-clear, anyone getting into the event would pass through a metal detector. Stella planned to arrive after the dogs, but would still have to get through the metal detectors. Her cameras, lenses, and lights should be an adequate excuse for her to pass through security.

Stella gathered her equipment and loaded it into her car. She checked her watch. 2:00 p.m. There was still time before heading back to Marcus's office to collect the package. Acting on a hunch, Stella slipped into her own office, determined to confirm the truth about Richard for herself.

Stella grabbed her private laptop out of her safe. She closed her eyes and took a deep breath to calm her racing heart. She pushed images of Caitlin out of her mind and focused on the job at hand.

All the work Stella and Fiona did last night to trace the timeline of the threats and what was going on in her life wasn't in vain. Max was right; it was important work—the only problem was they identified the wrong suspect. She thought back to what they'd discovered this morning and homed in on two things: the first message she got after the lunch meeting with Max, and the video she received after her meeting with Marcus.

Stella already knew the timing of the first message wasn't about Marcus's business card planting something on her phone. That could have been a coincidence. But the timing of the video was too precise to be a coincidence. Stella had taken photos of the surrounding area that day in case anything ever came up about their meeting. Now, she wanted to see those photos.

Stella kept anything she used specifically for her criminal activity on this computer. She didn't attach it to any identifiers, and kept it offline as much as possible. She saved up-close images of jewels people wore when she photographed events and faces of potential targets she wanted to learn more about. After she received the video threat, everything had gone haywire. She'd forgotten about the pictures completely.

Stella quickly found the group of images by date, knowing she'd met with Marcus on the eighth of December. She scrutinized each one. A few pictures had people in them, most of them far enough in the distance not to be of any concern.

But then Stella hit it.

In one photo, there was someone sitting on a bench at the other end of the park.

The person had a cup of coffee at their side, and they were reading a book. They wore a baseball cap and a green jacket that looked to be between a windbreaker and a winter coat. They looked like anyone else spending time outdoors during a Connecticut winter.

She hadn't thought anything about it when she originally snapped the photo. They were far away, and she was taking rapid pictures, more as a deterrent to anyone watching her than anything else. Now though, she could see this person had pulled the book in front of their face as she'd snapped the picture. She could see it now, still in motion from being raised up high instead of held in the lap like most people would. No one reads a book holding it right in front of their face.

Her instincts told her this was the one.

The longer she looked, the more she picked the image apart. The person dressed like a man but sat with their legs crossed. Women who crossed their legs normally shifted their hips a little, relaxing into the pose, often tucking their crossed leg behind their other foot. Men crossed their legs and sat up straight, keeping their hips straight, forcing one foot out farther in front of them. It was a chic version of manspreading. The person holding the book was a man.

Something else caught her eye, too. When she zoomed in on the photo, she spotted cufflinks. They stuck out from under his jacket, on display while he held the book to hide his face from the camera.

It was Richard. He'd watched her meet with Marcus.

Whether it was jealousy or worry that she'd take on a partner that wasn't him that pushed him to blackmail her, she didn't know. Either way, he'd been watching her. And right after that meeting, he sent her the video.

She grabbed the burner phone to call Fiona and tell her the news, then froze.

"No way." She sighed. "No. Fucking. Way." She pivoted and grabbed her personal phone; still glued to her side in case the kidnapper contacted her again. She unlocked the phone and searched for the Find My app, cursing herself the entire time.

The second she opened the app, she scrolled through the list of people whose location she tracked, and the people who tracked hers. Caitlin and Rita showed up at the same location, Caitlin's phone still at Fiona's house in the Hamptons with her mother. Max didn't allow anyone to track him, not even Stella, and she'd never tracked Fiona. But third in line listed Richard Medina.

She grabbed the burner phone and called Fiona while she ran upstairs to change her clothes. "It was me. I'm the one who led him to Evan. He's been tracking my new fucking phone, and I didn't know it." Stella yelled the second Fiona answered. "I also found a picture of him. He followed me to my meeting with Marcus. I caught him on film. He obscured his face, but you can see his cufflinks in the picture when you zoom in. It was definitely him."

"That bastard," shouted Fiona.

Stella saw red. "How could I have let this happen?"

"This is not your fault. You had no idea he was a psychopath. Don't let yourself spiral."

"I won't." With a sigh, she put the phone on speaker while she changed into the outfit she wore to photograph swanky events. "I'm too pissed to spiral right now."

"Good. I have news for you, too. I'm putting you on speaker," she said. "Marcus, Max, and Evan are with me. We think we've found where they're keeping her. Richard's family has a house about thirty miles outside of Philly. It's on sixty acres of land, pretty secluded. We're about to head that way."

"You can't go with them, Fiona. You could get hurt."

"You can't control everything, Stella, and you damn sure can't control me. I'm going."

Stella heard voices in the background, then Marcus spoke up.

"The question now, Stella, is do you want us to call in the cops? We're working on a hunch that they're holding her at the estate. My plan remains to put our team down there and trace the signal the second the bomb is activated, letting us pinpoint her location. We could be in the wrong place. But if there was ever a time to call in the authorities, this is it."

Stella stared at herself in the mirror as she spoke, needing to talk through this with someone, even if it was just her reflection. "My only care is to get Caitlin back safely before either bomb goes off. Nothing else matters to me."

"Agreed," said Marcus.

She'd hoped this moment wouldn't come. She didn't want to decide between Caitlin and the people at the hotel. "If we call the cops now, they'd cancel the gala, but where would that leave Caitlin? Richard will know the second the event is canceled. He'll kill her."

No one spoke. They let Stella talk herself through the scenario.

"I'm not convinced calling in the cops now would help. If we have the right location and they believe us, they'd swoop in with a fucking SWAT team and scare the people holding her. We know the bomb is under the bed, and we know it's remotely detonated. We also know it's going to go off if I don't blow up this one tonight. I might be wrong about this, but I don't see that helping us at all." Stella nodded to herself. This felt right. "What's your assessment? How confident are you in tracking her location when the bomb detonates?"

"I'm completely confident we'll trace her location. I'm less confident about the timing, but having the cops involved doesn't speed anything up. It might do the opposite."

Evan's voice spoke up then. "I've talked to my guys, and we're good to go. I'm bringing two people I trust, and another guy in Philly is hooking up with us there. We'll get her back."

"Stella, this is Max." Stella smiled at the sound of his formal voice, as if he needed to tell her it was him. "I know you're concerned about Caitlin. I promise you she's our only consideration. If I thought for one moment that calling someone in would give us a better chance of getting her home safely, I would call them myself. But I don't think it will help us. Not at all."

"I appreciate it. All of you," said Stella. "Marcus, the second you pinpoint Caitlin's location, can you shut down the bomb in the gala? I can't hurt innocent people."

"If the signal is set as a series, we can do it. We can get Caitlin to safety and shut down the other bomb. All we need is time."

Stella nodded to her reflection. She'd take care of that on her end. "Let's keep going. I'm heading back to pick up the device now and then going to The Pierre. Get your guys, Evan, and Marcus's team and head to Philly. Please keep me posted every second of the way."

"We'll be in communication with you the whole night," confirmed Marcus. "I've got your comms ready to give you when you get back here."

She thanked them all again and ended the call.

As she made her way back downstairs, Stella stopped by Caitlin's room, soaking in everything around her. The Taylor Swift posters on the wall, her stuffed polar bear on her pillow. It was clear she'd packed to leave in a hurry; her uniform for school lay in a heap on her floor. Everything about the room exuded Caitlin.

Stella sat on Caitlin's bed and picked up a picture of the three of them at Christmas last year from her bedside table. She ran her fingers over her daughter's beautiful face. "I'm so sorry, sweetie. I never meant for this to happen to you."

Stella looked around the room. "I tried so hard to give you a normal life. I wanted you to have the best education money could buy; family and friends who loved you. But I messed it all up."

Stella touched the pink down comforter on her bed and saw the cot she now slept on, a small green blanket the only thing to keep her warm. "I was so fucking selfish. I had to have it all. I got off on the adrenaline, and you're paying the price."

Stella had ripped her childhood from her, and if things went poorly tonight, that room would be the last place Caitlin would ever see. If it weren't for the slim hope offered by Marcus and Evan, Stella would lay down right here and die tonight, along with her daughter. "I'm so sorry, sweetheart. I'm so fucking sorry."

She picked up Cait's polar bear and inhaled the scent of her daughter that lingered on the stuffed animal, squeezing him tight.

"I'm going to try and bring her home," she told the bear. "Please, God, let me bring her home."

Stella wiped her eyes, set the bear down and went to her car. It was time to go.

34

S tella pulled her car up to The Pierre's valet parking and was greeted by a young man looking every bit like the thousands of other men his age in the city. He wore a mustache and beard, his long hair pulled back into a bun to look more presentable for work.

Stella looked at his tag and addressed him by name. "Mark, can you help me? I'm working the event in the Grand Ballroom tonight. I'm the photographer?" She raised her voice at the end, turning it into more of a question than a statement. "I've got a trunk full of equipment. Any chance someone can help me lug it in? Or hold the car here for me while I run the stuff back and forth?"

"No problem." He raised his hand to call someone else over. "Ethan, Nathaniel." He turned to address her while his friends ran to help. "They'll help you carry in whatever you need, and I'll park your car for you. We don't want to tie up traffic for too long. Lots of big wigs coming in tonight."

His friends arrived and opened the hatchback in time for Stella to meet them. She glanced at their nametags and cautioned them. "Be careful with this stuff. It's fragile."

"Got it, ma'am," Ethan said. He took the box full of lenses, and his friend grabbed the box with the lights.

"I'll take that one," said Stella, reaching for the box with the bomb in it. "Better I break this one than you." Nathaniel smiled and thanked her. She let him take her bag of lenses.

Mark gave her a ticket, and she slipped him a tip for his help. She gave each of his friends the same amount as they reached the ballroom entrance. "It'll take me a while to clear security with these; you can set them here," she said.

"We got you covered." He called over to one of the security guards. "Larry, can we get some help here?"

A man in a security uniform jogged over. "Don't you have anyone with you, ma'am?"

"Solo tonight. I think they want every available body in that room to be a donor," said Stella. Her heart skipped a beat when Larry nodded his understanding and grabbed the box from her hands. "I can get that," she protested.

"No problem, I've got it."

They followed Larry through the metal detectors, setting them off as they entered.

"What you got in here?" asked Larry. "Anything metal?"

"Everything is metal," Stella told him. "Lights, lenses, extra cameras—they all set these things off."

"Got it." Stella followed him as he guided her through the security system, the alarms buzzing in their wake. He raised the box to his counterpart, and the man waved him through. As Larry led her through the maze of tables to the back of the ballroom, Stella's eyes went wide. She snapped back to attention when Larry called to a woman at the back of the room. "Alexis, do we have a room for her equipment? She's the photographer."

Alexis took over as guide, leading the group to the staff area. Stella's heartbeat pounded in her ears. She was certain that everyone around her could hear it.

"There's a closet there you can store your boxes; anything that isn't needed out on the floor." Larry, Nathaniel, and Ethan delivered the equipment to the closet and set everything down.

Stella thanked them profusely for their help. She didn't need to act to look a little flustered from the whole ordeal. They bid farewell to her and jogged back to their stations.

Once the door closed, Stella let out a gush of air. The tablecloths. Instead of free flowing to the floor as they'd assumed, these were attached to the base of each table, pulled tight to ensure the table-cloth wouldn't move or present a tripping hazard. There was no possible way to stick something under a table with these blocking her path.

She'd have to improvise.

Stella worked quickly to get her equipment in order. She'd asked Evan to add strips to the bomb to let her quickly pull it out of her bag and stick in place as fast as possible. It had to work the first time, and it had to be sturdy enough to hold the bomb in place without setting it off. He'd assured her he'd take care of it.

Stella opened the box and removed the top layer of lighting, then dug through a layer of foam to pull out the box buried beneath. She studied the device as fast as she could, noting the changes she'd seen since this morning. They'd added the interceptor to it, and there were now three strips of adhesive added to the top of the device. She touched one with her fingertip and was happy to see it instantly adhered to her finger. That should work.

Stella tried to sear the bomb's dimensions in her mind. If it couldn't go under the table, Stella thought she might have to place it under a chair; she needed to know if it was thin enough to set it up without being visible to the entire room. Another option would be for her to slide her camera bag under the table and "lose it." A risky proposition with so many women putting purses under the table, but it might be her only choice.

She switched her materials around and moved the bomb to a smaller shoulder bag she could carry with her around the room. This held a lens and several different light meters, which allowed the bomb to blend in with the contents of the bag. If you glanced at it, you'd think it was some other kind of electrical equipment.

Stella checked her watch; the gala began in twenty-five minutes. She returned to the main ballroom and noted the entire room was perfectly arranged—tables set, chairs aligned, and flowers brightening every corner. After a full day of preparation, the staff had cleared out, leaving the space nearly empty. Only a few techs remained, running sound checks on their equipment.

Stella made a show of putting down her bag, pulling out her light meter, and checking the readings at the back of the room. She pushed the flash a few times, temporarily blinding anyone who happened to be looking her way. Then she knelt to switch out an item in her bag.

With her back to the stage, blocking the sound guy's view, Stella examined the chair in front of her. It was plush, top of the line, with a thick wooden trim around the base of the seat. She pretended to fumble with her light meter, using it as a cover to put her hand under the chair. There was a definite gap between the edge of the trim and the bottom of the seat. The material under the chair felt like polished wood; smooth and clean. It could work.

She rose and continued her lighting check around the room, noting the place cards at the tables she passed. They had each attendee's name etched in gold foil. Stella mentally compared the names she saw with the map of the event in her mind. They lined up perfectly.

She worked her way around the room, coming closer and closer to the stage. She was hoping the techs would finish their soundcheck, but they seemed in no hurry to leave. Stella checked her watch; it was now or never. She had to place the bomb soon or risk the room being overrun with people at any minute.

Stella made her way over to Table Three. She glanced at the place cards and saw his name etched in gold. Juan Castillo. Seated next to him was his mother, Melina Medina. She couldn't help herself; Stella planted the bomb directly under his chair. Surely, he wasn't going to show tonight, but she wanted it there for symbolism more than anything.

Stella dropped her bag by his seat, clicked the light meter a few times and then stooped to pick up her bag. She accidentally kicked the bag, spilling some of its contents onto the floor. She cursed, bent over to gather her things while she looked around the room as if embarrassed by her mistake.

No one was paying any attention to her. It was now or never.

As Stella reached into the bag, someone shouted her name. "Stella Meyers. Finally."

Pam fucking Fisher.

Stella pulled the bomb out and stuck it to the bottom of Richard's chair in one smooth motion.

"What are you doing over there?" Pam screeched.

Stella made a show of picking up the lenses from under the seat while she raised her head to locate Pam. "Hi, Pam. Finishing up a lighting check."

She put the lenses back in her bag and then stood, straightening the chair before she walked away. Stella saw Pam check her watch as she crossed the room to greet her.

"I've been wondering when you were going to arrive. I expected you hours ago."

"I'm here. Everything is set up and ready to go," Stella assured her. She blocked Pam's view of the table.

Pam sighed. "I don't know what to say."

"I believe the words you're looking for are, 'thank you,'" said Stella. She went on the offensive. "I would rather be anywhere other than here tonight. Therefore, I would appreciate it if you simply thanked me for stepping in and rescuing you."

"Well, I never—"

"No, you never say thank you," said Stella. "I need to finish setting my light meters. If there's nothing else?"

Pam tried to regain the upper hand. "You were not my first choice for photographers, Stella. I believe you know that." She checked her watch again, and Stella wondered if she had a compulsion to look at the time. "Please make sure you don't miss the big moment again. Blake Cameron will be speaking tonight, and the most powerful and influential people in the country will fill the room. This is not a school gymnasium. I expect your undivided attention on the task at hand."

"I assure you, nothing will pull my focus from the big moment." Stella tilted her head and raised her eyebrows, daring her to say anything else. They stood for another moment, sizing each other up. After a few beats, Pam gave up and turned her attention to the tech guys finishing their work. Stella sighed with relief, unsure if it was because she hadn't noticed the bomb, or because she was just grateful the bitch had left her alone.

Stella took more light tests, checking to see if the bomb was visible from different places around the room. She couldn't see it, and she knew what to look for.

Once the room filled with people and everyone was drinking, dining, and talking, Stella was confident no one would notice the bomb under Juan Castillo's seat. Maybe not even him, if he was dumb enough to show his face tonight.

She went back to the equipment closet to set up her camera. She put the earpiece Marcus had given her in her ear and sent her first transmission. "All set."

She heard a mix of voices, then Marcus's voice telling people to clear the comms. "Roger that, Stella. Our team is on location. No visual of the target yet. We'll keep you posted." They knew she couldn't answer, but every part of Stella wanted to beg them to get her daughter home safely. As if Marcus could read her mind, he said, "We'll get her home to you, Stella. Trust us."

She had to trust them. She had no other choice.

35

The doors opened promptly at 6:00 p.m. and a line of people queued to get through security and into the ballroom. Everyone wanted as much time as possible to see and be seen at the exclusive event. No one would be casually late tonight. The opening act took the stage while smiling servers poured wine and ferried hors d'oeuvres around the room, hoping for generous tips tonight.

Stella listened to the team update their progress as she worked, taking pictures of anyone and everyone in attendance. "We have eyes on the property. No one appears to be in residence at the main house. We're sending someone up to check." Stella wondered who would draw that straw and instantly knew the answer to her question. Fiona would gladly saunter up to the gate and see if anyone was home.

While she waited, Stella watched people claim their seats. She moved as far away from Table Three as she could, but it continually drew her eye. This was the best part of her cover, and the reason she wanted to attend the event tonight as herself. A server or event worker would only be in the room for brief periods of time, and they had to be actively serving guests. Stella's entire job tonight was to sit back and watch the evening unfold.

"We've confirmed no one is in the main house. We're checking the guest cottage next."

Stella recalled the estate they found belonging to Richard's family sat on over sixty acres of land and had multiple buildings on the property. She didn't expect her daughter would be in the main house, but it gave her a little hope that the home was unoccupied.

As the guests took their seats and settled in for the gourmet meal their $50,000 per plate donations had bought them, Stella noticed Melina Medina seated at Table Three. Striking blue eyes, a strong jaw, and thick wavy hair that looked almost white in the ballroom lights, she was unmistakably Richard's mother. She sat ramrod straight in her chair, her every movement conveying she was not a woman to be trifled with. As Stella took in her emerald necklace and matching earrings, she saw the woman turn her head up and speak to someone standing near her.

Gasping, she raised her camera to her eye and talked as quietly as she could, gritting her teeth. "He's here. Richard is here." She snapped some photos, taking in the entire scene. Richard wore a black tuxedo, tailored perfectly to his frame, not a wrinkle visible on him. She zoomed in on him, snapping more pictures, noting his signature cufflinks.

Max's voice filled her head. "You must not let him know you're on to him, Stella."

Stella watched him work the room. Richard smiled and shook hands with his fellow guests; he clearly knew everyone he was seated with, making his way around the table and beyond to make small talk before dinner was served. She heard Max speak again. "You must play along. If he senses anything is amiss, he could detonate the bombs early."

She imagined herself picking up a knife and stabbing him in the heart, much like he'd done to her. But she knew Max was right. She had to keep her cool.

He made a move to sit down. Richard leaned in to kiss his mother on both cheeks, the gesture there but not the sentiment. It was clear hostilities still ran deep between them. As he sat, his eyes lifted and caught Stella's gaze from across the room. She saw a flicker of doubt cross his eyes. He recovered quickly with a smile. For a moment, Stella thought she'd misread him.

He whispered something to his mother, then made his way to Stella. "This is a surprise," he said as he closed the distance between them. "What are you doing here?"

Stella held up her camera, trying to put a smile on her face. "The photographer canceled for tonight, and Pam asked me to fill in." She pulled him to the back of the room, keeping their conversation private. "I didn't know you were coming. I didn't see your name on the list of attendees they gave me."

She wanted to see how far he'd take the lie.

Richard chuckled. "I'm here on family business. My mother asked me to fill a seat. Apparently, it's unbecoming to have an empty seat at an event like this. He positioned himself to block Stella's view of the room, then ran his finger down the side of her blouse. "It's good to see you."

Stella shuddered at his touch.

"How is Caitlin? I assumed you'd be with her."

Stella's eyes went wide, but instead of responding, she searched his eyes to figure out what game he was playing. He knew he had Caitlin, but did he know Stella knew that? This was grandmaster chess, a game Stella normally won. But she was at a disadvantage tonight. This wasn't a game to her—not when her daughter's life was on the line.

Richard was more than a con artist; he manipulated and toyed with people to get what he wanted. And he'd wanted Stella. Stella could pretend to be someone else for a few moments, to play the game. His subterfuge was on an entirely different level. Richard lived a lie.

She didn't have his skills. She thought she might throw up right there in the ballroom. He repulsed her. For all her skills at lying and deception, she knew she couldn't fake this.

Richard leaned into her. Stella thought he was going to kiss her, claim her for himself in front of the entire gala. Instead, he passed her lips and whispered in her ear. "I wish you'd let me in. We would have made a great team."

"That's what you said," Stella said, her own voice barely audible above the sounds of the gala.

He turned and headed back to his table, with Fiona screaming in her ear.

"That motherfucker. I'm gonna kill him." Stella heard Max admonish her, and Marcus said to clear the comms again.

Stella was grateful her friend said what she couldn't. She needed something to fortify her for the night to come. Killing Richard Medina sounded like a great idea to her.

36

S tella kept her cool as best she could, watching the events unfold before her eyes in the hotel while listening to what was happening a hundred miles away in her ear. She tried to inconspicuously take pictures, but she found herself constantly drawn to Table Three to see what Richard was doing.

"Cottage is clear," Stella heard in her ear. "We're going to the outbuildings now."

Stella watched as the guests were served their desserts, coffee, and tea. She checked her watch. It was 7:00 p.m. Blake would be up to speak soon. Even if he wasn't the target, she knew they'd likely detonate the bomb while he was speaking to make it look like he was the intended victim. As the thought crossed her mind, Pam Fisher approached the podium.

"Ladies and gentlemen, thank you for coming out tonight to celebrate the rebirth of our nation, the opportunities facing all of us to help make America the greatest country in the world again." A round of enthusiastic applause echoed throughout the room. "We ask that you finish your desserts and refill your coffees, as our esteemed speaker, Mr. Cameron, will address us in the next five minutes."

Stella brought the camera to her eye and snapped pictures of Pam while she talked into her mic. "Did you hear that? He's almost up."

Richard rose from his chair, placing his napkin in the seat. "Richard's on the move," she whispered into her mic.

Stella looked up and caught his gaze. Richard smiled at her, a flood of broken promises in his eyes. She glared at him. He pulled out his cell and excused himself from the table, pretending to take a call. Stella saw him press a button.

Stella heard the phone ping, a beacon to her amidst all the noise in the room.

"Bomb is armed. Let's go." The voices came at her furiously, Stella unable to keep track of who was doing what. "Detonator is set. Countdown is at four minutes forty-five seconds."

Someone was tracking the detonator, someone was tracing the cell signal, and someone else was trying to sever the signal between the bombs. They planned to sever it manually, which would make Caitlin's bomb believe the other had detonated, and would shut hers down. Then they could shut down this bomb.

Stella had no choice but to listen to it all play out while she watched Richard leave the room.

"I've got a lock on Caitlin."

"Four minutes and counting," came a female voice. Stella froze, riveted to the drama playing out in her ear, unable to focus on anything else.

"We have a problem," said a male voice. "There's only one code." Stella didn't know what that meant, but she didn't have to wait long for an explanation. "These won't go off sequentially. They're set to detonate at the same time."

Stella didn't understand.

"If I attempt to sever the signal, they'll both blow."

Stella's heart leaped out of her chest.

"Can we disable one bomb remotely without detonating the other?" Marcus asked someone in Stella's ear.

"Please do that." Stella spoke too loudly, causing several people to turn and stare at her. She raised her camera again to hide her face.

"Three minutes, thirty seconds."

"Affirmative," said someone Stella didn't recognize. She didn't know what they were affirming.

Marcus jumped in to explain. "We are focusing our attention on disabling Caitlin's bomb, Stella. We're calling in a bomb threat to the gala. Get yourself to safety."

Another voice asked, "How far away are we?"

"Five minutes out."

"You've got two."

Stella's heart rate skyrocketed. Adrenaline coursed through her. She had to help buy them some time.

"Stella, this is Evan. I know you're scared. We're on our way to get your girl. She'll be safe. But you have to stay calm. He can trip this anytime he wants. If he thinks we're getting close to her, he can blow it up before the timer runs out. Don't let that happen."

Stella ditched her cover job and left the room to find Richard. If nothing else, she hoped to keep him from blowing the bomb early. She passed through security.

"She's in that building," came the voice in her head. "Let's go." Stella heard van doors slide open and people moving quickly, whispering commands to each other. They didn't know who might be guarding Caitlin and needed to proceed with caution.

"Three minutes."

Stella asked the coat check woman if someone had come and retrieved their coat in the last couple of minutes. She felt sure Richard would be off the premises when the bomb blew. The woman shook her head. "No one yet, ma'am. But Blake Cameron hasn't spoken yet; I'm not expecting anyone to leave until he's done."

"Bathrooms?" she asked the woman, who then pointed down the hall. She took off in that direction.

"They've cleared out. No one is there but Caitlin," said a voice Stella recognized. Celina.

"Two minutes, thirty seconds."

Stella saw the men's restroom up ahead. She froze in place, not sure if she should go in after him or wait outside. He wouldn't detonate the bombs early if he didn't understand they were on to him, would he? She'd guessed incorrectly about this man on every point. Regardless, her feet stayed glued to the floor.

"Door is padlocked," said a male voice.

"Get us in that building."

"Someone cut that lock off."

People were speaking all at once. Stella had no idea what was going on.

"Two minutes."

Stella saw Richard emerge from the bathroom. His expression morphed several times in quick succession: surprised, happy, confused, then resolved. This was the real Richard. Masks gone, game over.

"Please don't do this. Don't hurt Caitlin. She didn't do anything to you."

"I didn't do anything," said Richard. He gave her a half smile, squinting at her.

"I know you've taken her. I've done what you asked. I'll do whatever you want, just please keep her safe." Stella grabbed his arm, trying to steady herself or capture him, she didn't know which. He shrugged her off.

"One minute, thirty seconds."

"I told you, Stella. I didn't do anything. You did this." He stared at her, his eyes darkening. "I wanted a partner. Someone equal to myself. I thought that person was you, but I was wrong."

She grabbed him again, turning him to face her. "I'll partner with you. I'll do anything you want." Stella's hands shook as she held onto his coat, tears springing to her eyes. "I'm begging you; don't hurt her. She's a child. You're her teacher. She's innocent in all this."

"I don't want you anymore," he hissed. "My plans changed the moment you rejected me,"

"I don't understand why you're doing this. What did I do to you?"

"You disappointed me. I knew it would take a genius to get into Hayes's house. I set it up to see if there was anyone up to the task. Imagine my surprise when I saw you on that video. You didn't even break a sweat. So cool and collected." Richard ran his hands through his hair, frustrated. He bent to whisper in her ear then. "Do you know what we could have done together? With my access to the elite and your skills?" Stella watched him relive the fantasy he'd been creating in his mind these last several months.

She heard scrambling in her ear. They were trying to cut the padlock and get to Caitlin. With the clock ticking down, she didn't know whether to be relieved or terrified.

Richard was working himself into a rage. It was a side of him she hadn't seen before. "I did everything for you," he yelled, then got his voice back under control, looking around to see if anyone heard him. "I got that teacher out of the way, played my role as the perfect boyfriend, but you never let me in. You kept your secrets and refused to tell me who you really were. You gave me no choice, Stella. This is all on you."

Richard pushed past her, heading back to the ballroom. He checked his watch.

"One minute," sounded in her ear. It was an eternity, and yet no time at all.

"Why are you doing this?" She jogged to catch up with him, then whispered, "Why kill all those people?"

"I'm only interested in one person," responded Richard. He left her there, shaking her head, confused. Then it hit her—his mother. With her out of the way, he'd inherit the company. In one night, he could eliminate his rival and punish Stella, getting rid of the only two women who had challenged him.

Stella followed him, anxious to keep him in her line of sight.

She risked letting them know what was happening. "He's going back."

His pace was steady, neither fast nor slow. He knew exactly what was happening, had timed it to the last second. He'd be clear of the blast and suspicion all at the same time.

"We're in!" She heard several people running and scrambling, calling out Caitlin's name. Relief flooded Stella.

Stella walked into the ballroom at the same time everyone

assembled back in their seats, getting ready for Blake Cameron to speak. She looked at Richard standing near the back, chatting to someone as if nothing was happening. He was clear of the blast zone.

She saw security guards entering the room, but they didn't know where to look.

"Thirty seconds."

Stella saw a flash of light go off beneath Richard's chair. It must have been the timer. She moved quickly, still tracking the movements of the team at Richard's house.

"Mommy." She heard Caitlin screaming, pounding on a door. "Mommy."

Stella ran to the table and grabbed the chair, lifting it as she spun around the room and ran to the back door. The chair was heavier than she'd imagined. The thought that they'd spared no expense for these people flashed through her mind as she weaved through the gold-plated tables.

"Stand back, Caitlin. Step away from the door." She heard Evan's voice in her ear.

"There's a bomb," her daughter yelled.

Stella kept her pace steady; she didn't want to spook everyone. If she announced it was a bomb, they'd block her path in their panic to leave.

"Fifteen seconds."

Clearing the door, she ran down the hallway that fed several different event rooms. Stella had memorized the floor plan of the hotel. She knew exactly where she wanted to go. She just didn't know how long it would take for her to get there.

Sounds of security shouting orders and running after her filled the hall.

"Mommy!" Stella heard one final scream from her daughter, then the unmistakable sound of a door breaking down.

"I've almost got it," someone said.

Stella wasn't sure what that meant, but there wasn't time to ask. She ran into the side entrance to the kitchen. Chefs were yelling as food prep continued at every station. The room was packed with people.

"Bomb," she yelled as loud as she could. "There's a bomb!"

Her plan worked. This group was used to being under pressure and following commands. Each and every person stepped away from their stations and made for the exit, clearing the path for Stella.

"Three." Stella spotted her target and sprinted to the freezer.

"Two." Stella heaved open the freezer door.

"One." That was the last sound Stella heard as she threw the chair into the freezer. The bomb exploded the second it left her hands.

37

Stella felt like she was suffocating, her entire body pinned down. She swam in a sea of darkness, fog enveloping her body and mind. No sound or light could reach her. She felt her heart rate pick up, panic beginning to rise in her veins. She heard a faint beeping sound. The image of a timer came to her mind, causing her to wince. Everything in her wanted to shut down again and return to the darkness.

Images formed in her mind. Richard. Fiona. Caitlin. Her brain locked on that image. Caitlin. She was in trouble. Stella had to help her. She fought the darkness, tried to force her body to move. The beeping grew louder, and her heartbeat accelerated, throbbing in her chest. She had to get to her daughter.

"Mom," Caitlin yelled.

"I'm coming, sweetie." She willed her voice to work but it refused.

"She's waking up."

Stella's mind raced, searching for answers. Then she felt her daughter's hand; heard her voice clearly in her ear.

"Wake up, Mom. We're here. Please wake up."

Stella forced her eyes open and saw the most beautiful sight she'd ever seen—Caitlin's face inches from her own. She was okay. Caitlin was okay.

Stella smiled at her daughter, then looked behind her. The room was full of her favorite people. Fiona ran to her bed. Rita came up behind Caitlin and put her arms around her granddaughter. Max stood at the foot of the bed, a smile on his face. Even Evan was here, leaning against the back wall.

Caitlin moved in to hug her and Stella tried to return the gesture, but her whole body protested. Monitors beeped and the pain hit her like a truck.

"You're pretty fucked up," said Fiona.

Stella looked down at herself in the hospital bed and didn't disagree. The parts she could see were a mess—full leg cast on her right leg, her left arm in a cast below the elbow. Every part of her hurt when she moved.

If this was how she looked on the outside, she couldn't imagine what she looked like inside. She hoped there was no permanent damage.

Reading her mind, her mother gave her the medical report. "You're going to be fine. It's going to take a while, but you'll get there. They've operated on your leg. You've got pins holding everything together until your bones heal. There was some internal damage, but they took care of that, too. You'll pull through." Tears welled in her mother's eyes. "You gave us quite a scare."

"You're a hero, Mom," said Caitlin. Stella couldn't imagine how she was seeing her daughter standing in front of her, safe. And somehow calling her a hero. She was the villain in this nightmare if there ever was one.

She crinkled her nose at her daughter and protested, even though it killed her to do it.

"No, really." Caitlin protested her look. "They said you saved that man's life. A lot of people's." She bent down and whispered to her then, "Mine, too, but no one knows that."

"I think we have these people to thank for that," whispered Stella. "Them and a few more."

Caitlin nodded, then tears filled her eyes. She hugged her mother again. "I was so scared," she cried.

"I know, sweetie. So was I." She didn't know if Caitlin was talking about the kidnapping, the bombing, or her mother being in the hospital. It was all scary. "We're okay now. We're both going to be okay."

A nurse came into the room, breaking up the reunion. "Happy to finally meet you, Stella." Her loud voice infused the room with genuine joy. She moved around to the far side of the bed, displacing Fiona to check on the machines and the fluids in her IV.

"How long have I been out?" asked Stella.

Rita spoke up before the nurse could. "Two days. They kept you in a medically induced coma until they finished the emergency surgeries."

"You needed time to heal, sweetie," said the nurse. "But you're back now and on the mend." She turned to everyone in the room. "Stella needs her rest. All of you need to go."

Caitlin clung to her, and the nurse seemed to understand she was asking too much of Stella's daughter. She bent down and addressed Caitlin directly. "How about you stay a little longer? Watch over your mom for a bit? These fine folks can go get a bite to eat and maybe bring you back something?"

Caitlin nodded and squeezed her mother's hand. Stella squeezed it back.

"Step out with me for a second, Caitlin. Let your mom say goodbye to her friends. I'll get your food order and then you can go back in when we leave."

Caitlin agreed and headed out with her grandmother.

Max walked up to the side of the bed where Caitlin had been standing, leaned in, and kissed her on the forehead. It might be the only place that didn't hurt. "You really were very heroic. You planned that all along, didn't you?"

Stella nodded. Max knew she couldn't let other people get hurt because of her.

"Did he get away?" She looked at Max and then Fiona, both of them nodded.

"He made a runner," said Fiona.

"His mother was particularly grateful you spotted that bomb in time," said Max. "It seems she's softened somewhat to her son. Apparently, she reconsidered his leadership qualifications when she realized someone could have accidentally killed him attempting to take out Blake Cameron." Stella closed her eyes at the news. He'd gotten away with it and gotten everything he wanted to boot. Max kissed her hand and said goodbye, joining Rita and Caitlin in the hall.

Evan stepped up. "I won't stay. Just wanted to make sure for myself you were okay."

Fiona poked Stella in the ribs and Stella yelped. Fiona stage whispered loud enough for the nurses in the hall to hear her. "He's been here the whole time. Won't leave your side no matter what we say." She smiled at Evan, and he returned it, her charms already working their magic on the man.

Fiona stepped back to give them some space, but she could hear everything they said.

"Thank you for saving my daughter," said Stella. "I can never repay you for that."

"No debt owed," said Evan. "But I do have a gift for you. Marcus's people disabled that device at the last second; it never went off."

"I had no idea."

"Well, you wouldn't, would you?" interrupted Fiona. "Throwing the bomb in the freezer and blowing yourself up."

"Not myself, clearly," Stella countered.

"I kept it. Happy to destroy it for ya if you'd like," said Evan. "Or I can keep it. In case it comes in handy in the future." His smile reached his eyes. Stella felt her spirits lift a little higher.

"Once it's gone, it's gone. Might as well keep it in inventory." Stella smiled to herself. She knew exactly where she wanted it to go. Evan waved and left the room. She could hear him making Caitlin laugh in the hallway. At least there were a few decent men left in this city.

Stella turned to face Fiona.

Fiona made her way to Stella's side and stared at her for a moment, silent. "You lied to me. Like a billion times." Stella nodded. She couldn't deny it. "I don't deserve that. I've done nothing but be there for you and Caitlin."

"I know," whispered Stella. "I'm sorry."

"If you weren't lying in this bed in a coma all beat to shit for the last two days, making me think you were going to die, I would've killed you myself."

"I deserve that."

Fiona bent down to whisper in Stella's ear, tears glistening in her eyes. "I'm done with you."

Stella turned her head and closed her eyes, trying to keep the tears from falling. Losing Fiona was the last straw. She couldn't bear to think of life without her.

"If you ever lie to me again, even about the smallest thing, I will walk out the nearest door and never come back. Do you hear me?" Fiona's voice rose loud enough for the whole hospital to hear. "If I ask you if a dress makes my ass look big and you even hesitate to answer, I'm gone. I will not have a friend who lies to me. About anything. Got it?"

Stella chuckled and her ribs screamed in pain. "Yes, ma'am."

Fiona pulled back and gazed at her best friend, smiling and crying all at once. Stella squeezed her hand and shook her head, tears coming down her own face. "I'll never lie to you again. Promise."

Stella could keep that promise to Fiona; she was truly part of her inner circle now. Telling Caitlin the truth was another matter. It would be years before she could confess the truth to Caitlin about her abduction, if ever.

"We didn't get to kill him," she whispered. "After everything that bastard did."

"Not yet," said Fiona. She waved Caitlin back into the room to sit with her mom and keep her company, then turned and faced Stella again before she left. "You're my best friend, Stella Meyers. I know you better than anyone on earth." She smiled at her again, mischievous this time instead of sad. "You'll get your revenge somehow. I'm sure of it."

38

Stella turned the headlights off and drove the last quarter mile to the estate in total darkness, the full moon the only light offering her any visibility in the pitch-black night. This was country dark—no house lights, no streetlights, everyone tucked in for the night. Stella was more afraid of hitting a deer than being caught by a nosy neighbor, but she kept her profile low, regardless. She'd rented a late model black van that matched the owner's work van. If anyone spotted her traveling down the road toward the back of the sixty-acre estate, they'd assume she was staff.

Dos Lagos was a playground for its wealthy owners and their friends. The luxury estate boasted over 12,000 feet of living space in the main house, with an impeccably refurbished and modernized two-story guest cottage originally built in the mid-nineteenth century. There were two lakes on the property that gave the estate its name, as well as an indoor pool, full-size tennis court, and acres of beautifully landscaped gardens.

She pulled up to the buildings located at the far end of the property. These three buildings held the golf carts, tractors, plows, and heavy equipment needed to keep the multimillion-dollar estate running. They also held the mechanic's room that served as her daughter's prison for two days last winter.

Stella moved slowly around the buildings, her feet crunching on the gravel path the only sound of her presence. She'd studied everything about this property, poured over floor plans for weeks, and memorized every second of the video Marcus's team had captured during their rescue mission for her daughter.

Onyx had hacked into their security cameras and recorded their staff carrying out their daily routines in the lavish main house. They'd even eavesdropped on the home's owners, guests, and staff through bugs they'd planted throughout the estate.

Stella knew every inch of this place, but this was the first time she'd ever stepped foot on the grounds.

She moved to the main door of the garage, then bent down to pick the simple lock. The padlock they'd found on the door when Caitlin was kidnapped was long gone, there was nothing valuable to protect now. She was inside the room in under a minute, using a penlight to traverse safely across the garage to the smaller storage room they'd put Caitlin in during her stay.

The room had changed since Caitlin was here. The cot she'd slept on was gone, replaced with a snowblower and shovels not needed for the estate in the middle of summer. Caitlin had said they'd given her a portable toilet to use while she was here—the indignity of that was almost more upsetting than the entire experience.

Her therapist explained Caitlin had compartmentalized a lot of what happened to her that weekend, pushing some feelings to the back of her mind, but allowing others to flourish, giving them more weight than they might have otherwise deserved. The toilet was one thing that received Caitlin's full attention. Being in a small room with a bomb strapped underneath her cot wasn't something Cait could speak about yet, but she could rant about having to do her business in a portable potty in the middle of the room, terrified someone was going to walk in on her whenever she had to use it.

Stella was determined to help her daughter process what had

happened to her, to help the nightmare fade, if not disappear completely. Caitlin hadn't healed yet, but they were working on it.

Stella had her own way of dealing with the trauma Richard had inflicted. Tonight was her therapy.

She checked her watch. 3:23 a.m. Time to go. She backed out of the room and left the garage, locking the door behind her out of habit more than anything. She crept back to the van and opened the sliding door.

"You ready?" asked Evan. Stella nodded. She put on her backpack and took the black suitcase Evan held out to her. "Clock starts now," he said, pushing a timer on his watch while she did the same on hers. She had forty-five minutes to get her prize and meet him at the rendezvous spot. Stella slid the door closed, then began the trek to the main house.

Stella scanned the grounds, letting the moonlight guide her, looking for any sign of life on the property. The skeleton crew who ran the estate when its owner was out had been sent away for the weekend under the auspice of giving them a bit of time off to celebrate the country's national holiday weekend. Aidan had called them using Richard's voice print and dismissed them. Stella didn't want anyone to catch her on the property tonight.

She reached the guest cottage within twelve minutes. She set her suitcase down and pulled the pack off her back. The cottage sat to the west of the main house under its own cover of trees. Stella dug her nocturnal binoculars out of the backpack. Crouched, she moved to the edge of the trees and trained her binoculars on the main house. She swept the grounds, looking for a security guard or guard dog, anything she might have missed in her research, but there were no surprises.

She texted Evan the first code word.

Stella: Warranty

He'd relay that to Marcus's team, and they would cut the feed of the security cameras to the estate. She didn't want herself on film for this. She put her binoculars back in her backpack and waited for the all-clear. Her wrist buzzed and looked to see Evan's reply come through.

Evan: Guarantee

She was clear.

Stella moved quickly across the lawn to the main house now, small jabs from her leg and hip making her wince. She'd recovered enough from the explosion to complete this mission, but her body liked to remind her what she'd been through.

She reached the courtyard and slipped beneath one of the stone staircases that led from the upper level of the house to the grounds. She paused, scanning the shadows to be sure no one followed, then checked her watch—thirty-one minutes left.

Stella set down the suitcase and pulled her backpack off. She grabbed the UV light meter—the same one she'd used at Sebastian Hayes's house—and confirmed there were no lasers targeted to the doors. She texted the next code word to Evan.

Stella: Tranquility

Within a minute, her watch buzzed again.

Evan: Peace

Working with Marcus's team did have its perks. They had already disabled the alarms to Dos Lagos. She was free to go inside.

Stella picked the lock on the French doors leading into the home's lower recreation level. Technically a basement, it opened to ground level at the back of the house. Moving through the rooms from memory, she passed a pool table, a ping pong table, and a wine cellar glimmering faintly to her right. A quick glance at her watch showed she was ahead of schedule, so she detoured into the cellar, snatched a few dusty bottles of red, and stuffed them into her backpack without bothering to check the labels. Anything from this place was bound to outclass any wine she'd ever had. Then it was on to the kitchen.

Dos Lagos's main house had two kitchens—one on the main floor upstairs, and this one. She entered this one and saw the double ovens set inside a lovely navy-blue cabinet. She switched both on high and opened the oven doors, then turned to head upstairs.

Once on the main level of the house, Stella again moved through the darkness to find the primary kitchen. It helped that it was on the opposite end of the house from its counterpart. This kitchen had an elaborate gas range and another set of double ovens. As this was her primary target, Stella blew out the pilot light in the range and turned on all the burners, now lacking the igniter needed to set the gas aflame. She also opened the oven doors here and turned on gas to them.

She checked her watch—twenty-four minutes to go. She left the kitchen and picked her way through the dining room into the parlor. There, she accessed the gas fireplace and turned that pilot light off and opened the valve. Gas from the kitchen poured into the room, the smell consuming the room.

Now that Stella had gas actively accumulating in the house, she rushed to the other fireplaces in the residence to cut out their pilot lights as well. Any open flame near this gas would be a disaster. There were four fireplaces in all. She hit the fireplace in the formal living room first, blowing out its pilot light and opening the valves for good measure.

She checked the time. Eighteen minutes and counting until she had to be at the rendezvous site. With gas filling the house, she needed to be faster. She moved to the primary suite and repeated the procedure with the fireplace there. She could smell the gas flowing through the house now, forcing her to run into the owner's office and blow out the pilot light in the final fireplace before the gas reached it. Instead of opening the gas valves in that fireplace, Stella looked around the room.

She pulled the penlight out of her pocket and shined it on the mantle above the fireplace. Stella thought it was a risky place to put a multimillion-dollar painting, but she understood the appeal. The owner could marvel at the painting from any point in the room, especially the eight-foot chestnut desk opposite the fireplace. She smiled to herself as she looked at the beautiful dancers in their blue dresses. "There you are," she whispered to the ballerinas.

Never before had Stella been so moved by a piece of art. Maybe it was how hard she'd worked to acquire it—both times. Maybe it was that it represented the highest high and the lowest low of her life. Or it could simply be that the painting made her want to reach out and help the young dancers ready themselves for the stage. Whatever the reason, Stella was standing in front of the one piece of art she would take and never sell again.

Stella pulled what she now thought of as *her* Degas off the wall. As she touched it, her wrist buzzed, making her jump and then double over with laughter.

Evan: I'm in place.

She reached for the painting again, more than ready to take her prize.

Stella leaned the painting against the desk across the room, then opened the suitcase she'd been carrying. She was happy she'd never have to see this device again. It was the same one Richard had placed under Caitlin's cot. She could think of no better way to get rid of the explosive than returning it to the man who caused her so much grief.

Stella placed the bomb in front of the fireplace and turned the key to open the gas valves. Her mind grew hazy, the gas from the kitchens and other fireplaces reaching her easily now. She paused long enough to pull a gas mask out of her backpack and put it on. The last thing she needed was to pass out now.

The gas had been flowing in the house for a full ten minutes now. It should be enough. She dialed the cell number to arm the bomb.

As quickly and carefully as she could, Stella grabbed the Degas leaning against the desk and maneuvered her way through the house to the front door. If her shoes so much as sparked static on the Persian rugs, she feared the house would catch fire.

She made it to the front door. The moment she stepped out into the fresh air, she shut the door behind her, sealing the gas inside the house. She tugged off her mask and placed it back into her backpack.

Stella checked her watch again. Six minutes to meet Evan. She pulled her binoculars out once again and used them to survey the front yard, driveway, and sweeping lawns. The only thing visible in her binoculars was the black van stationed at the end of the driveway, ready to leave. There was no one else in sight. She put the binoculars away, grabbed the painting and headed down the steps to the circular drive.

Stella made it across the top of the driveway to the fountain at the front of the house. She checked her watch again, wanting to give the gas every opportunity to fill the house, but also not wanting to over-stay her welcome. The gas had been leaking in the house for twenty minutes now. That should be enough.

She pulled the burner phone out of her pocket and typed in the number to the phone attached to the device.

With one last look at the opulent mansion in front of her, Stella hit the send button on her phone. She heard the call connect and waited to see if her preparation had worked. Each second that passed felt like an eternity. She heard what she thought was the initial explosion of the bomb, but it could have been the gas in the office exploding. Whatever the trigger, there was a pulse that pushed from the center of the house, knocking Stella back a step.

The house erupted in flames, seemingly everywhere all at once. The heat hit her like a second wave, sweat pouring down her face, her black leather pants sticking to her legs.

Stella turned and walked to the waiting van, her silhouette dark against the blinding light of the flames, explosions erupting behind her as pockets of fuel ignited. She reached the van and climbed in as Evan pulled away. She set her prized possession against the wall. Then, as she closed the door to the van already in motion with a satisfied smirk, she turned and watched Richard's house burn. She loved this life.

The End

AUTHOR'S NOTE

Thank you so much for taking this adventure with Stella and me!

This story first came to me when I saw the perfect PTA mom in the school parking lot, and I wondered if it was all a ruse. What if behind the perfect husband, perfect kids, and perfect smile, she really lived a secret life? What if she broke the law every day and none of us knew it? Stella Meyers had a name and a life before I made it home. And once the idea came to me, it wouldn't let go. After several versions of this story written while I raised kids and traversed the country, I finally got to give Stella's story the time and attention it deserves. I hope you've enjoyed the ride!

If you loved Stella and want to support an indie author, please leave a rating and review on Amazon, Goodreads, StoryGraph, or Fable. Every recommendation helps authors find more readers and allows us to continue writing stories you love.

ACKNOWLEDGMENTS

I feel like Julia Roberts at the Oscars—thanking everyone who got me to this point could take a while! I'm indebted to all the people who have cheered me on, read a million versions of this story, and encouraged me to keep going no matter how many excuses I dreamed up to pull my focus from Stella and her thieving ways.

More than anything, I'm grateful to everyone who believed in me, no matter what.

Jan, Carrie Lynn, and Karyn were the first friends to read my work, often in the middle of the night when I just had to share it with them. David has never wavered in his belief that this day would come. Brett has encouraged me no matter what crazy direction my life has taken, and answered my many questions about life in New York City. (Any mistakes in this book are on me, not him.) Bonnie read an early version of this book and told me she couldn't put it down. Tim, Neha, and Melissa always cheer me on in anything I do. Bailey headed up my street team before I even knew what that was. Thank goodness for friends like these!

Thank you to Rachel, Emily, and the entire Tenacious Writing community, whose writing courses, mindset work, and endless support keep us going when the words fail to come. Thanks to the Dream Drafters, Erika and Kayla, and my critique partners, Cristy and Jay, without whom this book would not have seen the light of day. Bri, Molly, Annie, and Hannah also provided reader feedback, emotional support, and sage advice. And huge thanks to my Colorado writing group with Jayne, Kerry, Lisa D., and Lisa G. for supporting me and inspiring me to keep going. Thank you, all!

I've had lots of professional support creating this book as well. Carrie Nauyalis is the best creative coach around and held my hand as I made the leap from professional who wants to write, to professional writer. Huge credit to Lewis Jorstad for his incredible outlining and story structure courses, as well as holding my hand through the publication process. Rachel May gave the book her expert advice with an intense developmental edit. (Any remaining structural errors or plot holes are my fault, not hers.) Ashley Earley provided a detailed line edit of the novel, and her associate Ashlyn Harmon proofread it for me. And Sandra Maldo designed a cover more stunning than my fifteen years of dreaming about this book could have ever imagined!

Two people are no longer here to cheer me on, but they are with me in spirit. Christina Hruzek pressured me to keep going no matter what and was always there to lift me up. Olivia Winter caught me writing on a break from work and said I was living my best life (she was always right). She also whispered in my ear as I wrote, cursing like a sailor.

My deepest thanks go to my loved ones, who put up with me from my earliest days. Bill Bankston and Fran Talbott have encouraged me in every conceivable way, including throwing me a launch party for this novel! Darla Jones holds me up when I falter and won't let me quit. Tracy Roberts tells me how proud she is of me every day. And though Erin Pecci is the newest addition to our clan, she shares her wisdom and encouragement with her mother-in-law daily.

Last in this list, but first in my heart, my life would simply not be worth living if not for my husband and children. Chris has supported every dream of mine for over thirty years, while filling our lives with love and laughter. Merrill and Mark have literally grown up watching me write during play dates, vacations, and soccer practices, telling me they couldn't wait to see my book on a shelf. It's been my greatest joy to spend my life with you.

In every way that matters in life, I am rich beyond my wildest dreams. Thank you all.

Scan me!

www.kendrapecci.com

Thank you for taking this journey with me. If you'd like more adventures, scan the QR code to sign up for my newsletter! You'll hear stories from the writing trenches, learn about upcoming releases, and get insight into the mind of a former adrenaline junkie who now lives vicariously through her characters.

ABOUT THE AUTHOR

Kendra Pecci lives for the thrill—both on the page and in real life. She spent her younger years jumping out of airplanes, then chased the ultimate high by becoming a mother.

Now she gets her adrenaline fix by writing heart-stopping stories centered around strong, imperfect women who live life on their own terms. When she's not putting her characters into complicated situations that get her own heart racing, she's immersed in a Stephen King novel, deconstructing her father-in-law's meatball recipe, or chasing her next adventure in the Colorado Rockies.

If you'd like more adventures, sign up for Kendra's newsletter! You'll hear stories from the writing trenches, learn about upcoming releases, and get insight into the mind of a former adrenaline junkie who now lives vicariously through her characters.

www.ingramcontent.com/pod-product-compliance
Lightning Source LLC
Chambersburg PA
CBHW050032120726
47903CB00006B/2014